B↑

"*Sanctuary Island* is a novel to curl up with and enjoy by a crackling fire or on a sunny beach. It's a beautifully told story of hope and forgiveness, celebrating the healing power of love."
—Susan Wiggs, #1 *New York Times* bestselling author

"I didn't read this book, I inhaled it. An incredible story of love, forgiveness, healing, and joy."
—Debbie Macomber,
#1 *New York Times* bestselling author

"A heartwarming, emotional, extremely romantic story that I couldn't read fast enough! Enjoy your trip to Sanctuary Island! I guarantee you won't want to leave."
—Bella Andre, *New York Times*
bestselling author of the Sullivan series

"Well written and emotionally satisfying. I loved it! A rare find."
—Lori Wilde, *New York Times* bestselling author

"Redemption, reconciliation, and, of course, romance—Everett's novel has it all." —*Booklist*

"Richly nuanced characters and able plotting . . . Everett's sweet contemporary debut illustrates the power of forgiveness and the strength of relationships that may falter but never fail." —*Publishers Weekly*

ALSO BY LILY EVERETT

Sanctuary Island
Shoreline Drive

AVAILABLE FROM ST. MARTIN'S PAPERBACKS

Homecoming

The Billionaire Brothers

LILY EVERETT

St. Martin's Paperbacks

This is a work of fiction. All of the characters, organizations, and events portrayed in this work are either products of the author's imagination or are used fictitiously.

HOMECOMING: THE BILLIONAIRE BROTHERS

Copyright © 2014 by Lily Everett.
"The Firefly Café" copyright © 2013 by Lily Everett.
"The Summer Cottage" copyright © 2013 by Lily Everett.
"Island Road" copyright © 2013 by Lily Everett.
"One Year Later . . ." copyright © 2014 by Lily Everett.

For information address St. Martin's Press, 175 Fifth Avenue, New York, NY 10010.

ISBN: 978-1-250-05449-4

Printed in the United States of America

St. Martin's Paperbacks edition / August 2014

St. Martin's Paperbacks are published by St. Martin's Press, 175 Fifth Avenue, New York, NY 10010.

10 9 8 7 6 5 4 3 2 1

For Rose
Thank you for always encouraging me,
supporting me, believing in me, and
pushing me to stretch myself as a writer.
You're the best editor in the world!

Dear Reader,

Many of you have written and told me how much you wish Sanctuary Island were a real place and that you could live there! I feel exactly the same way, which is why I couldn't resist the chance to spend more time on the windy beaches with the wild horses and the warm, welcoming people who've made this magical island their home.

That's why I wrote *Homecoming: The Billionaire Brothers*! It's the story of three wealthy, sexy, charming brothers who each wind up following his heart to Sanctuary Island . . . and discovering there's more to life than money and power.

Originally published as three individual e-book novellas, *The Firefly Café*, *The Summer Cottage*, and *Island Road*, this trio of short, interconnected romances really can be read as one long story. Each picks up where the last one left off, and each revolves around the timeless themes of healing, family, forgiveness, and love.

I'm thrilled that these stories are now available to those of you who prefer to read print books, and I hope you enjoy returning to Sanctuary Island with me. And if this is your first visit, welcome! *Homecoming: The Billionaire Brothers* can be read entirely on its own. It's set in the same world as my full-length novels, *Sanctuary Island* and *Shoreline Drive*, but you don't have to read them first to enjoy *Homecoming*.

And for those of us who wish we lived someplace as friendly, peaceful, and beautiful as Sanctuary Island, just remember that daydream is never further away than the turn of a page . . .

xoxox,

Lily Everett

The Firefly Café

Chapter One

June 2013

Dylan Harrington popped the kickstand down and swung his leg over the seat of his hand-restored fifteen-year-old BMW sport bike. Tugging off his helmet, he stared up at the fairy tale of Victorian gingerbreading and white clapboard at the end of the boxwood-lined walkway.

This may have been a mistake.

Or maybe that was just the hangover talking, and all of this stately colonial business would look better after a strong pot of coffee and a pile of greasy cheese fries at the one restaurant he'd passed on his way in. Even a tiny, picturesque seaside joint called the Firefly Café would serve cheese fries, right? Right?

Dylan pinched his eyes shut around the throbbing headache. Walking his bike onto that tin can masquerading as a ferry boat hadn't helped the sickness roiling in his gut, and the way he'd turned heads with the growl of his bike as he rode through the town square sure hadn't done much for his state of mind. But he was here now, and what the hell? His grandparents' vacation home was as good a place as any to lay low until Miles got over his temper tantrum.

Dylan wasn't a moron. He was well aware that he was wasting his life partying, getting into bar fights, and taking a different woman back to his penthouse every night. He didn't need his perfect, responsible, judgmental eldest brother to lay it all out for him.

Miles looked at me like I was a complete stranger.

Shoving down the angry shame that choked him at the memory of his brother's disappointed frown, Dylan set his jaw. Miles made his choice a long time ago, and it hadn't been to stick with the family and be there for his brothers.

This was just another in a long line of lectures about his lifestyle, Dylan reminded himself. Yet another argument with Miles about missed opportunities and what their parents would think if they were still alive. No reason to get bent out of shape. It certainly wasn't why Dylan had impulsively jumped on his bike and started riding south.

Dylan was bored with the city, that was all. Same scene every night, same gallery openings, same women in tight dresses looking at him with that same edge of calculation from under their fake eyelashes. He needed a break from being the "Bad Boy Billionaire," as the scandal rags had tagged him.

Sanctuary Island, though? Might turn out to be more of a change than he could handle.

Realizing he'd been standing on the sidewalk in front of the house for a good five minutes, Dylan shook his head to clear it. The way his pickled brain sloshed against his skull made him regret it instantly, but at least it got him moving.

He slung his leather duffel over his shoulder before starting up the walkway to the wraparound porch. Morning light glittered off of the house's navy-blue-shuttered windows, and Dylan shivered a little and zipped his leather jacket a little tighter to his chin, even though it was warmer here than he was used to.

Back in New York it was still in the sixties almost every morning, but tucked away off the coast of Virginia, Sanctuary Island already felt like high summer. Pink and white dogwood blossoms nodded at him from the small trees lining the path, and deep magenta azalea bushes crowded the flowerbeds below the porch.

He glanced over his shoulder to remind himself that, yep, the house really honestly faced out on an old-fashioned town square, complete with gazebo and bandstand set in the lush green sprawl of the grassy park.

It was beautifully serene, almost idyllic. Dylan felt as if he'd blundered into a Thomas Kinkade painting. Rubbing a hand over his suddenly dry mouth, he grimaced at the rasp of stubble against his palm.

Just like that old song from when we were kids . . . one of these things is not like the others.

Despite feeling viciously out of place, even a jaded cynic like Dylan could appreciate the appeal of this place. No wonder his grandparents, Bette and Fred Harrington, had loved this island. They'd spent summers on Sanctuary until their deaths, one following the other as closely as they always had in life, five years ago.

The edges of grief had smoothed over time, like stones tumbled on the riverbed, and Dylan breathed through it as he contemplated how to get into the locked vacation house.

He probably should've planned ahead, gotten the key from whoever his family employed to oversee their various properties around the world. Now he'd have to bust in a window or something, which sounded like a lot of trouble in his hungover state, after ten straight hours on his motorcycle.

Dylan was tired, his bones almost aching with it. Of course, that was why he'd come to Sanctuary Island in the first place.

If he was honest, Dylan was tired of the life he'd chosen, the reputation he'd deliberately cultivated.

The pretense of it all, paddling around the shallow waters of the New York art scene, made him sick. He couldn't remember the last time he'd looked a beautiful woman in the eye without catching the edge of calculation as she wondered what she could get out of him.

Grimacing, he dropped his duffel on the porch and prepared to jam his leather-jacketed elbow through the diamond pane of decorative etched glass flanking the front. Before he could do more than crack his knuckles, the heavy wooden door swung open.

A woman appeared in the doorway, pushing a strand of dark chestnut hair out of her eyes. She was small and delicate looking, with softly rounded cheeks that were flushed a healthy pink that had nothing to do with cosmetics.

She couldn't look more different from the magazine-ready models he usually dated, so the sudden shot of desire caught him off guard. Already off balance from nearly getting caught in the act of breaking into this woman's house by accident, Dylan stood there silently while the woman closed those wide hazel eyes and clasped her hands in front of her.

"I thought I heard someone out here," she breathed. "And thank the sweet lord, because my shift starts in half an hour and I can't afford to be late. Come on in, the toilet's this way."

"Toilet?" *Wrong house. Man, I even manage to screw up my vacation.*

Somewhere, his brother Miles was laughing his ass off.

Obviously clocking his confusion, the angel flushed and brushed a self-conscious hand down her front. "Right. The uniform. I know, it doesn't look right, and I swear I don't usually wear it around the house."

For the first time, Dylan noted her getup, which looked like a costume for a diner waitress in a fifties movie, complete with a sea-green skirt that bared long, slender legs and a tiny white apron emphasizing the curves of her waist. THE FIREFLY CAFÉ was embroidered in pink over her left breast.

"You look just fine to me," he told her honestly. Dylan was no stranger to beautiful women, but this woman, with her messy, tumbled-out-of-bed hair and slightly tired eyes unaccentuated by makeup sparked something in him. Something he hadn't felt in a long time.

She managed to look so *nice,* even while rolling her eyes; maybe it was the good-natured twist to her pretty pink mouth. "You're sweet. A liar, but sweet. And I've got a plumbing issue that needs to be fixed or the Richie Rich one percenters who own this place will throw a hissy."

Dylan frowned—was she talking about his family? Maybe this was Harrington House, after all. But what was this woman doing here? Stalling for time to figure out what the hell was going on, he said, "I'd like to help you out, but I'm not sure I'm the guy you want."

The smile that lit her face heated Dylan's blood faster than the most seductive pout. "Oh, you're definitely the guy I want."

Arousal, all the stronger for being so unexpected, tightened his belly. "Is that right?"

Pink bloomed over her cheekbones and down her neck, but instead of getting bashful, she lifted a flirty brow and said, "That's exactly right, sugar. So long as you can snake my pipes."

His bark of laughter surprised even Dylan. "Is that my cue to make a crack about showing you my tools?"

"Don't strain yourself, sugar." She waved a cheerful hand. "I work the night shift at the only restaurant on this island that serves alcohol. Trust me, I've heard every dirty joke there is. Now get in here, the clock's ticking and the plumbing isn't the only issue. I've got a whole list."

When Dylan hesitated, reluctant to own up to belonging to the family she'd rolled her eyes over before, a slimly toned arm shot out and grasped the lapel of his leather jacket. With a laugh, she hauled him over the threshold and into the dimness of the house.

Half a second later, Dylan Harrington, third son and heir to the multibillion-dollar Harrington fortune, stood in a small white-tiled, paisley-wallpapered bathroom staring down at the plunger in his hand.

Glancing up, he caught a glimpse of his own bemused expression in the gilt-edged mirror above the pedestal sink. The wry half-grin tugging at the corner of his mouth gave his face an unfamiliar lightness, but it felt good.

So much for a vacation from women who wanted something from him.

But somehow, as he faced down a misbehaving toilet and whipped out his smartphone to search the Internet for tips on plunging, Dylan admitted to himself that this was something different.

The mystery of who this woman was, and why she was living in his grandparents' old vacation house, roused Dylan's curiosity. But the bigger mystery was why he found himself attracted to a woman whose clean, fresh looks screamed "good girl."

Dylan gripped the handle of the plunger, his rusty laugh echoing off the bathroom tiles. For the first time in a long time, his life had taken a sharp turn . . . and he couldn't wait to find out what was around the corner.

Chapter Two

Penny Little smoothed her palms down the front of her oft-mended uniform, fingertips automatically worrying the frayed buttonhole at the collarbone, and breathed deep to calm her racing heart.

When she phoned her employers for help, Penny had been expecting Grady Wilkes, the local handyman, or one of the Hackleys who ran the hardware store on Main Street. Not some tall, muscled, motorcycle-riding, scruffy-chinned vision of hotness on her doorstep.

"Bad Penny," she muttered as she escaped to the kitchen to fix a pitcher of sweet tea. "Quit thinking about borrowing trouble. You're full up already."

And a man like the one who'd peeled off his leather jacket to reveal a white T-shirt straining across broad shoulders was nothing but trouble. A dark band of ink circled one muscular bicep, and Penny'd had to stop herself from asking where else he was tattooed.

Still, trouble or not, good manners dictated that she offer him a glass of something cold, Penny told herself as she headed back down the hall to the sound of muffled curses from the bathroom. Good manners. That was all.

But she recognized that for the dirty lie it was the instant she cracked open the door. Her breath caught at the sight of trouble leaning over the toilet in a way that molded those sinfully tight jeans to his lean hips and . . . well. Penny wished she had a hand free to fan herself with.

His surprisingly high-tech phone buzzed from the side of the sink, and he frowned down at it as he reached to heave the lid off the tank. The muscles in his corded forearms bulged briefly, drawing Penny's gaze to the tanned skin dusted with hair a shade or two darker than his light brown buzz cut.

Setting the lid down with a clang, he twisted at the waist to consult his phone again, pulling that T-shirt tight across his chest.

"Is that for me?"

The deep voice startled Penny into bobbling the glass. Ice sloshed and cold tea dripped onto her hand as she dragged her gaze up from the mesmerizing play of muscles under his clothes.

He was smiling at her again, the devil grin that heated Penny's blood and sent it racing through her body like a runaway horse. When he reached to take the glass from her, their fingertips brushed.

A jolt of electricity zipped up her arm, and the slippery glass dropped and shattered on the floor.

"Oh, shoot!" Penny grabbed the hand towel from the sink and moved to wipe up the spilled tea before realizing most of it had drenched the front of his T-shirt before dripping down onto his jeans. She'd actually been about to cop a feel, with only thin terry cloth and wet, clinging denim between her hand and his—

"I'm so sorry," she gasped, feeling her neck and face go hot with embarrassment. Okay, embarrassment and lust, but the lust was a little embarrassing, too, so, yeah.

"No big deal." He smiled and raised her core temperature by another ten degrees when he reached for the hem of his soaked T-shirt and drew it up and over his head. "I was due for a shower, anyway."

Penny blinked. Granted, it had been a few years since she'd been face to chest with a half-naked man, but even considering that, she was pretty sure she'd never seen anything to compare to the golden-tan planes and ridges of this man's perfectly sculpted torso. He looked like a movie star or an underwear model, one of those guys whose whole job rested on their ability to strip down and render ordinary women speechless with desire.

Well, being a handyman required plenty of heavy lifting, she reasoned dazedly, her eyes glued to his pecs. And a flexible schedule that probably left plenty of time for the gym.

Mmm, flexible . . .

"If you bring me another glass of tea, I promise I won't throw it on the ground."

Penny's gaze snapped up to his face. He sounded repentant, but the look on his face was anything but. Wicked amusement danced behind his shockingly blue eyes. This man had a very clear understanding of his body and its effect on women.

Natural contrariness stiffened Penny's spine. She wouldn't be another notch on this gorgeous handyman's tool belt. "Sorry, no second chances," she said, the words as automatic as breathing. "House policy."

Confusion narrowed the sky-blue eyes. "House policy?"

Kneeling to carefully pick up the larger pieces of sharp glass, Penny snorted. "Okay, no. Not house policy, as in imposed by the rich folks that own this place. From what I've heard, they're pretty permissive when it comes to family members misbehaving. No, the one-strike-and-you're-out stuff is all me. Call it a personal philosophy."

A lesson she'd learned well and thoroughly, at heavy cost.

"Sounds like a tough way to live. Everyone deserves a second chance, now and then."

His low, husky voice startled her out of her reverie. Finger jerking, she nicked herself on the corner of a glass shard and pressed her lips together as a droplet of blood welled to the surface. "Not everyone. Trust me."

Glass crunched softly under his black motorcycle boots as he crouched down to her level. "Okay, you win." He smiled easily, a man used to using his charm to get what he wanted. "I'll live without the iced tea."

Right, they'd been talking about spilled tea, not her life story. Cursing the riptide of her memories for sucking them into these deeply personal waters, Penny smiled back and let him help her to her feet. "Thanks. Give me a second to grab the broom, and I'll get the rest of this cleaned up."

Every inch of her was so hotly aware of his smooth, hard body a mere breath away from hers. Shivering, Penny backed toward the door and the relative safety of the hallway.

He stopped her with another quick smile. "What you said about the family that owns this place. How much do you know about them?"

"The Richie Riches?" Penny blinked. "Not much, except that they have enough money to leave this gorgeous old place sitting empty for years on end. Such a waste. At least they cared enough to hire a caretaker."

His face cleared as if she'd slotted the final piece into a jigsaw puzzle. "Right, a caretaker. That's you."

She laughed. "Of course! What—did you think I was squatting? No, I'm paid to stay here and make sure the house doesn't fall down while the Harrington boys live the high life in New York City."

"The high life." He said it absently, turning back to the partially dismantled toilet, but Penny caught a glimpse of his slight frown in the sink mirror. He looked upset, maybe annoyed.

She could sympathize. "I know. When you work hard for a living, it's aggravating to be reminded there are playboy types out there who can afford to do nothing but drink and dance the night away. I've even heard ... oh, listen to me gossiping! Never mind, I'll get that broom."

"Wait. What have you heard?"

Thoroughly embarrassed, Penny winced, but when she made reluctant eye contact with the handyman again, there was no judgment in his lean, handsome face. Instead, he looked curious, if still a little tense.

She unbent enough to quirk a half-grin. "Well. I've heard one of the Harrington brothers is actually so famous for his partying that he has a nickname in the press: the Bad Boy Billionaire."

He twitched a bit, clearly as repulsed by the moniker as she was. "Sounds like a douche bag."

That shocked a laugh out of her. She leaned against the doorjamb and admired the play of light over his muscles. It was so sweet of him not to have put his damp shirt back on. "I don't know the man personally—gosh, I can't even remember his first name. But apparently he's quite popular with the ladies."

"I hate this guy."

Penny grinned at him. "Don't sweat it. Any woman who's worth having would prefer a man like you, who makes an honest living working with his hands, over a guy who cats around enough to be a breeding ground for sexually transmitted diseases."

His eyes went wide, and Penny felt herself flush. Could she be any more awkward and obvious about her attraction?

"Anyway, I'll let you get back to work! And, shoot, I'd better get to my other job. I wait tables at the Firefly Café," she explained. "Hey, if you get peckish later, you should come over to the restaurant. The food isn't fancy, but it's delicious."

"Sounds great." He stood there, bare chest gleaming and so, so distracting, with a smile lurking in the depths of those ocean-blue eyes.

"Okay. Great," Penny echoed, flustered by the way she couldn't seem to look away from him. "So maybe I'll see you later, um . . ."

She stopped, shocked at herself. "Wow. Here you are, half nekkid in my powder room, and I don't even know your name."

"Dylan," he said at once. Sticking out a large, square-palmed hand, he cleared his throat. "And I can put my shirt back on, if it makes you uncomfortable."

"Penny Little," she replied. "It's nice to meet you. And please don't put your shirt on!"

The hint of a smile graduated to full-on wicked smirk. "No?"

Face flaming with heat, Penny soldiered on. "I mean, because it's all wet. At least let me wash it for you first."

And if he had to stay shirtless while his tee was stain treated, laundered, and dried on the line in the backyard, well. Sometimes life was hard.

Grinning, Dylan picked up his shirt from the pedestal sink and stepped close enough to drape it around her shoulders, since her hands were still full of glass shards.

"Thanks. Careful though," he said, hoarse and deep. "It's my favorite."

The dark scent of sweet tea and working man surrounded her, and Penny drank it in gratefully. "I'll treat it like it's one of my bosses' custom-tailored wool suits," she promised.

"No worries," he said, flashing that charming grin. She didn't want it to be as effective as it was. "It's been through worse than a tea bath. It'll survive."

Great. The shirt would survive. But as Penny hightailed it out of the powder room and gasped in her first breath of non-Dylan-scented air in minutes, she wondered.

Would she survive this house renovation with her sanity—and her heart—intact?

Chapter Three

The moment the front door closed behind Penny, Dylan had his phone in hand, fingers frantically touch-typing out a query to his middle brother's frighteningly efficient personal assistant. If anyone had the scoop on the caretaker in charge of the Sanctuary Island house, it was Jessica Bell.

But when the ringing of the phone clicked through to voice mail, it was Logan's voice in his ear.

"*Jessica can't come to the phone right now,*" his brother intoned solemnly. "*She's too busy inserting herself into every aspect of my life and making sure I waste time eating and sleeping instead of working in my lab. When she's ready to stop annoying me, she can have her phone back. Until then, leave a message, I guess. I certainly won't be checking them or passing them along to her, though.*"

Dylan hung up before the beep. No extra info from Jessica, then. Fine, he'd have to figure out what Penny Little's deal was the old-fashioned way—with a generous dose of charm.

He didn't question his desire to spend more time here, in this house with this woman, and without the heavy baggage of the reputation he'd recklessly built back in New York. Penny Little was interesting. Working on the house was surprisingly interesting, or at least satisfying.

The whole thing felt like a vacation from the boring, predictable cynicism of his real life.

So yeah, he hadn't come clean about who he was. But seriously, what if he admitted to being the Bad Boy Billionaire Penny despised? That would end things in a hurry. No, he'd decided on the spur of the moment to play this out a little longer, and even though he felt an uncomfortable tickle of guilt at lying to Penny, he shrugged it off.

He wasn't hurting anyone. In fact, he was saving Penny from the embarrassment of realizing she'd bad-mouthed him and his entire family right to his face. Plus, Penny was getting the help she needed with the house repairs. Everybody won.

Syrupy afternoon light was pouring through the newly polished windows by the time Dylan had made his way through the first quarter of the to-do list Penny had left. Some of the tasks were self-explanatory—it didn't take a genius to wash a window, just a good ladder and a guy with zero fear of heights. For the rest, well, thank God for Google. And the local hardware store.

He'd gotten a fair number of tips from the tall, athletic woman behind the counter. For instance, apparently crumpled-up newspaper was the only way to get glass clean with no streaking. She'd talked herself out of a sale with that one, since Dylan had been about to buy a bundle of microfiber cloths, but she didn't seem to mind.

This whole island couldn't be more different from the urban rush of Manhattan. And Dylan had yet to see more of Sanctuary than the quaint "downtown" area bordering the town square where his grandparents' house stood.

As he located the leaky pipe under the kitchen sink—number five on The List—Dylan rolled his sore shoulders and admitted to himself that as unusual as the situation was, he'd needed this.

Man, when he got back to Manhattan, he was asking for a refund from his personal trainer. The strenuous daily gym routine hadn't prepared him for a full day of manual labor. Dylan's muscles ached. But it was a good ache, a clean, pure soreness that let him know he'd used his body well today, and he'd likely sleep well that night.

And something about the blend of mindless, repetitive actions like hammering the loose floorboards on the front porch back into place combined with figuring out the intricacies of nineteenth century plumbing had allowed him to completely tune out all the stress and drama he'd left behind in New York.

With a contented sigh, Dylan wedged his shoulders into the under-counter cabinet hiding the leak and started tinkering.

A thud from out in the kitchen behind him startled

him into cracking his head on the edge of the cabinet. "Crap!"

"What the hell are you doing?" The sharp male voice had Dylan backing out of the cabinet on his hands and knees, wincing against the sting of his bruised temple.

A teenaged boy stood next to the oval eat-in kitchen table, hands on his hips and backpack on the floor beside his scuffed sneakers. That must have been the thud Dylan had heard.

Who was this kid?

"Well?" the boy said, narrowing his light hazel eyes and putting his big puppy paws on his skinny hips. Whoever he was, he was packing way more attitude than his lanky frame could back up. He had the weedy, gawky look of someone whose body was growing and changing so rapidly, he was having a hard time catching up to it.

Dylan remembered how that felt. Remembered, too, the horrible awkwardness of being caught between childhood and manhood, teetering on the cusp and trying desperately not to fall on his face. The memory of how he'd coped with it all—badly— prompted Dylan to stand up straight and wipe his hands on his jeans.

Holding out his still-smudged right hand, man to man, he said, "I'm Dylan. I'm the handyman. And you are?"

The kid slowly reached out and shook Dylan's hand. His scowl lightened a bit as he unconsciously squared his shoulders.

"Answer my question first," the kid said stubbornly, crossing his arms over his chest.

Dylan tugged the creased, water-spotted list out of his back pocket and waved it in the air. "I'm the guy who's been working his way through this list for the last seven hours. Does Penny Little know you hang out here when she's at work?"

Dylan and his high school buddies used to break into empty apartments to smoke and raid the absent owner's liquor cabinet. This kid, in his baggy polo shirt and too-short khakis didn't exactly look the type, but you never knew.

Giving Dylan a look that clearly communicated searing scorn, the kid said, "Uh, yeah. Since I live here."

The snark made Dylan bite down on a smile—sarcasm didn't sit well on the young, unlined face, with those bright green-gold eyes. Eyes the same unusual color as Penny Little's.

With a sense of dawning comprehension, Dylan said, "You're Penny's . . . brother?"

Another look of withering disgust. "No. I'm her son. Matthew."

Dylan blinked. "Wait. She's married?"

"Divorced." Matthew again crossed his arms over his thin chest belligerently. "You're pretty slow."

"Hey! Give me a break. You're what, sixteen? Penny looks—well, she can't be old enough to have a teenaged son."

Those eyes he'd inherited from Penny became narrow and suspicious. "I meant you were slow because it's taken you seven hours to get to the leaky sink."

Ah. Awkward. Dylan kept his expression serious with an effort. "I take pride in my work."

Raising his brows, Matthew said, "Oh, man. You are totally perving on my mom."

"What? No, I'm not," Dylan denied, feeling his cheeks heat even though he didn't know what he had to be embarrassed about.

Clearly unconvinced, Matt made a grossed-out face. "Yeah, you are. You called her Penny, you noticed how she looked, asked if she's single. I'm not an idiot."

"Look, kid." Dylan raised his hands in surrender. "Sorry if it freaks you out, but your mom is an adult. I'm pretty sure she doesn't need you to protect her honor."

"It doesn't matter anyway." Matt jerked his chin in the direction of the door. "Since you're leaving."

"What?"

"You can go now. I'll take it from here."

Dylan raised his brows. "Yeah? Your mom didn't say anything about that to me. I wouldn't want to leave the job half-finished."

"Not even half," Matthew sneered. "But Mom isn't here."

It sounded like he was grinding his teeth, and his deep voice cracked a little on *here*. Flushing angrily, he tilted his chin up in a way that reminded Dylan vividly of Penny.

Raising his voice, Matthew grated out, "I'm the

man of the house. Which makes me your boss, and I say you're done."

A gasp from the other end of the kitchen had them both turning to face Penny, standing in the doorway. The starched pleats of her uniform had wilted over the course of the day, but her curly hair was as bouncy as ever.

"Matthew Emmett Little! I didn't raise you to be rude to guests in our home."

Matthew deflated like a pinpricked balloon, but his mouth went hard and flat. "It's not our home, and he's not a guest. He works here. Like you do."

Something around Penny's tired eyes went taut, but her voice was calm as she said, "Even more reason to keep your sass to yourself. Dylan is here to do a job, and you will treat him with the same respect you'd expect in return."

Dylan shifted his weight, wishing he could crawl back under the kitchen sink to escape the awful tension strung between mother and son.

But when Matthew broke and dropped his gaze away from his mother's inflexible stare, he looked straight at Dylan. "I apologize," Matthew said. "You're just doing your job. But we don't need your help."

"The Harringtons sent Dylan down here," Penny told her son, coming into the kitchen to stand shoulder to shoulder with Dylan. "They hired him. It's not up to us."

Matthew struggled visibly for a second, anger and embarrassment at war on his open, young face. "It should be. We're the ones who live here most of the time! And I told you I would take care of all the stuff on this list, Mom. I can do it. And if I needed help, I could call Dad."

"Matty . . ." Penny pressed a hand to the bridge of her nose as if she felt a headache coming on.

"Don't call me Matty," Matthew shouted, deep red suffusing his cheeks. "I've told you a million times, I hate that stupid baby name."

With that, he grabbed his backpack off the floor and all but ran out of the kitchen. Heavy footsteps pounded up the stairs and down the hallway, punctuated by the slam of a door.

Penny winced, then blew out a breath. "Sorry about that. I'll see what I can do about getting you combat pay."

"Don't give it another thought. Believe me, I've seen worse." Dylan gave her an easy smile, wanting to lift some of the weight off of her slumped shoulders. "In fact, I *was* worse. Way, way worse."

"Matty—I mean, Matt." She pressed her lips together as if chastising herself. "He's a good boy. But ever since the divorce . . ."

She cut herself off with a little laugh. "Listen to me rattle on. You don't want to hear about our problems."

"Don't stop on my account. I can't promise any sage advice, but I'm happy to listen if you want to talk about it." Shockingly, Dylan realized it was the truth. He saw a lot of himself in Matthew's troubled eyes. And Penny—she tugged at something in him.

"You don't have to, just to be nice. I know there's still a lot of work to finish."

"I'm never nice. Besides." Dylan hitched his hip up on the kitchen counter beside the sink with a winning grin. "I'm due for a break. And maybe another shot at that iced tea? Although if we fumble this one, too, I'm out of luck. This is my last clean T-shirt."

Penny's gaze sharpened on his face as if he'd just come into focus. "You're not fooling anyone, you know."

Freezing, Dylan's brain went into an immediate, frantic tap dance trying to come up with a way to keep this going.

"What do you mean?" he asked, stalling.

A slow smile lit Penny's round, apple-cheeked face as she sank down into one of the kitchen chairs. "I don't care what you say, you're the real deal. An actual nice man, hallelujah and praise be."

Relief and guilt made for a dizzying cocktail. Dylan grimaced at the galloping of his pulse. He was just starting to slough off the dirty skin of the Bad Boy Billionaire. He wasn't ready to go back to being a Harrington yet—but even though it wasn't hurting anyone, didn't matter in any real way, he still didn't like lying to Penny.

"No," he said quietly, meeting her warm, kind eyes as she handed him a glass full of sweet amber liquid. "I'm really not."

Chapter Four

Under the cover of the table, Penny slipped off her shoes and flexed her exhausted feet. It wasn't even four o'clock yet. Plenty of daylight left to get through the endless mountain of laundry and dirty dishes generated by a teenaged boy. But before her second shift started, Penny decided she'd allow herself a few moments to enjoy the strange intimacy that had sprung up between herself and this gorgeous stranger.

"So you were saying, about your divorce?" He went back to tinkering with the kitchen sink, which somehow made it easier for Penny to open up.

"It happened a few years ago now, but Matt's still angry at me. The marriage didn't just break up—we also left the town we were living in to start fresh here, on Sanctuary Island. The transition was hard on him."

"But not on you?"

"It was my choice to leave." Although there hadn't been a choice. Not really. "Matt doesn't understand why his whole life had to be uprooted, or why I cut off all contact with his father. Not that his father makes any effort to keep in touch with him, anyway—which, of course, Matt blames me for."

"He's at a rough age." Dylan shrugged, sympathetic and pragmatic at once. "You're an easy target for all those hormones and emotions rocketing around his system, because you're the one who's here for him. Believe me, when I was his age, I was sure everything would be better if my older brothers would just come home and pay attention to me. It's only now, looking back, that I see how wrong I was. And boy, do I regret being such a jackass to people who were doing their best to look after me."

"So you're saying to wait it out, and in ten years Matty will realize I wasn't a crappy mother, after all?" Penny laughed, and was surprised to notice that the belly-twisting tension of yet another fight with her son had almost completely dissolved. "I actually feel better. You delivered on the sage advice, after all!"

He laughed. "Well, I was once a teenage boy. I know how they think. I wasn't so different from your son, in a lot of ways." The smile slid off his face and those blue eyes turned serious. Speaking carefully, as if unsure how much to tell, Dylan said, "I was younger than Matt when I lost my father. Both my parents, actually."

"I'm so sorry," Penny croaked around the sudden lump in her throat. It was her worst nightmare:

that something would happen to her, and Matty would be left all alone.

He shrugged. "I was lucky—my brothers and I had relatives who took us in, and they were wonderful. It could have been a lot worse. But I remember how it felt to be that age and looking around me to try to see what kind of man I wanted to be."

"That's a huge part of why I left my husband," Penny said, the truth pouring out of her. "Because I didn't want Matty to look up to him as an example of how to be a man."

"I get that. Having no male role model is way better than having a bad one. Maybe I was lucky my brothers weren't around more when I was a kid. I can't imagine what I would have learned from them. My middle brother is a genius, but a total workaholic loner. And my oldest brother— well. I guess he could've taught me how to close off all emotion and go through life like a machine while trying to control everyone around me. Nah, I was better off making it up as I went along."

He snorted as if to say he was still making it up, and was pretty sure he was getting it wrong. Penny wanted to hug him so badly, she had to sit on her hands to keep from reaching out. "It seems to me like you did a pretty good job with that."

Dylan tilted his head from side to side, cracking his neck, then shrugged again. "I made a lot of mistakes. Wasted a lot of years drinking too much and pretending to be the life of the party, like that would make up for the fact that I was drifting without a purpose."

"What changed?"

His gaze shifted to the side for a second, the corner of his mouth quirking up. "I got a job. I've always been lucky. But my point here is that Matt's lucky, too. He has you."

Distracted from her curiosity about this brief glimpse into Dylan's past, Penny sighed and rested her aching head on one hand. "Matt's not going to learn a lot about how to be a man from me. And all he learned from his father was how to be a bully."

In the pause before Dylan turned around, Penny tasted the sour anger of her own words on the back of her tongue. She swallowed it down.

"Sorry," she said quickly. "That probably sounds pretty bitter."

"Don't apologize." Bracing his hands on the counter, Dylan stretched his legs out, all long lines and lean muscle. "Seems like you've got plenty of cause for bitterness."

"Maybe, but I don't have to give in to it." Dredging up a smile, Penny stood and smoothed down her skirt. Yuck, she was still wearing her stale, maple syrup and strawberry jam–stained uniform. "I'm going to run upstairs and change out of this. Thanks for listening. And hey, if you haven't made other plans—and if you can stand to spend any more time than you have to with a sullen teenaged boy—you're welcome to join us for dinner."

Dylan crouched to pluck a wrench out of the plastic sack of tools at his feet. "I don't have any plans at all. Thanks for the invite."

The way he said it, head ducked and eyes hidden,

set off Penny's radar. "Did the Harringtons arrange for a place for you to stay?" she asked slowly.

A dull red flush suffused the back of his neck. "Not exactly."

Righteous indignation turned her voice sharp. "I can't believe they sent you to do a job without making sure you were taken care of! The lack of consideration—"

"It's fine," he interrupted hastily. "There must be a hotel around here where I can get a room."

"On an island this size? Bless your heart. No. You'd have to take the ferry over to Winter Harbor, which would be a pointless waste of time. You'll stay with us. We have more than enough space here—I'll make up one of the guest rooms."

When Dylan looked up and met her eye, a distinct twinkle had taken over for whatever embarrassment he'd felt. "People don't say 'no' to you very often, do they?"

Penny shrugged. "I'm a mom. And I deal with the lunch rush at the Firefly Café every day. The only way to get through it in one piece is to maintain total, unflappable confidence at all times."

"It's a good trick," Dylan told her. "And . . . that was a 'yes,' in case I wasn't clear. A 'yes' and a 'thank you.' I really appreciate it."

For some silly reason, the way he looked at her gave Penny a shiver of delicious heat all down her spine. Trying not to flutter, she said, "You're very welcome. Now get that kitchen sink finished up so I can fix dinner."

She turned to beat a hasty retreat before the warm shine of his eyes made her visibly flush, but his voice stopped her.

"Penny. I realize I don't know you very well, but do you want an outsider's take on what your son can learn from you?"

The flutters got worse, moving up from her belly to squeeze at her lungs. Her voice was embarrassingly breathless when she whispered, "Sure."

Dylan held her gaze, the force of his ocean-blue stare drawing Penny closer. "In a single day in this house, I've seen a woman who doesn't back down, who takes charge of her life and works hard to make it the best life possible, for herself and her kid. I see a woman who could let the toughness of that life get her down, but who chooses to smile instead. I see graciousness and hospitality—enough to welcome a stranger into your home, and to make him feel like . . . well. You make me feel like we've known each other longer and better than should be possible when we've only just met. It's actually freaking me out a little."

Penny had to laugh. It was that, or cry—the emotion struggling up from her chest had to come out somehow. And given the choice, Penny would always pick laughter over tears.

So she laughed, and held out her hand, and let herself enjoy the tremor of feminine awareness when his strong, callused fingers enfolded hers. "Considering the way Matty and I forcibly dragged you into our issues, I'd say you're no stranger. So welcome to the family, Dylan—" She cut herself off, and this time the laugh was less shaky. "You know what? I don't even know your last name!"

His fingers tightened on hers for a brief, convulsive moment. He stared down at their joined hands, silent. The pause lasted one heartbeat, two—then Dylan looked her directly in the eye and said, "Workman. Dylan Workman."

Chapter Five

"Dylan Workman," Penny echoed, smiling. "How appropriate, for a man in your line of business."

Dylan dug deep for a carefree expression, even though, inside, he felt a little sick. What the hell was he doing, lying to this pretty woman about who he was? He knew it was wrong—and just then, he'd come so close to blurting out the truth that his heart was still pounding.

Whether it was with relief or regret that he'd kept the deception going, he wasn't sure.

"I'd better finish up here so I can get out of your way," he said, reluctantly letting go of her hand. Shorter and more curvaceous than the glamazon models Dylan usually dated, Penny Little had small hands, roughened in places by hard work. He found he liked the realness of her skin, the way her glow came from within rather than from a battery of

expensive beauty products full of crushed diamonds and gold dust, or whatever.

He liked Penny Little, period.

Which was the problem, of course. He liked her,
as a person—and he wanted her to like him back
in exactly the same way. No preconceived no-
tions based on his bank account, no weird inequal-
ity because she was technically his family's employee,
and definitely no chance that Penny might look at
him and remember everything she'd heard about
the Bad Boy Billionaire.

He wanted her to get to know the real him. Just
Dylan, no bells and whistles. And maybe he'd dis-
cover that wasn't enough for her, but he needed to
find out if a woman like Penny could want him for
himself alone. He'd never have a better opportunity.

Dylan listened for her light footsteps on the stairs
as he ducked back under the kitchen sink to confront the leaky pipe. He removed and patched the
problematic section of pipe with half his brain; the
other half was focused on the woman upstairs.

The woman whose brilliant smile in the face of a
dark, murky past lit up the entire house, and whose
no-nonsense attitude made her a force of nature.

The woman who was currently unbuttoning that
sea-foam-green waitress uniform and pushing the
fabric off her creamy shoulders and down to her
lush, rounded hips . . .

A drip of cold water from the pipe splashed
down on Dylan's cheek, and he shook it—and the
vibrant images in his mind's eye—off with a gasp.

Wiping his damp cheek on his T-shirt-covered

shoulder, Dylan forced himself to concentrate on the plumbing. Luckily, it turned out to be fairly straight-forward, and in ten minutes, he was tightening the segment of repaired pipe back into place. Shimmy-ing out from under the cabinet, Dylan leaned over the sink to turn on the faucet and test the repair.

"Looking good," Penny said from behind him.

Dylan jolted, suddenly hyper aware of how low his jeans were riding on his hips after crawling around on the floor and wriggling into the tight space under the counter. "Tell me I don't have plumb-er's crack."

"Not that I'd be uncouth enough to mention it if you did," Penny said, laughter sparkling in her voice. "But I meant the pipe."

"Sure you did," Dylan teased. He couldn't stop thinking about the way she reacted every time he flirted with her. Even the gentlest flattery, the most G-rated, Disney-approved joke, brought a pretty pink flush to her cheeks.

He liked seeing it, wanted to see more of it. He wanted to see more of her, in general.

In just about every way, she was the polar op-posite of . . . Dylan cut off the thought before the image of his ex-fiancée could form in his mind.

Monique Gallo had been quick to respond to Dylan's charms, too—but every giggle, every sigh, every moan had been a deliberate move in a game Dylan hadn't known they were playing until it was almost too late.

Penny's responses were so unstudied, no artifice or fakery to them at all. And when she looked at him the way she was looking at him now, hazel eyes lit up with happiness and Cupid's bow mouth quirked into a secret, feminine smile, Dylan knew she meant it.

The knowledge went to Dylan's head like a shot of smoky sweet bourbon. It brought out conflicting urges in him—made him reckless and hungry with the need to push for more, but it also gave him the less familiar urge to protect her, to move slowly and carefully to keep from bruising this tender thing between them.

Caught between desire and restraint, Dylan stood paralyzed as Penny blushed and self-consciously gathered her dark brown hair into a messy knot on top of her head. Pushing up her sleeves, she snagged a plain blue apron from a hook by the stove.

She whipped it over her head and cinched the tie around her trim waist as she moved toward the cabinet to the right of the fridge, her movements quick and a little jittery, as if Dylan's presence sparked her nerves.

That was fair, he considered, since she sparked plenty of strange new reactions in him, too.

The loud clatter as Penny removed the pot she wanted from the bottom of a pile of heavy cast iron and aluminum cookware startled Dylan into realizing he'd been standing like a lump, staring at her silently for the past minute. No wonder she was nervous—he was acting like a looming, lurking weirdo.

Shaking his head at himself, he knelt to pack his new tools back into their super fancy carrying case, a plastic shopping bag with a yellow smiley face and HAVE A GOOD DAY printed on it.

"Oh!"

Penny's sudden exclamation made Dylan look up just in time to see her tripping on the hammer he'd left lying on the floor. She pitched forward and he stood up in a rush to try and catch her, but all he managed was to get his arms around her and turn so that when they hit the ground, he took the brunt of the fall on his back with a solid "Oof."

"Sorry," they both said at the exact same time. Dylan broke off sheepishly, kicking one booted foot at the offending hammer, but Penny laughed. Her soft chuckles vibrated through his chest where they were pressed together, moving her lithe, wriggling warmth just enough to remind him that, hello, a beautiful woman was lying on top of him.

"I'm such a klutz," she groaned, still smiling even though her cheeks were an almost feverish red. "First the iced tea, now this! You're going to be eligible for combat pay *and* hazard pay."

"It's my fault. I shouldn't have made such a mess while I was working."

"Hmm. At least I can get a look at the job you did from down here." She craned her neck slightly, making a show of seriously examining the sink's undercarriage. "Yep, dry as a bone. You do good work, Mr. Workman."

The fake name he'd given her hit him like a slap to the back of the head. Her eyes widened at the pained noise that escaped his throat before he could choke it back.

"Oh my gosh, I must be crushing you! Let me just . . ."

She squirmed deliciously, trying to find her balance, and every muscle in Dylan's body went taut and throbbing with expectation. When Penny got her knees under her, straddling his waist, and moved to prop herself up on her hands, Dylan's arms tightened around her automatically, holding her in place.

"What?" she breathed, staring down at him all pink cheeks and tousled hair. Her mouth was so pink, the bottom lip so delectably plump, it looked as if he'd already kissed her.

Unable to bear it another moment, Dylan reared up to capture that tempting lip between his. He breathed Penny's gasp into his mouth, and Dylan's shocked brain finally caught up to his body. He was still for a frozen moment, the hardness of the linoleum at his back and the soft weight of Penny's body all that kept him tethered in place.

Then she kissed him back. Hesitant, at first, as if she wasn't sure she ought to be doing this, but when he released that succulent lip and opened his mouth to the tentative sweep of her tongue, Penny caught fire.

Clasping his head between her hands, her fingers tightened so that he felt all ten points of pressure, tilting his face to the best possible angle. He groaned deep in his chest at the clean, freshwater taste of her, with a hint of spearmint, as if she'd brushed her teeth before coming back downstairs.

Dylan shifted his hips to cradle her body between his legs, the resultant squeeze and friction good enough to make his eyes cross. The little breaths Penny hitched against his chest dazzled him. He was pretty sure no one had ever breathed so perfectly, with so much unconscious seduction, in the whole history of the world before.

A door closed somewhere in the house, jarring them apart. Penny stared down at Dylan for a long heartbeat, and the way she looked at him cut him off at the knees.

Eyes wide, cheeks flushed, chest heaving—Penny looked stunned, as if she couldn't believe this was happening.

Dylan swallowed, throat clicking loudly in the heated silence between them, and she pushed up off his chest. For a guy who didn't believe in guilt or regret, Dylan found himself taking a dive right into it.

What was he doing, making out with this woman in her kitchen, with her kid right upstairs, and this huge lie between them? This was not a woman to be toyed with and cast aside, Dylan knew.

"Penny," he said hoarsely, "there's something I have to tell you."

The sound of a throat being cleared had them leaping to their feet instead, untangling their arms and legs in a disheveled flurry. Matthew stood in the doorway, angular face dark with anger.

"I knew it," he said, pointing an accusing finger at Dylan, who could only be grateful that the close shave with spilling the truth about his identity had killed his erection.

"Mom, what are you doing with this guy? Tell him to get lost!"

Shooting Dylan an apologetic glance, Penny hurried forward. "Now, honey. I know this is probably weird for you, but Dylan and I . . . it was only a kiss. Not anything for you to worry about."

Matt twitched away from her, sidestepping so he could keep his glare focused on Dylan, who stood there feeling helpless and crappy. "I never meant to cause any trouble here."

"Well, you are, so why don't you fuck off!" Matt shouted.

"Matthew!" Penny looked as if she ached to grab the kid by the scruff of the neck and shake him. "There's no call for that kind of language! Apologize to Mr. Workman, right this minute."

"I'm not apologizing," Matt sneered, though his lips trembled. "And if he's staying, I'm leaving."

He turned to go, and a note of iron entered his mother's voice. "If you walk out of this kitchen right now, you're grounded for the next month. End of discussion. No second chances, Matthew."

Dylan winced, reading Matt's answer to that in the defiant set of his rigid shoulders.

"So what," the kid snarled, eyes unnaturally bright with unshed tears of anger. "You think I care about being grounded? I don't have any friends on this stupid island, anyway. I hate it here. I wish we'd never moved away from Charlottesville. I wish I could go back and live with Dad instead!"

Penny gasped and fell back a step as if her son had planted a hand in the center of her chest and shoved her. Frozen into pale silence, she watched Matt turn on his heel and run from the kitchen. He bounded up the stairs, and the slam of his bedroom door made her flinch as if she'd been slapped awake.

She started after him, but Dylan caught her wrist, heart hammering and guilt churning in his belly. "Let him cool down, and tomorrow . . . I'll talk to him, man to man. It's my fault he's so upset, let me try to fix it."

A sharp tremor ran through her. "It's not your fault, it's mine. I don't know how to deal with him when he's like this. He's so angry, all the time, but if he knew the truth . . ."

Dylan frowned, the phrase tugging at his memory. There was more to the story of why she'd taken her kid and run from her ex, but this wasn't the time to dig deeper. "If I'm going to stay here, even for a few days or weeks to finish off your to-do list, Matt and I need to come to an understanding."

Penny bit her kiss-swollen bottom lip, clearly torn between the need to make sure her son was all right, and the hope that Dylan would be able to get through to him. "Okay, but I apologize in advance for how rude he'll probably be. And Dylan?"

She grabbed his hand and brought it to her mouth, pressing a shaky kiss to his knuckles. He felt it like a brand.

"Thank you," she said.

She wouldn't be thanking him with stars in her eyes if she knew he'd been lying to her since the moment they met, Dylan thought, heart sinking. But maybe getting to the bottom of whatever was troubling Matt would cancel out his deception, or at least balance the scales enough that Dylan would be able to face himself in the mirror.

And even though he knew he didn't deserve Penny's gratitude, he had to admit it felt good to be looked at like that, to feel like he was helping her. The way she made him feel like there was hope for him yet, like he could be a better man—it was addictive.

Even if it was all built on a lie, Dylan wasn't ready to give it up.

Chapter Six

"Heads up, burning hunk of man meat has entered the building."

Penny nearly fumbled the pitcher of ice water she was pouring from. Her friend, Greta Hackley, shielded her lap with the Firefly Café's laminated menu and gave Penny a mischievous look. "Careful, there. I know it's been a while since either of us had access to a man we didn't go to kindergarten with. The fact that he's ridiculously sexy—and dropped a bundle of cash on top-of-the-line tools at my store—as well as mysterious is just a bonus, really. But I'm not so overheated about it that my crotch needs an ice bath."

"Keep your voice down," Penny hissed, using a corner of her apron to mop up the water she'd dribbled onto the table. Without even turning around, she knew who Greta had seen walk through the café door.

She didn't need to turn around . . . but she couldn't quite help herself.

Sure enough, a quick glance over her shoulder showed Dylan at the hostess stand in his dark jeans and white T-shirt, his hard jaw rough with just enough stubble to make him look like he'd rolled out of some lucky woman's bed. His bright blue eyes scanned the restaurant, and Penny tilted her head in the direction of the corner booth where Matt was hunched over a book.

Giving her a nod, Dylan headed toward the back of the restaurant, and Penny sent up a silent prayer that she was doing the right thing.

When she dropped her gaze back to Greta's expectant stare, Penny pressed her lips together. "Don't make a fuss. He's just a man."

A man who was about to have a heart-to-heart with her son.

"Riiiiight." Greta's dark eyes snapped with curiosity. "And a Ferrari is just a car."

Penny leaned her hip on the edge of the booth, lowering her voice. "He drives a motorcycle."

Greta moaned. "You're killing me, here. If you try to tell me Dylan Workman gives you no special feelings in your lady parts, I'll have to call Dr. Fairfax to check you for a pulse."

"He's hot, okay, yes," Penny admitted, frustrated and on edge. "But it's not that simple."

"It could be," Greta said hopefully. "Dylan could be exactly what you need to break your dry spell."

Penny laughed, but it sounded harsh to her own ears. "Dry spell. More like total lockdown. Ever since Trent, the instant I get close to a man, all I can think about is . . ."

She broke off, swallowing back the tinny taste of adrenaline and fear, the instinctive flinch.

"I know, sweetie." Greta's strong-boned face went soft with understanding. "What happened to you was awful, scarring—and I can't imagine how hard it is to trust another man, after that. But Dylan isn't Trent."

"You're such a closet romantic," Penny said, shaking her head. But the comparison helped. Dylan wasn't Trent. For one thing, Trent had never shown much interest in spending time with his own son—and here Dylan was, attempting to mend a fence he wasn't even responsible for breaking.

Dylan was . . . unlike any man she'd ever known, actually.

"Yes, I have a slight romantic streak," Greta hissed, glancing around with alarm. "Don't spread it around, I have a reputation to uphold. My brothers would never let me hear the end of it."

Breathing in a deep, calming breath, Penny said, "Want to hear something romantic? Dylan kissed me last night."

Greta gasped. "Girl! You are docked at least a hundred friend points for not leading with that information. How was it?"

A shiver of remembered passion gripped Penny for a delicious heartbeat. "Wonderful, while it lasted—which is basically the story of our whole potential relationship. I mean, what relationship? He's only here on the island until he finishes the work on the house! I'd be crazy to open myself up to the pain of being left behind."

"Sweetie. I say this with love and understanding, but you are one of the most closed-off people I've ever known. Your life motto is No Second Chances. If this guy makes you want to take a chance and open up, even just long enough to experience a little joy and pleasure?" Greta cocked her head. "You'd be crazy *not* to get with him. Yes, for however long it lasts."

Before Penny could argue or agree—she honestly wasn't sure which—Greta's gaze snagged on something behind them.

Glancing over her shoulder, Penny saw that Dylan had installed himself in the corner booth, across from Matt. A weird pang hit her heart at the sight of their two dark heads leaned close across the table, the expression on Dylan's face as serious and intent as if he were speaking to the president of the United States.

"Maybe I should go over there. Should I?" Penny fretted. "Not that it would help. Matt hasn't said three words to me all day. I had to threaten to withhold his comic book allowance to get him to come with me to the restaurant today, but I wanted to keep an eye on him."

Greta's dark blond brows lifted almost to her hairline. "If you want to keep an eye on him, you better look quick. They're leaving. Together."

"What?"

Penny whirled around in time to catch a final glimpse of Matt preceding Dylan out the back door of the café. The back door led out onto a sea-side patio deck, usually empty during the heat of the summer noon. What on earth was going on?

"I'd better go check on them, make sure Matty's okay," Penny said.

"Not so fast," Greta muttered, jerking her head toward the kitchen where a tall, bald man was glaring balefully at them over a pile of dishes waiting to be served. Chef/owner of the Firefly Café, Alonzo Chappelle was a marshmallow to work for—most of the time.

Rushing up to the pass-through window, Penny apologized profusely as she gathered up the rapidly cooling plates of food. "I'm so sorry, Lonz! I'll straighten these orders out, I promise. And then—can I maybe take my afternoon break? Please! I have to talk to Matty."

Lonz scowled, but waved her away. "Sure, for Matty. Go, go."

Balancing orders for five different tables on her arms, Penny went, as carefully but as quickly as she could.

Her mother senses, which had been tingling for months, were suddenly clamoring like a fire alarm. Something had been up with Matty for a long time, something more than the regular stresses of adolescence, but this felt different.

Her son was in trouble.

But no alarm on the planet could've been warning enough for what Penny saw when she finally squared away her tables and slipped out the back door.

Across the deck, next to the stone wall that separated the patio from the wide, blue ocean, Dylan and Matt faced off like boxers in the ring.

And as she watched, horrified, Dylan drew back one brawny arm and let fly with a punch toward her child's face—and Penny was plunged suddenly into the nightmare she'd left her husband and their entire life behind to avoid.

"Get away from my son."

The low, terrible voice from behind him had Dylan pulling his punch before he meant to, stumbling forward just in time for Matt to prove he'd learned the new block by executing it directly into Dylan's jaw.

Matt's knuckles cracked hard into Dylan's chin, and they both said, "Ow!" simultaneously.

Seeing stars, Dylan shook it off, vaguely aware of Penny brushing roughly past him.

"Mom, look what you made me do!" Matt exclaimed, looking half apologetic and half thrilled at getting a shot in.

"He'll be lucky if that's the worst he gets," Penny snarled, and Dylan gave her a sharp look.

Her cheeks were whiter than the sand on the beach, but her eyes burned with a poisonous green rage that sent a chill through Dylan's blood.

"Wait." Dylan's hands dropped lifelessly to his sides. "Do you honestly think I was about to hit him?"

"I know what I saw." Penny's voice was hard and brittle, like ice cracking over a frozen pond.

Betrayal and fury strung every muscle taut as she faced him down, ranging herself between her child and the man she suddenly perceived as a threat.

Fighting an answering surge of betrayal, Dylan deliberately stepped down and made himself less imposing by sprawling into a nearby café chair. "I guess it looked bad, but Penny, come on. Is that honestly what you think of me?"

Something flickered in her gaze, but before she could reply, Matt spoke up from over her shoulder. "Mom. Come off it. Dylan was just showing me a couple of moves."

"Moves?" Penny's spine was so stiff, he could've used her as a battering ram.

Working his jaw from side to side, Dylan tongued at the sore spot where his teeth cut into his lip. "Yep. He's a natural. But don't expect a block to work like that every time. You usually have to throw a fist on purpose to get a solid hit."

"That's enough." Penny's chest heaved, spots of dark red appearing high on her cheekbones.

Dylan stared. She was still pissed, even though he obviously hadn't been beating up on Matt. "What is your problem?"

Her throat worked. "My problem," she said slowly, "is with you teaching my son violence and aggression. I don't know how you live your life, but my son doesn't need to know how to 'throw a fist' or get a 'solid hit.'"

The palpable disgust in her voice when she echoed Dylan's lesson made him recoil slightly. Feeling attacked, he came back with, "Oh yeah? Maybe you should talk to your son, instead of assuming you know what he needs."

Penny blinked. Over her shoulder, Matt was frantically shaking his head and making "Abort, abort!" gestures. Dylan raised his brows. He wasn't about to get caught in the crossfire on this one.

"What do you mean . . ." Penny twisted to face her son. "What is he talking about? Is there something you want to tell me?"

Wiping all expression save a blank innocence off his face, Matt shrugged. "No, not really."

Oh, kid. Dylan got it, he did. This was a sensitive subject. But Penny needed to know what was going on with her son.

Luckily, this wasn't Penny's first rodeo. Clearly unimpressed with Matt's innocent act, she propped her hands on her hips and stared him down until he squirmed.

"Fine." He rolled his eyes. "I asked Dylan for a few tips on fighting. Just in case."

Hmm. Not exactly the way Dylan remembered the conversation, but okay.

"In case of what?" Penny demanded, her gaze darting suspiciously between her son and her handyman.

Dylan held up his hands. "I think maybe this is my cue to bow out. Seems like this is a family matter, and you probably want privacy."

To his surprise, Penny squeezed her eyes shut in a full-body flinch. "A family matter," she repeated, her voice a thready whisper. "Oh, God. Matty . . ."

Matt's face darkened, his hands clenching. "I've

asked you a billion times to quit calling me by that dumb baby name. It's like you don't even hear me! I hate it!"

I hate you.

He didn't say it, biting his lips closed on the words, but they hung in the sea-swept air like a gull riding the wind.

Visibly shaken, Penny tried to pull herself together. "Don't try to make this about a nickname."

Dylan couldn't stand to watch another second of this train wreck. But instead of beating a retreat back into the diner, he found himself leaning forward in his chair and resting his elbows on the patio table. "But that is what it's about, at least partly."

The kid shot him an agonized look, but Dylan shook his head. "Tell her. Or I will."

"Ugh, fine!" Matt threw himself down to sit on the low stone wall separating the deck from the shore. "Some stuff went down at school, last semester. I got in a couple of fights. Dylan said he could show me how to win, so I took him up on it. End of story."

"No way, that's nowhere near the end of the story." Penny looked as if someone had bashed the back of her head with a rock. "Honey, what were you fighting about? That's not like you!"

Some of the sulk drained out of Matt's expression, leaving a weariness behind that Dylan hated to see in a kid his age. It reminded him too vividly of himself.

"Mom, come on. I have no friends. Everyone at that school thinks I'm a fat loser."

"You're not fat," she said fiercely.

Matt rolled his eyes. "Not anymore, and thank God for growth spurts. But you know what they call me at school? What they've called me ever since we moved here?"

She covered her mouth with the fingers of one hand, as if she knew what was coming.

"Fatty Matty," the kid said, pulling his long legs up onto the wall and wrapping his arms around his knees. "They make fun of me, Mom."

"Why haven't you told me about this before? If someone is bullying you, I'm not going to stand for that, I'll call the principal, we can fix this!"

"And that's why I never said anything," Matt said quietly. "I don't want you to feel like it's your fault, or your problem. It's my problem, Mom, I have to deal with it."

"Not by hitting anyone!"

"What if someone hits him first?" Dylan couldn't help interjecting. "I'm not saying Matt should start fights, but he damn well ought to know how to finish one."

For the first time since Matt's confession, Penny met Dylan's stare. He was stunned by the depth of pain haunting her hazel gaze; in less than two days, he'd gotten used to seeing her eyes bright with laughter.

"The only true way to finish a fight," Penny said quietly, "is to walk away. And never look back. Matt, come with me. Now."

Responding instantly to the steel in his mother's tone, Matt jumped off the stone ledge and hurried after her as she turned on her heel and strode back into the café.

Dylan watched them go, face turned up to the sun and the ocean breeze, and wondered where he went wrong.

Chapter Seven

After that day at the Firefly Café, life at Harrington House settled into a new rhythm. Penny tried to talk with Matt about fighting, and how uncomfortable it made her to see him solving his problems with his fists, but she could tell he didn't really get it.

In fact, Matt spent most of the following two weeks nearly glued to Dylan's side, helping him with the repairs around the house. Penny watched them working together with a pang in her heart. She wasn't sure if she ought to be jealous that her prickly teenager was bonding with another adult, worried about what said adult might be teaching him, or just grateful that Matthew had someone he felt he could open up to.

Oh, who was she kidding? She was a mess of emotions, none of them sensible. But the overriding feeling clutching her heart at the moment was the need to apologize.

It had been two weeks since that searing hot kiss in the kitchen, and since she'd walked away from their argument at the café, but instead of growing more comfortable around each other, the air between them seemed to be getting heavier. As if the unresolved tension between them had its own density and weight, a gravitational pull that kept Penny constantly orbiting around Dylan in a dizzy circle. They needed to clear the air.

She waited until Matt left for his volunteer job at the library, on her one day off per week, before going to confront Dylan. She found him outside at the foot of a ladder, staring up at the fresh coat of navy-blue paint on the wooden shutters flanking the second-floor windows.

"I can't believe how much better the whole house looks!" Penny said, hiding a wince at the false brightness of her tone.

Dylan barely looked at her. "Matt's been a big help," he muttered.

Tension throbbed between them like a pulse. "Thanks for letting him tag along after you," she said quietly, crossing her arms over her chest.

Dylan shrugged. "It's the kind of thing I always wished my dad were still around to do with me, or one of my older brothers. I was an oops baby; my brothers are older. They were both leaving for college the summer our parents died, and they didn't have time to babysit their stupid kid brother."

"It's been good for him. I haven't seen him this happy in a long time."

"You're not afraid I'm warping his fragile young mind and turning him into a crazed, violent thug?"

The hurt below Dylan's sarcasm cut her sharply. "No," she said firmly. "I've been meaning to talk to you about that. I know I . . . overreacted that day. Blaming you. But there are things you don't know, about me, about my past . . ."

"You don't have to tell me." Dylan busied himself with shortening the ladder from its fully extended length, the loud clang of the metal rungs running like a knife cutting through the moment. "None of my business, and in a few more days, you'll get your wish and I'll be gone. No harm, no foul."

Regret tightened her throat. "Dylan, I don't wish you gone."

The skeptical look he leveled at her through the rungs of the ladder, held before him like shield, reminded Penny she'd spent the past two weeks avoiding Dylan as much as possible.

"Sorry," she said awkwardly. "That's all I really wanted to say, anyway. I'm sorry for how distant I've been, when you've been nothing but kind to Matt and me. You deserve better."

An emotion she couldn't name flattened his handsome mouth into a thin line, but the lines around his eyes smoothed enough to let Penny relax.

Until Dylan replied, in the gentlest tone she'd ever heard him use, "No need to apologize for pushing me away. Even if it weren't your default setting, it would still be the smart thing to do with me."

"What?" Penny sputtered, rearing back and nearly tripping into an azalea bush.

"Because I'm leaving soon," Dylan explained, breaking eye contact to heave the folded ladder onto his shoulder.

Penny shook her head, trying to get her heart rate under control. "Not that. What do you mean, pushing people away is my default setting?"

Wrapping her arms around her torso, Penny held her breath against the urge to run away from the ghost of her past that seemed to finally be catching up with her.

Out of the corner of his eye, Dylan watched her brace for his answer as if she were expecting a blow, and his stomach roiled at the confirmation of his worst fears.

Debating how much to say, how hard to push, Dylan trudged down the garden path toward the shed, with Penny shadowing him. "I'm sure you have your reasons," was what he settled on as he nudged open the shed door with one booted foot and deposited the ladder inside.

"My reasons," Penny echoed flatly. All the life and joy had drained from her pretty face, and without it, she looked older. Old enough to have a sixteen-year-old son and a failed marriage behind her. "What do you know about my reasons?"

There was that tinge of bitterness again, the acid

note that only crept into her voice when she was thinking about her ex-husband. Treading carefully, Dylan closed the shed door behind him and leaned against the rough, chipped wood.

"Nothing," he told her. "And you certainly don't have to tell me—but I think you ought to tell someone, because secrets eat you up from the inside out. Trust me on that."

She gave him a weird look, but didn't remark on the fervent tone. "It's not a secret because I'm ashamed of what happened."

Dylan plastered on a supportive smile, even though his knuckles already ached to find her ex-husband and cram his teeth down his throat.

Carefully uncurling his fists, Dylan said honestly, "I can't imagine you ever doing something you'd need to be ashamed of."

With a wry smile, Penny wandered over to sit on the stone bench alongside the garden path. "Oh, I don't know. What about saying 'I do' to a man I didn't love, because my parents couldn't conceive of another option beyond marrying their teenage daughter off to the guy who knocked her up?"

Dylan breathed out through his nose and pressed his hands flat to his thighs. "That sounds more like a regret than something to be ashamed of."

Staring down at her fingers, twining restlessly in her lap, Penny admitted, "I wish I'd been stronger back then, more willing to stand up under pressure. I knew, with every fiber of my being, that marrying Trent was a mistake. But I did it anyway, and I stayed with him until . . ."

She broke off, her whole body freezing into the alert stillness of a prey animal scenting danger.

This was it, Dylan knew. This was the steel at the core of Penny Little's spine, the darkness at the back of her eyes. It seemed oddly incongruous to be having this conversation in a sunlit garden, surrounded by the drone of bees and the heavy perfume of roses. But when Penny tilted her face up, eyes closed and lashes trembling under the warmth of the afternoon sun, Dylan realized this conversation could only happen here.

On Sanctuary Island, in his grandparents' perfect cottage garden, with the bright sun pouring down to chase away the shadows.

Pushing off the shed, he walked closer to her, taking care to move slowly and not spook her. But he needn't have bothered, he realized the moment he reached the bench.

Without opening her eyes, Penny stretched out her fingers to touch the back of his hand. "You know what my grandmother used to say?"

He shook his head mutely, grief for his own departed Gram tugging at his heart.

Her lashes fluttered open, and she stared straight up at him with damp, clear eyes. "A very wise woman, my grandmother. If she'd still been around when I got pregnant with Matt, everything would have been different."

Dylan straddled the bench beside her, facing her head-on and studying every line of her pretty face. "What did your grandmother used to say?"

Penny breathed in deep, then let it go. "She said,

'A man might hit me once . . . but he'll never hit me twice.' "

He'd suspected before this—from her reaction to seeing Matt fight, among other things—but to know beyond a shadow of a doubt. Dylan swallowed down bile. "Your ex-husband," he grated out. "That's why you left him. He hit you."

Giving him her profile, Penny gazed out at the garden. "A man might hit me once, but he'll never hit me twice. Because I won't stick around to give him the chance."

"No second chances," Dylan said, another puzzle piece clicking into place.

"It's a clean way to live." Penny touched her fingertips to the drowsy, bobbing head of a full-blown red rose on the nearest bush. "If you lie, you're a liar. If you cheat, you're a cheater. And if you raise a hand to your wife . . ."

"You're an abusive asshole who ought to be put down like a rabid dog," Dylan snarled.

"No second chances." Penny murmured it like a mantra, and beneath his anger at her jackass ex, Dylan was aware of a yawning chasm of despair opening up in his chest.

All along, in the back of Dylan's mind, he'd taken it for granted that if and when he ever came clean to Penny about who he really was, she'd be okay with it. It wasn't as if he was hiding a wife in the attic or something—he was hiding the fact that he was a billionaire! Who'd be mad about that?

Okay, yes, he was also hiding the fact that up

until he came to Sanctuary Island, he'd been a shallow, directionless playboy who'd done nothing with his life beyond partying and cultivating a bad reputation. But the billionaire thing was bound to be a plus, right?

Except sitting here now, looking at this woman who'd pulled herself out of hell and left it behind without a backward glance, Dylan wasn't so sure.

If you lie, you're a liar . . .

When Penny found out the truth, she was never going to trust him again.

But that was the future. Right here in the present, Penny had trusted him with a terrible piece of her personal history. And Dylan Harrington, who'd never had a conversation with a woman he dated about anything more serious than where to go for drinks after dinner, was damn well going to get this right.

For Penny.

"Thank you for telling me," he said. "I know how much easier it is to shove everything down into the dark, to try and forget about it."

Sympathy washed over her pretty face. "You get it. That's part of what gave me the courage to open up to you. The other part, of course, was to explain that when I walked out of the Firefly and saw you with your hand raised to my child . . ."

"It triggered all these feelings," Dylan realized aloud. "Of course, that makes perfect sense."

"Once memories like these come to the surface, it's hard to sink them deep again," Penny said, fiddling with the hem of her simple sundress. "But I shouldn't have lashed out at you. You were only trying to help Matt. I'm sorry."

The yellow cotton was bright and happy against her lightly tanned skin. When she ducked her head and smiled up at him from beneath her dark lashes, Penny was like a beam of sunlight come to life.

Licking lips gone suddenly dry, Dylan swallowed down the surge of wrongness at Penny being the one to apologize to him. "I shouldn't have assumed you'd be okay with Matt learning to fight. And, geez, I hope I didn't trigger any bad memories for him, too."

"Oh." Penny's smile faded. "About that. Actually, it would be best if you didn't mention this conversation to Matt."

Confused, Dylan cocked his head. "Why?"

"He doesn't know about what happened with Trent. I mean, he's aware on some level that his father wasn't very nice to us, that what time he did spend at home was mostly in front of the game with a beer."

"But you didn't want to tell him his father is an abusive asshole."

"Who ought to be . . . what was it? Put down like a rabid dog?" Faint humor glimmered in Penny's eyes. "No, I don't think it would be good for Matt to hear something like that about his father. It's better if he doesn't know."

"Even though that means he blames you for the divorce."

Penny shrugged, her gaze shifting sideways. "Someday, he'll understand."

Not if he doesn't have all the facts, Dylan thought, but he didn't say it. How could he? When he was every bit as guilty of selective truth telling.

But he couldn't stop thinking about it, all through the afternoon's repairs to the garden path's paver stones, and the easy dinner that followed. Even through the fun of watching Penny and Matt relax enough together to joke around, and the joy of being included in the warm circle of light surrounding this little family, Dylan couldn't stop pondering the reasons behind Penny's refusal to tell her son why she whisked them off to Sanctuary Island to start a new life.

He was still thinking about it hours later, staring up at the ceiling over his bed, when a muffled shout of terror from down the hall tore through the night.

It was Penny.

Chapter Eight

Without conscious thought, Dylan was on his feet and moving silently down the darkened hallway toward Penny's room. Every sense was alert to possible danger, but the only creaking boards he heard were under his own bare feet.

When he reached the door to the bedroom he'd visited just once, to change the light bulb in the tiny closet, he paused to listen.

All he heard were the comfortable sounds of an old house settling. And then, a tiny whimper from inside Penny's room had him pushing open the door and slipping inside.

Dylan scanned the room for anything out of place. But it was the same as in his memory: tidy and pretty, if a little bare of personal touches. Penny considered the room she lived and slept in to belong to the Harringtons.

Still, a woman with Penny's vibrant spirit couldn't

help but leave clues about her personality scattered throughout the room. He'd grinned at the froth of royal purple lace spilling out of a half-open drawer, and ran a furtive palm over the hand-stitched quilt folded at the foot of the queen-sized bed. There was a framed photo of Penny with a younger, chubbier Matthew, faces squished together happily and shot from the improbable angle achieved by Matt holding the camera at arm's length.

Dylan had looked at all of that and recognized traces of Penny in the impersonal, tastefully decorated room—the value she placed on fun, her pride in her family and its history, her hidden sensuality.

Another high-pitched noise from the bed got Dylan moving. Penny made a small lump under the covers, and as he approached the bedside, that lump thrashed against the blankets as if caught in a net.

"Penny," he whispered urgently, his hands hovering. He didn't want to startle her awake to find a man looming over her bed, but he couldn't let her stay trapped in a nightmare, either.

The thrashing continued until Dylan had the bright idea to switch on the small antique Tiffany glass lamp on her bedside table. Amber light flooded the queen-sized bed, picking up the dull gold threads in the patterned duvet cover as Penny finally stilled.

"Wha—?" She pushed the blankets down as if they were suffocating her, breath still coming hard and heavy, and blinked up at him sleepily.

Dylan's blood leapt, then rushed south. Penny may have been having a nightmare, but this situation was entirely too close to one of Dylan's better dreams. The glory of her chestnut hair spilling over the white pillows, the hazy sweep of her lashes and the sleep-warm flush of her skin . . . Dylan swallowed.

"Sorry, you were having a bad dream," he whispered, backing up a step to keep himself from reaching out to her. "I'll go now. Do you want me shut out the light, or leave it on, or—?"

"Dylan," Penny breathed, and she lifted her arms in mute appeal, her hazy eyes filling with tears.

Powerless to resist, Dylan sank down on the edge of the bed and let himself fold her close. She tucked her nose into the side of his neck and breathed damply for a moment, long enough for Dylan to realize with a shock of heat that she was wearing nothing more than a flimsy cotton tank top and a pair of plain white panties.

Which was more than he had on, since he'd hustled out of his room in boxer briefs. He was damn lucky there hadn't been an actual intruder.

Dylan huffed out a laugh, and Penny's arms tightened around his neck for a second before she sat back against her pillows. "Lord. It's been a long time since I had one of those."

Feeling useless and a little bereft without Penny in his arms, Dylan subtly twitched the corner of her blanket over his lap to hide the evidence of exactly how messed up he was.

Penny was in pain, upset and emotional, and here Dylan was—as Matt would say—perving on her. He sucked.

"Bad dream?" he prompted when she fell silent.

She nodded. "About Trent. I used to have this same dream all the time when we first moved here."

"About the day you left?" Dylan held his breath, not sure he wanted the answer, but Penny huffed out a small laugh.

"Actually, no. In the dream, Trent is my boss at the Firefly Café. I drop a tray full of glasses and they shatter all over the floor, and he yells at me in front of everyone on the island, the whole lunch crowd. No one says anything, they all just watch. I know, it doesn't sound that awful . . ."

"No, it does." Dylan could practically smell the fear and shame still radiating off her, the horror of being in Trent's power, and finding no help from the people she trusted. Exactly the nightmare she'd lived through, when her parents forced her to marry a cruel man.

"The dream was a little different this time," Penny said, her hazel eyes shining in the dark. "You were there."

Dylan's heart thumped loudly in his ears. "Did I just sit there and watch, like everyone else?"

"No." There was wonder in her voice, and a soft smile spread her pink lips as she curled her knees under her and leaned toward him. Dylan kept still, afraid any sudden movement would break the spun-sugar tension of the moment. When she was a breath away, she braced her hands on his shoulders and turned him to face her.

"You stood up for me. You told Trent to shut his mouth before you shut it for him. And you helped me clean up the glass."

"I helped you." Everything inside Dylan thrilled toward her, and what she offered him—the chance to be a better man, because Penny believed in him.

She nodded, tugging him closer, and Dylan followed her down to the mattress eagerly. "You could help me more, if you wanted," she murmured, the words soft and hot against his cheek.

"Anything," he promised roughly, entranced by the delicate shape of her shoulder blades beneath his palms as he cradled her.

"Help me forget the past," Penny said, arching up to him in a fluid curve that nearly blew the top of Dylan's head off. "Help me live in this moment, right here, right now."

She was like a flame, in constant searing motion, and Dylan fell into her without hesitation. Taking her lips in a deep, hungry kiss, he filled his head with her scent, her sounds, the feel of her kicking the thin sheets to the foot of the bed and bringing their lower bodies into heartbreakingly perfect alignment.

Two kisses weren't enough to get Dylan used to the idea that he was allowed to touch Penny, to press himself against the lush, welcoming softness of her curvy little body and sink into her.

The fact that she was trembling too made him feel better—he wasn't in this alone, overwhelmed and overloaded. Penny was right there with him, pushing hard into his arms and snuggling her face into the bend of his neck, where she fit perfectly.

There was an astonishing innocence to Penny, despite what she'd been through. She made Dylan remember what it was like to be young and eager, too inexperienced to realize that every woman who hopped into bed with him had visions of dollar signs and diamonds dancing in her head.

"You make me feel like I'm not any older than Matt," Dylan growled, nipping sharp little kisses along the line of her jaw. "Desperate for it, and having a tough time believing I'm about to get it . . . oh no. Matt."

"Don't worry about him. He's a teenager—he could sleep through a volcanic eruption." Penny tilted her chin back, baring her throat in a clear request for more biting, sucking kisses. Dylan was happy to oblige.

"I'll show you a volcanic eruption," Dylan muttered, just to make her laugh. The sight of her, head thrown back and smiling mouth open on a sigh, fed some hunger deep inside just as surely as the greedy clutch of her thighs around his hips fed his physical desire.

But even in the midst of the most passionate, intimate lovemaking Dylan had ever known, even as both of them clung to the present moment and immersed themselves in it and in each other, Dylan felt the future barreling down on him.

Penny had opened herself to him completely. He couldn't keep lying to her.

She'd made him believe he could be a better man. The kind of man who would tell her the truth . . . and once he did, Dylan knew he would lose her.

No second chances.

Chapter Nine

Penny blinked her eyes open with a start of disoriented wonder. Watery morning light filtered through the lace curtains, and she should be shivering under the thin cotton sheet, but instead it was approximately four million degrees in her bed.

A slow, luxurious stretch revealed the culprit behind the humid heat, and the twinge in certain seldom-used muscles.

Dylan Workman. The tall, muscled handyman who had—wow, really lived up to the hype about being good with his hands.

One of those broad-palmed, blunt-fingered hands was still cupped around her hip, as if he hadn't wanted to let go even in sleep, and Penny closed her eyes to enjoy the way her heart fluttered.

With a sharp intake of breath, Dylan stirred awake beside her. "Time's it?"

Penny glanced at the antique silver alarm clock

next to the bed. "Nine fifteen. We should get up, Matt will be awake soon. And I need to get ready for the lunch shift at the Firefly."

Dylan shifted, but only to sling a leg over Penny's bare calves and trap her more thoroughly on the mattress. "Not yet. Plenty of time."

Humming with pleasure, Penny relished the sticky slide of their naked skin, the crispness of Dylan's chest hair and the combined scents of their clean sweat and satisfying lovemaking. "We don't have plenty of time. But I'm not ready to get up yet, either."

A sweet, comfortable silence descended over the room, broken only by the dip and sway of the trees in the light breeze and the bright chirping of birds. Here in the heart of downtown Sanctuary, they were at least half a mile from the beach, but if Penny closed her eyes she pretended she could almost make out the sound of the waves lapping at the shore.

"This island," Dylan said, hushed and almost reverent. "It's not like any place I've ever been— and I've been all over the world."

Penny frowned a little. How did a handyman have money for international travel? But he'd probably backpacked across Europe or ridden that motorcycle of his across Asia or something. "Sanctuary Island is special," she agreed. "I've loved it ever since we moved here. I knew right away that it was the place to make our new start."

"The rest of the world isn't like this." He sounded almost angry, voice harsh and clipped.

"What do you mean?" Penny asked.

"Happy and peaceful all the time." Dylan's hand tightened on her hip.

Forcing herself to relax, Penny breathed deep. "Well, Dylan, I don't know how to break it to you, but not everyone on Sanctuary Island is blissfully happy, every minute of their lives."

He snorted. "Could've fooled me."

Dylan had been consistently bewildered by the friendliness of the townspeople he'd met, from her best friend Greta Hackley offering discounts at the hardware store when she saw how much he was spending on getting Harrington House fixed up, to random people walking their dogs in the park by the town square. It was endearing, if a little sad that he was so unused to basic human kindness.

But Penny had a larger point to make. "You talk a lot about how different we are here on Sanctuary, how much has changed for you since you got here—but Dylan, don't you see? It's the same for us, for Matthew and me. We were okay before, we were fine. But then you showed up, and you changed everything."

She could feel it when his heart picked up speed to slam against his rib cage. The whole bed shuddered with it.

"Penny . . ." His hoarse voice and clutching hands made Penny sit up to get a better look at his face.

All angular jaw and sexy scruff, his sky-blue eyes were piercing even in the soft morning sunlight. He looked lost. Chest clenching, Penny cupped his cheek in her hand and met his gaze with every ounce of calm and certainty she possessed.

"I know you're only here for a job, and that this is temporary—a moment out of your life. But I want you to understand what you mean to us." Pressing her lips together briefly, she amended, "To me. You're the only man in, well, years, who has made me feel brave enough to take a chance on opening up. And last night, you showed me how wonderful it can be to trust another person, with my heart and my body."

Penny wasn't prepared for the shattered look that washed over Dylan's tense face. "Penny," he said helplessly, and she rushed to reassure him.

"No, no—I'm not trying to put pressure on you about staying on the island. I know that's not the deal, and don't worry, you never gave me the wrong idea about that. You know that I don't do this kind of thing all the time, so obviously there's something special about you . . . and I don't want you to leave here without knowing how I truly feel. Because you deserve to know that wherever you're off to next, wherever life takes you, there are people here on Sanctuary Island who love you."

His eyes pinched shut as if she'd slid a steak knife between his ribs, his whole body jerking with the wound, and Penny's heart shriveled in her chest.

"You shouldn't," he said, the words harsh as gravel in a blender.

This wasn't going at all the way she'd imagined.

Dylan was so stoic—not much of a talker, more of a doer. But Penny saw beneath the cocky grin and the hard-clenched jaw. She saw a man with a past like a wound that kept breaking open, never healing right. She saw a man who understood what it meant to be lonely, and she'd wanted to give him something to take with him and keep him warm the next time he found himself all alone in the wide world.

Instead, she seemed to have broken him.

"Listen, Penny," he began, voice hoarse and eyes shadowed.

What was he going to say? Fear momentarily cut off the flow of oxygen to her brain—all she could do was sit there and stare at him, naked in her bed, with her grandmother's quilt pooled around lean hips still imprinted with the shape of her clutching fingers.

The sound of her cell phone blaring out Diana Ross's "The Boss" cut him off. Scrambling for the phone buried under the clothes they'd shed earlier, Penny held it up with an undeniable sense of relief, even as she frowned apologetically.

"Sorry, I have to take this. It's Harrington family business, I'm always supposed to be on call. I wonder what they need."

The tensing of every muscle in Dylan's body was all the more painful after being so recently melted into a puddle of happy goo.

Penny loved him. Or, more accurately, she loved Dylan Workman, the Sanctuary Island version of Dylan—who was nothing like the man he'd been back in New York.

He had to tell her. Now.

Tuning back in to the one side of Penny's call that he could hear, Dylan drummed impatient fingers on his raised knee and waited for her to be done.

"Jessica, hi! No, it's fine, I can talk."

Penny's gaze lifted to his for a moment, her brow furrowing as she listened to Jessica Bell, his brother Logan's assistant. "You are? That's—well, that's great! I'll look forward to finally meeting you in person."

Horror crawled down Dylan's spine. Crap. Jessica was coming here. He was about to be outed as part of the wealthy family who paid Penny's salary.

"Alrighty then," Penny said, determinedly cheerful even though Dylan could read the panic in her white-knuckled grip on the phone. "When should we expect you?"

The words were no sooner out of her mouth than the doorbell chimed its deep, mellow tones through the house.

Dylan's lungs seized. No. This couldn't be happening.

Beside him on the bed, Penny turned around, panicked eyes on Dylan. "Oh," she said faintly. "I see."

The phone fell away from her ear.

"The door," Dylan said through numb lips.

It wasn't a question, but Penny nodded, still shell-shocked. The doorbell chimed again, insistently, and Dylan experienced a moment of intense irrational rage at himself for fixing the damn thing five days ago.

The second bell catapulted Penny into action. She leapt off the bed and into her clothes, hair flying behind her like an unfurling flag. "Get dressed! Where are my socks? Who cares—I don't need socks. I do need a bra, though, oh thank goodness . . ."

Any chance Dylan had to tell Penny the truth was draining away like sands through an hourglass. He stood up and tried to catch her shoulders and make her stand still for a second, but it was like trying to catch a sunbeam. She slipped through his fingers, a constant whirl of frantic motion as she rushed over to the mirror and moaned at the sex-tousled state of her curls.

"Penny, please," he said, hating the desperation so naked in his voice, but unable to cover it up.

She glanced at his reflection in the mirror, jaw working. "Put some clothes on, I'm begging you. Unless you want to meet my boss in your birthday suit."

"I will in a second, Penny, but first just let me—"

The doorbell echoed through the house once more, making Penny squeak and rush for the door. "No time! I promise, we'll talk later! I have to answer the door."

And with that, she was gone, taking with her most of Dylan's hope for a way out of this mess he'd created.

Unless . . .

Jerking his pants up over his thighs and zipping them, Dylan dug through the pockets for his phone. Maybe, he thought crazily as searched, maybe he could text Jessica, explain the situation, get her to promise not to say anything . . .

Except his phone wasn't there.

Dylan cursed fluently while tugging his shirt over his head. He snagged his boots and jammed his feet into them to pound down the stairs toward the last place he remembered having his cell phone, in the kitchen. If he could get to it in time, before Penny opened the door and welcomed Jessica Bell in—but he was too late.

He skidded to a stop at the bottom of the staircase just as the heavy front door swung open. Over Penny's head, Dylan made eye contact with Jessica first—her perfectly manicured auburn brows arched into an infinitesimal lift as she took in his disheveled appearance.

But that wasn't the worst of it.

Behind Jessica stood her boss, Logan Harrington, pale and swaying in a rumpled three-thousand-dollar suit. Before Dylan could do more than plead with his eyes, Logan cocked his head and said roughly, "What the hell is my kid brother doing here?"

Chapter Ten

Penny kept her welcoming smile firmly in place, sure she must have heard wrong. Or Mr. Harrington was making a mistake—reading between the lines of Jessica's unusually tense manner when she'd called, and the gray-faced, wild-haired, lanky man on the front porch, Penny was pretty sure this Mr. Logan Harrington was about a heartbeat away from exhausted collapse.

"Y'all come on in, you must be tired from your trip. Just let me freshen up the master bedroom. Won't take me but a second," Penny said soothingly, darting a commiserating glance at the tall, svelte redhead whose voice Penny recognized from the phone as her liaison with the Harrington family.

Jessica, who'd been frozen on the welcome mat since Mr. Harrington's crazy question, unthawed and moved forward briskly. "Thank you very much, but that won't be necessary. I took the lib-

erty of accessing the house plans, and I saw that
there's a garden cottage behind the house. That
will do perfectly well for Mr. Harrington."

Penny blinked. Accessed the house plans? Who
did that? Well, apparently the perfect assistant did.
Mind racing with the list of tasks she'd need to ac-
complish in order to get the cottage ready for
occupants—Lord, she going to have to call in sick
to the Firefly, there was just no way to be done before her shift—Penny turned to lead the two guests
into the foyer. She stopped dead when she all but
collided with Dylan.

Standing at the foot of the stairs in an unbut-
toned shirt with his jeans sagging low on his hips
and his boots unlaced, Dylan stared at Mr. Harrington with his shoulders squared and his jaw set,
as if he were bracing for a punch.

As she glanced back and forth between the two
men, her heart began to race.

After a couple of weeks of working outside, Dylan's
skin was a healthy, burnished gold, unlike Mr. Harrington's weary pallor. Dylan's hair was cropped
close to his skull while Mr. Harrington's was long
enough to stick up as if he'd been running his fingers through it. But both men had light brown
hair, broad shoulders and muscular arms, although
Mr. Harrington was built along slightly leaner
lines. They both had sharp, angular cheekbones
and jaws.

But what really sent Penny's heart leaping into
her throat was the realization that hidden under
the heavy lids and deep purple shadows wrought

by exhaustion, Mr. Logan Harrington's eyes were the blue of a glorious summer sky.

The exact same shade she'd become so fond of in the last few weeks.

Behind her, Mr. Harrington was still confused and getting cranky about it. "Damn it, is this another intervention? Tink, you're fired. Dylan, go away, I'm fine."

Penny shuddered in a gasp that sounded horribly like a sob, and because she couldn't close her eyes against the train wreck of her own life, she saw the moment when Dylan realized that she knew.

His shoulders went even more rigid, until his entire body was as stiff and defensive as a suit of armor. "I tried to tell you," he grated out harshly, almost sounding as if he were angry at Penny for the way things had gone down.

"You had two weeks to tell me the truth," Penny hissed. "Fourteen days and nights . . ."

"Okay then!" Jessica spun into motion, taking charge of the situation with an effortless ease that Penny could only numbly admire. "First of all, Harrington, you can't fire me because you don't pay my salary. Harrington International, aka your older brother, Miles, does. So here's what's going to happen now."

She herded Dylan and a feebly resisting Penny toward the empty front parlor no one ever sat in. "You two kids clearly need to talk. I'm going to take Mr. Big Mouth out back to the cottage and get him settled in—no, don't worry about towels or clean sheets, a bare mattress would be a step up for Logan at this point, so long as it's horizontal."

"There's nothing worse than a woman who thinks she can manage the entire world," Logan growled, but out of the corner of her eye, Penny noticed that he didn't put up much of a fight when Jessica led him back out the front door and closed it gently behind them.

And then Penny was left alone in the parlor with the man to whom she'd given her body and her heart . . . before she even knew his real name.

"I'm sorry," Dylan said. He wasn't sure what to say to keep from getting swallowed up by the black hole of guilt and regret in his gut, but he definitely owed Penny an apology. Might as well start there.

As expected, it wasn't anywhere near enough. Penny shook her head in disbelief. "You're sorry. You mean, you're sorry your brother showed up here and exposed your lie."

The bitterness in her voice pierced him like broken glass. "No, Penny . . ."

But she wasn't listening. Dropping onto one of the overstuffed chintz love seats, Penny covered her face with trembling hands. "Your *brother,*" she groaned. "Lord almighty. Dylan *Harrington.* I feel like such a fool. You must have laughed yourself sick over how easy I was to seduce. Some silly, gullible waitress to play around with because she doesn't know any better. Are you going to go back to all your rich friends and have a good chuckle over your latest sexual exploits as Dylan Workman?"

"Of course not." Dylan stood in the center of the perfect, fussy little room full of touches that reminded him of his grandmother, and knew without a doubt that Bette Harrington would cry if she knew how the boy she raised had turned out. "It wasn't like that," he tried to say past the thick lump in his throat. "I never wanted to make a fool of you, Penny, I swear. And nothing about you is easy or gullible."

"No?" She raised her face to his, and though he'd braced himself for tears, her eyes were dry, burning with a fierce light. "'Kid brother,' Logan said. That makes you the youngest of the Harrington brothers, the one who refused to take any responsibility for the family company. The playboy. Oh, God—the Bad Boy Billionaire."

It stung to hear his whole life, decisions he'd agonized and suffered over, reduced to a single biting summation, but he couldn't deny it.

When he stayed silent, Penny swallowed and shut her eyes briefly. "Two weeks. That's all it took to make me fall in love—and into bed—with you. Tell me, Mr. Harrington, is that a record for you?"

Every word stabbed him like a knife, but Dylan forced himself to stand there and take it. He deserved whatever Penny dished out, and worse. With her tender, generous heart, there was no way she'd dole out a punishment severe enough to fit the crime.

But still, he had to try to explain. He couldn't let her compare herself to the models and celebutantes he'd casually slept with and discarded ever since he'd called his wedding off three years ago.

"Honestly," he told her, "no. Two weeks is an eternity for me to stay focused on one woman."

She winced, laughing thinly. "Great, so I guess I should be flattered. What was it that made me so special? Was I a novelty to you, Dylan? A single, working-class mom, someone so far beneath you it made me exotic?" She shook her head with a sad smile. "There I go flattering myself again. I'm sure you sleep with all the help, don't you?"

"Of course not," he said firmly. "And you're not 'the help,' Penny. You're the most amazing woman I've ever met. You're strong and warm and kind. You're an amazing mother. You're beautiful inside and out, and I don't think you even realize it. If you believe nothing else I ever tell you—and I wouldn't blame you for that—at least listen and believe this. What happened between us was real. I didn't tell you everything about myself, but what I did tell you was true. And I never lied about what I felt for you, or about how much I wanted you."

After a long moment of silence, during which Dylan imagined every possible response ranging from Penny falling into his arms to ordering him out of the house, she said quietly, "I think you can see how I'd find it difficult to put my trust in that."

At least she was listening. Pressing his advantage, Dylan sat down on the love seat with her, careful of the nearly visible wall of empty space she'd erected around herself. "I get that, and I'm not making any excuses. It was a stupid, childish stunt . . ." He paused, hearing himself, then shook his head. "Which, if you ask my oldest brother, Miles, is a fair characterization of my entire life."

"Miles Harrington. The head of Harrington International," Penny said, as if she were still trying to get all the players in this awful farce straight in her head.

"That's right."

"He—and that man out in the summer cottage—those are the brothers who went off to college and left you to deal with your parents' deaths alone? So Logan is the workaholic loner, and Miles is the controlling robot."

Startled that she remembered what he'd said about his brothers that first night, Dylan shook his head. "No. I mean, yeah, they weren't around much, but I wasn't completely alone. I had my grandparents, who were great. Although, like I mentioned before—I wasn't the easiest kid to raise."

She changed tack. "And when you said you spent years drifting through life aimlessly until you finally got a job—you meant until you decided on a whim to impersonate a handyman to fix up your own family's property."

Against his will, Dylan stiffened. "Yep. I ditched college and turned down every one of Miles's offers to come work for the family company, thereby breaking his heart—or whatever piece of well-oiled machinery he uses in place of a heart. You're now part of a very elite club, Penny Little: the Society of People Who Expected Better from Dylan Harrington and Were Disappointed."

"Stop that," she said sharply, getting to her feet and hugging her arms tightly around her rib cage. "You don't get to make me feel sorry for you. This is hard enough already."

Dylan blinked. "I wasn't trying to—but okay. Fine. Look, Penny, I'll make this right however you want. Just tell me what to do, and I'll do it."

Lifting her chin, a challenge glinted in Penny's hazel eyes. "I have to go to my shift at the café now. I want you out of this house before I get home. And if you ever come back to Sanctuary Island, I swear I'll quit this job, because I never want to see you again."

Chapter Eleven

"What are you doing?"

The tense young voice jolted Dylan from his mechanical stuffing of dirty work clothes into his duffel bag.

Matt stood in the doorway of the guest room, arms crossed tightly over his wiry chest and looking so much like his mother that Dylan went light-headed for a humiliating instant.

He turned back to his packing and hoped Matt didn't notice the way his hands shook. "I'm leaving."

"Why?"

Dylan pinched his eyes shut, hanging his head over the bag sitting on his bed. "No one told you."

"That your name is Dylan Harrington and you're related to the people who pay us to live in this house? Yeah, I know all that. I heard everything that went on downstairs." Matt marched into the room and grabbed Dylan's shoulder, jerking him around until they were face-to-face.

"What I don't know," Matt continued, thrusting his chin out pugnaciously, "is why you're running out on us like . . . like a coward."

The kid was trembling with the force of emotions too strong for someone so young to have to handle, and it hurt Dylan to see it. "Matthew. I lied to you and your mother. She doesn't want me around anymore, and you can't blame her."

Matt made a frustrated noise, his dark blond brows like thunder. "I *don't* blame her. I blame you, for not getting it."

It was as if his rib cage had grown rows of lethally sharp spikes. Every breath hurt. "She told me she never wants to see me again. She was very clear. One strike and I'm out. What, Matt? Tell me what I'm missing."

Sending him a pitying look, Matt shook his head. "It's totally obvious. Don't you see it? Everyone leaves. She doesn't want you to go. So she's testing you, to see if you'll fight to stay. And you're about to flunk, man."

With that, Matt stalked out of the room and down the hall to slam his own door shut, leaving Dylan alone and staggering with his thoughts.

What if Matt was right? What if Dylan hadn't completely blown all his chances with Penny—but was about to, by skulking off the island with his tail tucked between his legs?

The rough terrain of Dylan's heart was too rocky

to support a tendril of hope, but even in the midst of his overwhelming certainty that Penny would never deviate from her No Second Chances policy to forgive him, there was still a spark of desire to make sure she understood why he'd lied. But was that an entirely selfish impulse to salve his conscience, and nothing more?

He needed a ruling on this. Staring down at his hands wringing the thin cotton of the white T-shirt that still sported a faint brown iced tea stain from that very first day, Dylan set his jaw.

His brothers were never there for him when he was a kid. Logan could damn well offer up some advice now.

He strode down the path whose creamy smooth paving stones he'd placed himself, and rapped on the door of the cottage at the back of the garden. Within seconds, Jessica Bell appeared on the front porch, with a forbidding expression on her perfectly made-up face.

"Keep it down! If you wake him up—"

From inside the cottage, a ragged voice rumbled. "Who's at the door, Tink?"

Without taking her accusing glare off of Dylan's face, she called, "I'm handling it. Go back to sleep."

Dylan let himself into the screened-in porch, since Jessica was just standing there scowling at him. "Tink, huh?"

It was only meant to be something to say, a quick tease to get her to smile instead of frown, but instead, she blushed. Fascinated, Dylan tracked the progress of the red flush through her pearly redhead's complexion.

"That's Jessica to you," she said severely. "Miss Bell if you're nasty."

"What does Tink even mean?" Dylan had to ask.

"Tink. Tinker<u>bell</u>? Hi, nice to meet you, I'm Jessica Bell, personal assistant to the modern incarnation of Peter Pan." Rolling her eyes, she sauntered over to fold her long limbs onto the floral-patterned glider. "Never mind. You're here for romantic advice, right? I'll be better at that than your brother, anyway. Once I get over laughing myself sick at the idea of a Harrington doing manual labor."

Taken aback for a moment at how quickly Jessica seemed to have put the pieces together, Dylan decided beggars couldn't be choosers. Jessica wasn't family, but she knew the Harringtons better than most—her advice would have to do.

The whole story poured out of him as he paced the cozy confines of the little porch whose screens he'd patched himself. In the garden, bees meandered from hydrangea to rosebush, and the summer heat was like a humid blanket over the world.

He finished with, "So what do I do? Should I leave, like she asked? Or should I stay?"

Jessica gave a thoughtful look, but before she could answer, a rough voice came from the doorway into the cottage. "As the immortal philosopher collective, The Clash, noted: if you stay, there will be trouble. But if you go, it will be doubled."

Popping off the couch like a jack-in-the-box,

Jessica waved her arms at Logan as if he were a bird who'd flown into the house. "Go back to bed! Do I have to tie you down to get you to stay put?"

The scorching heat that entered his brother's eyes at that made Dylan wonder if Logan had finally found something to distract him from his lab work. But instead of diving through the perfect opening she'd left him, Logan leaned one wiry forearm on the wall of the house and addressed Dylan.

"Sorry if I messed up whatever scam you were running on the hot diner waitress."

Dylan was on his feet, fists clenched, without making a conscious choice to stand. "Don't talk about her like that. And it wasn't a scam, okay?"

Satisfaction stretched Logan's wide mouth into a wry smile. "Okay. But I'm not the one you need to convince."

Slumping, Dylan kicked at the leg of the glider to make the thing swing back and forth. It squeaked. He should fix that—except now he might not get the chance to fix anything else around here. "I told her already. I mean, I apologized."

"Did you *explain*?" Jessica asked. "Or did you give her the patented Harrington puppy eyes and expect her to fall all over herself to forgive you?"

Dylan ground his teeth. "I don't expect forgiveness," he gritted out.

Jessica, who was an expert at reading between the lines of the taciturn Harrington men, blew out a rude raspberry. "Psh, and you won't get it, either, if you don't even try to tell her why you lied to her."

"But I . . ." Dylan broke off, his head swimming. "I don't know what to say to her."

"Yes, you do." Jessica cocked her head, considering. "She opened herself up to you, stripped herself bare, but you were hiding behind a fake identity the whole time. Now it's your turn. Lay it all out for her, and hope she likes what she sees."

"That's the problem," Dylan croaked, his throat achingly tight. "I kind of hate Dylan Harrington, Bad Boy Billionaire. How can I expect someone like Penny to fall for him?"

"You're more than the Bad Boy Billionaire," Logan said suddenly. Dylan glanced over to find his brother watching him with the kind of laser intensity he usually reserved for his gadgets, eyes burning in his rough-jawed, angular face. "You know that, don't you?"

Bitterness soured the back of Dylan's tongue. "Right, I'm a Harrington. Spare me the lecture on what that entails, I've already heard it from Miles."

"No." Logan made an impatient slashing gesture with one long-fingered hand. "I meant that you're smarter than you give yourself credit for, and a harder worker. And of the three of us, you were always the one who charmed people, who made friends the easiest."

"Because I have money."

"Because you're a good person," Logan snapped. "You're fun to be around, you care about people, you aren't afraid to show your emotions—cripes, you're like the hero of one of those racy books

Jessica thinks I don't know she reads. But most of all . . . you're my brother."

Dylan's palms felt sweaty as he took a step toward Logan. "I haven't felt like any of those things in a long time."

Pain tightened the lines at the corners of Logan's eyes, but his smile was fierce, a challenge. "Well then. I think it's about time you reclaimed your birthright, don't you?"

Hope and gratitude expanded Dylan's chest like helium blowing up a balloon. He glanced over at Jessica, who arched a brow and said, "What are you waiting for? Go strip naked for Penny Little. Show her what you got. I have it on good authority that Harrington men are pretty damn near irresistible, when they put their minds to it."

Chapter Twelve

The ding of the bell over the diner's door shattered Penny's concentration. She nearly dropped her tray.

Shooting her an alarmed look through the pass, Alonzo Chappelle wiped his hands on his white chef's jacket. "You have been all over the place today. Do you need a break?"

"No," Penny said sharply, wincing when her boss stared at her. "I'm sorry. I'll get it together, I promise. I need the tips."

I need the distraction.

Lonz nodded and went back to slinging hash, too backed up with orders to keep worrying about his wait staff.

Balancing the tray carefully, Penny smiled at the man who'd ordered the steak and eggs. Grady Wilkes was the big, rough, silent type—a bit of a loner, but a talented carpenter. And there was a kindness in those eyes, the deep green of the maritime forest where he'd built his cabin, that made Penny wish suddenly and fiercely that she'd had the sense to fall for the local handyman instead of an imposter from Manhattan.

A tremor in the air made her pause, as if the very molecules she breathed in carried messages her heart could read. With a sense of inevitability, she turned to see Dylan Harrington standing at her shoulder.

Undeniably, the first emotion that rushed through her was a terrifying thrill of joy—but it was followed closely by a comforting rush of rage. Tamping down the part of herself that wanted to drink in the sight of him in his hip-hugging jeans and battered black motorcycle jacket, Penny set her jaw. "So much for doing whatever I want. But then, you've never been very interested in what would make me happy, have you?"

A muscle ticked in his temple, his eyes going dark, but he nodded. "I deserved that. And if you still want me to go after I've explained, I will. But please let me at least try to make you understand why I lied to you."

Penny hesitated, heart beating faster than a hummingbird's wings. *No second chances,* she reminded herself. "It won't make any difference, but if it'll get you out of here without a scene, go ahead."

Brows lifting, Dylan tucked his hands in his back pockets as he glanced around the nearly full diner. Most of the patrons were staring back at him, with varying levels of avid curiosity. This was basically the most interesting thing ever to happen during the lunch rush.

"Oh." Dylan cleared his throat. "Do you have a break coming up? We could go out to the deck."

The deck, where he'd proven how well he understood her son, and offered to help him. But that memory threatened the foundations of the anger that was keeping her going, so she shook it off.

Propping her tray on her hip, Penny stood her ground. "Nope. We're doing this right here. These people are my friends, my family. Anything you have to say, you can say to me in front of them."

Deep inside, a sad voice whispered, *There. Now you've done it, you've pushed him far enough. He'll leave and you'll be safe again.*

But Dylan didn't leave. Instead, he planted his feet and tilted his chin down decisively, hardening his jaw until he looked like a stone monument to courage. All conversation in the diner had ceased by that point, every eye in the place trained on the confrontation between the stranger they'd befriended and their favorite waitress.

Penny waited, her breath caught somewhere between her lungs and her throat.

"I lied to you," Dylan said again, not shying away from the reality of what he'd done. "But I never meant to hurt you. Which I know isn't the same thing as having your best interests at heart—as you pointed out, from the beginning, I've been more concerned with what was best for me. What I wanted. And what I wanted, more than anything, was to see where things went between us, if you had no idea that I've got money."

Sucking in a breath, Penny felt her cheeks go hot. "Look, just because I work two jobs and have to scrimp to keep my kid's college fund going—that doesn't automatically make me a gold digger!"

Eyes widening, Dylan lifted a hand. "No, that's not what I meant. When I first met you, I didn't know anything about you other than how gorgeous you are, and how hot and fun the sparks between us were."

Great, now Penny's blush was never going to fade away. She was permanently pink in the face.

"What I didn't understand," Dylan continued doggedly, "is that Sanctuary Island is nothing like the rest of the world. Where I come from, anyone who hears my name immediately looks at me differently. They care more about my bank account, my pointless tabloid fame, my connections—than they do about me. But I should have known that Sanctuary Island isn't like that. Whatever magic you people have here, it makes everyone more real, more open. I should have trusted that. But I couldn't, at first."

Penny didn't want to be moved, but she was. Maybe Dylan's name wasn't what she'd thought, but he still looked and talked like the man she'd fallen for. It was more than a little confusing.

Taking a deep, visible breath, Dylan laid it all out. "I couldn't trust that I would be enough, just me, without the money, because three years ago, I found out that the woman I loved and wanted to spend the rest of my life with—all she wanted was a rich husband. You know I have a . . . difficult relationship with my oldest brother. Part of it, I already told you about, but the rest . . ."

He paused, visibly steeling himself. "He got me to listen in on a phone call with Monique, to discuss the pre-nup I'd argued she didn't need to sign. When he pressured her, she immediately asked how much he'd be willing to pay to make her go away. She never really wanted to marry me at all, you see. All she wanted was cash."

Penny swallowed. The lines on his face, the rigid way he held himself—she could see how much it cost him to share this awful piece of his past. And it explained so much about him. She could feel herself weakening, the walls she'd built crumbling like sand, and it scared her.

"I don't care how much money you have," she said, frantically shoring up her defenses against the vulnerability in Dylan's strong face. She lifted her chin. "There's a name for people who lie down for money and nothing else, and it's not gold digger. But I'm not sure I can forgive you for not seeing that I would never be that person. Not at first, maybe, but after everything we shared . . ." Her throat closed, and she stopped talking.

He flinched a little, and she tightened her fingers around the tray until the plastic edge cut into her palm.

"I get that," Dylan said, straightening his shoulders. "And I understand your stance on second chances, but that's exactly what I'm asking for. A chance to spend time with you, with no lies between us, no secrets."

Fear and temptation shuddered through her, all her limbs weighed down with the paralysis of wanting to simultaneously fling herself into his arms and push him away. In fact, she'd stopped paying attention to her tray, which abruptly tilted far enough for the last remaining plate to slide off it and shatter on the café floor.

China cracked and grits splattered everywhere. For a breathless instant, Penny flinched in horror, the old familiar nightmare rushing over her.

But no loud, angry voice shouted from the kitchen. Trent wasn't here; he couldn't ever hurt her again. And when she started to stammer an apology to Grady Wilkes, whose jeans leg was now speckled with sticky globs of white, he didn't look at her coldly and impassively like the faceless café patrons in her dream. He leaned in and said kindly, "You're fine, no harm done. Look, your friend there has it almost all cleaned up already."

Penny whirled to see Dylan on one knee beside the mess, carefully collecting the sharp pieces of broken plate.

He looked up at her, the strength in every line of his body at odds with the humble pose. And when he said, "Don't push me away," there was no plea in his tone—it was all firm, gentle understanding.

"You have every reason to be cautious," Dylan said quietly. "But there's a fine line between protecting yourself and Matt, and hiding from life."

Lord, he was right. No second chances—she wasn't

only denying Dylan if she stuck to her policy. She'd be denying herself, and her son, the possibility of a future with this handsome, flawed, deeply loving man.

"Maybe I'm not the man you should take that next step with." Dylan's shoulders slumped. "You make me want to work hard to be better, for you and Matt. But I'm not there yet. At least I know better than to try and woo you with fancy cars or luxury homes, dinners out at gourmet restaurants and jewels for every finger . . . and crap, is that terrifying. Because without that, what's left? What do I have to offer?"

Penny's heart cracked down the middle at the honest desperation and confusion in Dylan's ragged voice. The fact that he truly didn't know if she'd be able to love the man underneath the money battered down the last of the walls around her heart.

"You dummy," she said, getting a good grip on the collar of his leather jacket and hauling him to his feet. He dropped the pieces of plate he'd gathered. "Don't you get it? What's left is all that matters."

She stepped forward, slipping on a smear of spilled grits and swooning into the arms Dylan opened automatically to catch her. Wrapping her own arms around his shaking back, she held on for dear life. "If you offer me your heart and nothing else, I'll take it. And consider myself the richest woman alive."

The entire Firefly Café erupted in applause and cheers, with a few cheerful wolf whistles thrown in for good measure. It was like fireworks going off all around them as Dylan dropped his forehead to rest against hers.

"Penny," he whispered brokenly. "You and Matt welcomed me into your family when you thought I was a penniless handyman. Is there a place there for a reformed Bad Boy Billionaire?"

Worry speared through her. "Oh, Matt. I told him you lied to us, that you were leaving—we need to call him . . ."

"No, we don't." Dylan pulled her closer, locking them together. "Matt knows exactly where I am. He's the one who convinced me to stay and fight for you."

"He knows about us?" Penny groaned, hiding her smile against Dylan's shoulder. "That's a little embarrassing."

"Why? The kid's smart, he gets people. He sees things other people don't," Dylan said, pride touching his voice with warmth. He nudged a hand under her chin and tipped her face up to his. "For instance, Matt could see how much I love you. And in spite of what I'd done, he saw that if I left without telling you, I'd regret it for the rest of my life."

"Remind me to thank him." Penny stood on her tiptoes to brush her lips over Dylan's.

A second round of applause and catcalls, boots stomping on the floor and silverware clanging on the tables reminded Penny suddenly that they were still standing in the middle of the café.

Grinning wide enough to split her cheeks, she

pulled away and called in the direction of the kitchen, "I think I'll take that break now!"

"Go on, get out of here," Lonz yelled back, laughing.

Dylan and Penny tumbled out of the café and onto the sun-warmed deck, unwilling to let go of each other. The ocean breeze and the sound of the waves, the screeching gulls and the far-off blast of the ferry's horn were a symphony of all the things Penny loved about island life.

And when Dylan tugged her to his chest and covered her mouth with his, she added a new love to the list.

When they came up for air, she gasped and shuddered with the excess of happiness flowing through her blood. "In case you haven't figured it out yet, I love you, too, Dylan. No matter what your name is or what your family is like—I love the essential Dylan, the man who fixed my kitchen sink and told me about his childhood and taught my son about self-defense. I love you."

Sinking down to sit on the stone wall at the edge of the deck, Dylan clenched his big hands at her hips and drew her close to stand between his denim-clad thighs. Resting his forehead against her collarbone, he said, "I don't deserve you."

"There's your mistake," Penny said fondly, running her fingers through the soft bristles of his buzzed hair. "Thinking you get to decide what we deserve. Silly man. But don't worry, Matt and I will help you learn to believe."

"This love thing is pretty new to me. And I was always a crappy student." He mouthed at the tender skin of her neck. "It might take a while for the lesson to sink in."

Joy lit Penny up from within. "That's okay. We have a lifetime."

The Summer Cottage

his head on his hands. "I hate it when you call me 'sir.' "

Which, of course, was why Jessica did it. To remind them both that their relationship might be full of banter that skirted the edge of unprofessionalism, but at the end of the day, Logan could never be more to her than that.

Logan Harrington was her job. Nothing more. And, certainly, nothing less—Jessica took her job extremely seriously.

Hell, at this point, she could write the definitive manual on the care and feeding of brooding billionaire geniuses.

Burrowing his long, agile fingers into his tousled brown hair, Logan tipped back in the chair and blew out a sigh at the ceiling. It was completely unfair, Jessica reflected. As the person whose job it was to bully Logan into sleeping and eating like a normal human being, she knew for a fact he hadn't slept more than three hours at a time in months. Ever since he started the new clean energy project, Logan's idea of a well-balanced meal was a stale pot of coffee with a vodka chaser.

By all rights, he should be gaunt and pale, with bags under his eyes and stubble on his cheeks. Instead, with his broad shoulders, powerful physique, and expensive haircut, Logan Harrington looked more like a male model than a mad scientist.

"Why did you bring me here?" he said, all mischief and humor drained from his tone, leaving behind nothing but wire-taut exhaustion. "I have work I need to be doing. The lab . . ."

"The lab will not fall apart without you," Jessica said briskly, moving to the sink to take stock of the cottage's kitchen amenities. "They'll call me if they run up against anything they can't handle, but you left them a nearly finished project. If your techs can't take your copious notes and run them into the end zone, we seriously need to start a headhunt for better techs."

There was no dish towel hanging by the sink, nor were there paper towels on the counter. Jessica hitched up her tailored linen slacks and crouched to investigate the cabinet under the sink for supplies.

The incident at the board meeting the day before had shoved Jessica into High Alert mode, and she'd hustled Logan out of town before he was recovered enough to put up a fight. So they'd arrived at his grandparents' vacation home unexpectedly, giving the caretaker no time to prepare the summer cottage for guests.

But it turned out that Logan's younger brother, Dylan, was already staying up at the main house, and knowing Logan's love of privacy, Jessica was determined to make the cottage work.

Jessica stood and opened the quaint, vintage refrigerator in the corner of the kitchenette. As she'd suspected, it was completely bare.

"End zone." Logan perked up. "A football reference. You like football? You grew up with older brothers, or maybe you were close to your father . . ."

Before he could spin one of his elaborate imaginary histories for her, Jessica cut him off. "It's only an expression. I could just as easily have said 'hit it out of the park' or 'ride the wave.' "

Logan scowled. "Doesn't it ever bother you that you know every intimate detail of my life, while I know nothing but your basics?"

"No." In fact, that was the way Jessica liked it.

"Anyway, that's not the point," Logan grumped, setting his clenched fists on the table. "Project Reactor might be done, but there's always more. If I'm not there to direct the lab, who will—"

"The work will still be there when we get back, after you rest. It's time for a break." Jessica kept her voice firm. Logan would attack any sign of weakness. "This island is perfect for that. Look at it rationally. If you run yourself into the ground, the quality of your work will suffer. You need to refill the well."

"I don't buy into those studies," Logan snapped. "And I certainly don't need to refill some mythical, metaphorical well. You're my assistant. You take orders from me, and I'm ordering you to get on the phone and call the company plane to come pick us up. Now."

Pushing back from the table with a screech of wooden chair legs on linoleum, Logan made to stand up, but Jessica stopped him with a hand on his shoulder. "Logan, be reasonable. There's no place to land a plane on an island as small as Sanctuary."

"The chopper, then." Impatience crackled around Logan like a force field.

"I'm not calling the helicopter!"

"That's it," Logan snarled. "You're fired."

Jessica gritted her teeth. "For the millionth time, you can't fire me. I work for your brother—I take my orders from him. It's my job to take care of you. Let me do my job."

"Your job is supposed to be making my life easier, not dragging me off to some backwater island with no decent Internet access or cell service," he complained.

His shoulder was rock hard with tension under her light touch. Blowing out a breath, Jessica played her trump card. "Logan. You collapsed in the middle of a presentation to the entire board of Harrington International. You are going to take the time you need to get healthy. Period. If I have to sit on you to make you slow down for a while, I will."

A glimmer of interest lit Logan's intense blue eyes. "I could be into that."

She ignored him and continued, "I don't ask for much from you. But I'm asking now. Please, give Sanctuary Island a chance."

He glanced aside, jaw working, and Jessica's heart quickened. He was close to giving in, she could feel it.

But when he met her eyes once more, head canted to one side in sudden calculating consideration, her blood froze. She knew that look.

Logan Harrington had one of his genius ideas.

"How much is it worth to you?" he asked. "Me here on this island, soaking in all the mind-numbing serenity and wasting days of my life when I could be working. What would you be willing to give me in return for my time?"

The rush of heat to her core was as shocking and confusing as it was unwanted. Jessica dropped her hand from Logan's shoulder and backed up a step.

Anger mixed with disappointment curdled in her stomach. As much as Logan flirted, as many times as he'd come on to her, she never thought he would stoop to emotional blackmail.

"I'm not going to sleep with you to get you to do what's right for your own health," she snapped.

Genuine surprise flashed across his expressive face. "What? No, Tink, that's not what I meant."

Jessica stared into his wide eyes and felt her anger dissolve. She believed him. And that nickname—Tink, a play on her last name, Bell, and the fact that Logan considered her fine-boned features pixie-like—gave her the usual, undeniable thrill.

She hid how much she liked the nickname with the ease of long practice. "What did you mean, then?"

Arching a brow, Logan warned, "You might not be any happier about this. But here are my terms: for every day I waste on this island, you answer one personal question."

Jessica sucked in a breath, an instinctive denial on the tip of her tongue. Before she could say anything, Logan held up a hand. "I'm talking full and complete answers, to my standard of satisfaction—no simple yes or no. I want details, specificity."

What Logan was asking was dangerous—to her mental health, if nothing else. Jessica knew him. He wasn't going to be satisfied with inane questions about her favorite color. If she gave her insatiably curious, demanding boss this opening, he'd make the most of it. He wouldn't be happy until he knew all the secrets she'd worked so hard to bury.

But . . . Logan needed this. He needed to rest, and he also needed a puzzle to solve, something to keep his brain just stimulated enough without overloading his system.

"So. What do you say?" He crossed his arms over his chest, drawing her gaze to the play of muscles under his T-shirt. For a guy who rarely took time off to hit the gym, Logan was ridiculously ripped. Must be all the heavy machinery he lifted in his lab, building his prototypes.

Tilting up her chin, Jessica planted her feet and mirrored his stance. "One question per day—and in that day, you eat what I tell you to, sleep when I tell you to, and in all other ways follow my instructions to rebuild your strength, or that day's question is revoked."

Those wickedly arched brows quirked up, and she knew she'd surprised him. Good. She was surprising herself, too. But this was a chance she had to take. If she could get him to listen to her, the way he rarely did back in New York . . . if she could get him to let her in enough to help him . . .

"You're actually agreeing," he said, wonder lightening his voice.

"I promised your brother I'd take care of this situation." *Take care of you,* Jessica added silently. "You know me. I do whatever it takes to get the job done. Sir."

His reflexive frown at the honorific lifted Jessica's sprits. She could do this. She could bare a bit of her soul and her past to keep Logan on the island long enough to heal, without forgetting the essential truth.

Logan Harrington was her job. Nothing more, nothing less. And if anyone knew the dangers of mixing business and pleasure, it was Jessica Bell.

Chapter Two

When Logan agreed to Jessica's terms, he hadn't counted on his old pal, insomnia, showing up to make it impossible to keep his word about sleeping on command.

But here he was, staring up at the sloping ceiling above the loft bed, eyes dry and burning and sleep nowhere on the horizon. The silence of the empty cottage pressed in on him like a weight. And his preferred methods for shutting off his brain long enough to get to sleep—sex and alcohol—were unavailable for the moment.

Frustration at his inability to conquer his own body, to simply give in and let sleep knock him unconscious, seethed through his veins like an unscratchable itch. To distract himself, he considered the most enticing dilemma he'd faced in quite some time.

What question should he ask of the elusive, mysterious, impenetrably professional Jessica Bell?

He considered what he knew of her already. Over the years since she first appeared in his lab and laughed at him when he ordered her to stop tidying and get out, Logan had discovered shockingly little about what made his personal assistant tick—other than her dedication to efficiency and competence.

In fact, he barely knew more than he'd gleaned from hacking into the Human Resources department's secure servers and reading her résumé.

Jessica Anne Bell, twenty-eight years old, bachelor's degree in communications from Illinois State, previous work experience as the personal assistant to the CEO of a chain of luxury boutique hotels.

Then there were the details he'd observed over time: long naturally red hair with a slight wave to it, green eyes in a fair-skinned, oval face. High, clear forehead, straight nose, pink mouth shaped for smiling. His gaze frequently caught on her pert chin with the tiny indentation in the center—a genetic trait inherited from one or both of her parents.

Which was the sum total of what he knew about her family. He didn't even know where she'd grown up—her deliberate, thoughtful speech patterns contained no discernible accent.

Jessica didn't cake on the makeup like some women Logan knew, but she wasn't a bare-faced natural girl, either. She favored classic, sophisticated fashion, preferring to fill her wardrobe with little black dresses and well-fitted pantsuits in jewel tones rather than chasing the latest trend, and since she was tall and slender as a model, everything looked good on her.

It was possible Logan had devoted quite a bit of time to gathering information on his assistant.

Only because she's a mystery, he consoled himself as he laced his fingers together behind his head. *She's the one puzzle I haven't been able to solve. And once I get the answers to some burning questions, I'll never be distracted by her again.*

Downstairs, the cottage door swung open, letting in the scent of roses on the warm evening breeze. Jessica was back from her exploration of the island, and from the rustle of plastic bags, Logan surmised she'd also stopped in to whatever quaint general store this island boasted, to secure provisions.

He tracked her progress from the cottage door, across the bare hardwood floor of the miniscule living room to set the grocery bags down on the kitchenette's tiny table. She spent some time unloading whatever she'd bought, cupboards opening and closing, the refrigerator making a soft whir as it clicked on. It was oddly relaxing. Logan felt his muscles soften against the mattress as some unnamed tension flowed out of him.

Until he heard the light click of Jessica's heels on the stepladder leading up to the loft above the living room, where Logan was supposed to be sleeping.

Before her head cleared the top of the ladder, he'd turned onto his side and shut his eyes, evening out his breathing into a slow, deep rhythm. Jessica paused for long enough to get Logan's heart pounding with the possibility that she'd call him out for faking it and refuse to answer a question later.

But finally, he heard the soft tread of her retreat down the stepladder, followed by the quiet snick of the downstairs bedroom door closing. Excellent, he'd fooled her. Smiling to himself, Logan settled in to wait a reasonable amount of time before coming back downstairs to demand his daily Q & A session.

The next time he opened his eyes, bright morning sunlight suffused the loft, along with the smell of fresh-brewed coffee.

Hauling himself up off the mattress was surprisingly difficult. He'd slept straight through the night for the first time in he didn't even know how long, but he didn't feel nearly as rested as he would have hoped. Instead, his body ached as if it had been tied in place for the past nine hours, his limbs weighted down with stones.

He managed to get down the stepladder without falling and breaking his neck, but it wasn't easy. When he finally felt the cold hardwood floor under his bare feet, he exhaled a grateful sigh.

"I told you I should be the one sleeping up there." Jessica's no-nonsense voice from behind him sent a pleasant shiver up Logan's spine.

"Tonight," she declared, "we're switching. You can take the bedroom, I'll take the loft."

Logan shrugged, not wanting to start the day with an argument. He'd be sleeping in that loft, though. Just because he hadn't reliably slept through the night since his parents died, that didn't make Logan a child to be coddled and ordered around.

Dropping into the nearest kitchen chair, Logan dredged up a winning smile. "You made coffee. That's why you're my favorite, Tink."

"I'm your favorite because your brother pays me well to make sure your needs are met," Jessica corrected absently. Most of her attention was focused on the frowning scrutiny of Logan's face.

He rubbed a hand over his whiskery jaw, hiding a wince at the thought of how rough he probably looked. Meanwhile, he realized sourly, Jessica was pressed, perky perfection in her fitted cobalt-blue fleece sweatshirt and a pair of black spandex workout pants.

Hoping to induce her to turn around so he could get a peek at the hind view, Logan picked up the coffee cup set out with the plates and silverware in the center of the table. He waggled it beseechingly, making his best puppy dog eyes.

But instead of filling the mug with the sweet nectar of life while bending over the kitchen counter in those tight black pants, Jessica said, "You actually slept last night. I checked on you."

"Yeah, so?" It wasn't a lie, Logan reasoned, since he had actually dropped off.

"So why don't you seem refreshed and rested?"

Logan shrugged. "When I go through long periods of having trouble sleeping, I kind of acclimate to not sleeping. Then when I do finally manage a full night, my body doesn't know how to handle it. I wind up groggy, still tired."

"That's awful! Is that normal?" Worry created an adorable crease between her brows. It probably didn't say anything great about him that he loved that look on her face.

"Might not be normal, but normal is boring." Logan shrugged. "Anyway, it's been happening since I was a teenager. It used to bother me, but I've lived through it every other time. I'll live through it this time, and next time, too. No need to call out the National Guard."

Jessica whirled, finally giving him a view of her delectable backside, but she didn't move to grab the coffeepot. Instead, she filled a teakettle with water, set it on the four-burner range and turned up the heat under it.

Logan cocked his head, intrigued. "You're having tea? You always drink coffee."

She gave him a strange look. "No, you're having tea. Herbal, in fact."

He snorted. "The hell I am."

Jessica ignored him, the way she always did when she'd made up her mind to drive him completely insane. "Until I research the do's and don'ts of chronic insomnia, you're not having any caffeine."

Dismay turned his voice into a low growl. "Now wait a damned minute."

Twirling to face him, Jessica braced her hands on the counter behind her. "You agreed to follow my instructions regarding your health," she said tensely, eyes flashing. "Are you going back on our deal already, over something as small as a cup of coffee?"

That shut Logan up for a second, long enough to weigh the cost-to-benefit ratio of pushing this. Yeah, he loved his morning espresso, but did he want it more than he wanted to know Jessica's secrets?

"Fine," he snarled, slamming away from the table. Hey, nothing in the deal said he had to be a good sport about any of this. "But I'm not drinking tea. Tea is just water boiled with sticks and leaves. I'd rather drink out of the toilet."

"If that's what you prefer, be my guest," Jessica said calmly. "Just so long as it's not caffeinated toilet water."

Damn it, now he was biting down on a grin. She was uncomfortably good at shaking his bad moods loose. "Got it. So what else are you prescribing for me today, Nurse Jessica?"

Her green eyes took on a glittery sheen of satisfaction. "A healthy breakfast. Do you think you can deal?"

Logan nodded. "Speaking of deals, I think we should count yesterday as the first day of our agreement. In which I held up my end of the bargain by sleeping straight through the night—and that means you owe me."

Pausing in the act of opening a carton of eggs, Jessica swallowed audibly. Staring down at the fragile white shells, she said, "Fine, but you're coming with me for a walk around the island. You can ask your question while we get a little light exercise."

Logan was so cheered by the prospect of delving into the locked box of Jessica's past, he didn't even want to argue about the exercise. "Sounds great. I assume you packed me a pair of sneakers."

He only said it to elicit his favorite Jessica

look—the single arched brow and silent lip curl that carried a strong subtext of *bitch, please.*

"Obviously," she muttered, turning back to the stove.

Oh yes, the cracks are already starting to show, Logan mused, almost whistling as he sauntered through the cottage in search of his packing case. The unflappable Jessica Bell was more than a little flapped.

Curiosity, the burning fire that guided Logan's life, the best distraction and comfort he'd ever found, crested in his chest. When he finally got to peer behind the opaque curtain of Jessica's professional distance, what would he find?

And the question of why he cared so much, why Jessica stirred his insatiable curiosity in a way no other woman ever had? Well. That was easy enough to ignore.

Chapter Three

Jessica's brain obsessively ticked over the list of information she'd compiled about sleep disorders. The instant she had breakfast under control, she started Googling like a madwoman. There was far less research available than she would have expected for such a basic human need, but Jessica was confident in her problem-solving skills. She was determined to figure this out.

She made a mental note to look into whether trauma affected sleep patterns. He'd said he first started experiencing insomnia as a teenager—was that around the time of Phillip and Marilyn Harrington's tragic car accident?

The resignation in every weary line of Logan's face as he'd revealed the extent of his insomnia had torn at Jessica's heart. More than anything, she wanted to be able to promise him that he didn't have to live like that, in a constant cycle of exhaustion and frustration. She had more research to do, but she was cautiously optimistic enough to make up for the niggling worry over the question Logan was about to pose.

Glancing down at the route she'd mapped on her smartphone, Jessica said, "Turn left up ahead, at . . . yes, at Main Street."

"Of freaking course, this place has a Main Street. And my grandparents' house is on what, Island Road? Very creative, this town's founders were."

Normally Jessica, a New Yorker by choice if not by birth, would wholeheartedly join in the sophisticated eye rolling at small-town cutesiness. But as they skirted the lush green lawn of the town square and shared friendly greetings with an elderly couple walking a tiny poodle, Jessica couldn't find it in herself to look down her nose at Sanctuary Island.

"You'd prefer something more fanciful?" She blinked at him innocently. "I would have thought you'd like the simple directness of Island Road."

"I prefer my avenues numbered, orderly and logical, thank you very much." Logan tucked his hands in the pockets of the brand new track pants Jessica had bought him, sharp gaze taking in every detail of their surroundings.

He sauntered down the sidewalk, broad shoulders brushing hers on every other step. It was another glorious summer day, early enough to be warm rather than hot, and the constant gentle breeze cut the humidity nicely. Logan tipped his head back as they walked, and Jessica caught her breath silently as an expression she'd never seen crossed his handsome face.

With the sun beating down and an ocean wind ruffling his brown hair, Logan Harrington looked content.

The clench of her heart convinced her once and for all that she'd done the right thing in bringing him to Sanctuary. She'd always enjoyed her monthly check-in call with Penny Little, the caretaker of the Harringtons' vacation home, and getting the news of the slow-paced, friendly island.

When Logan collapsed in that board meeting, his older brother had decreed an enforced vacation was in order. At once, Jessica had felt a tug on her heart telling her to whisk Logan away to Sanctuary Island.

He could heal here. That was worth the discomfort of answering a few probing questions.

With that in mind, she led them left on Main Street, away from the town square. The clusters of houses grew sparser the farther they walked, the quality of the road deteriorating from smooth pavement to rough gravel over the next mile. She kept an eye on Logan, whose main form of exercise was generally accomplished naked and horizontal, but he didn't appear to be struggling as their walk stretched longer. In fact, a healthy color bloomed in his pale cheeks for the first time in weeks.

And still he didn't ask his question.

Relaxing a bit, Jessica thumbed in the changes to her GPS map that would take them on the longer route past the stretch of public-access beach along the eastern edge of the island. Her advance prep on this place had turned up an interesting tidbit about why it was called Sanctuary Island, and she wanted to check it out firsthand.

In strangely companionable silence, they crested a small hill lined with loblolly pines. At the top, they paused to get their breath back and stared out over the vista spread at their feet.

From the break in the trees atop their hill, the ground sloped down in a tangle of wax myrtle and sorrel to the edge of a wide salt marsh. Dark green patches of tall cordgrass waved in the breeze and the scent of salt hung heavy in the air.

Jessica's heart leaped as she caught movement from the corner of her eye. Grabbing Logan's elbow in a reflexive gesture of excitement, she couldn't stop herself from pointing and bouncing like a giddy child.

"Look," she whispered. "Can you believe it?"

Logan followed the angle of her arm, eyes widening as he saw what she was pointing at. "Huh. Looks like some farmer's ponies got out of the barn."

Jessica shook her head, gaze locked on the small band of rangy, shaggy horses grazing lazily among the cordgrass. "They're wild. The entire island is a wild horse sanctuary—there are no fences anywhere, and all the residents look out for them."

"That's insane." Logan stared down at the horses with a perplexed smile. "Huh. I don't think I've ever seen a horse that didn't have a mounted police officer on its back, or a carriage for tourists strapped to it."

"They're beautiful." Jessica sighed, caught by the indefinable air of freedom the feral animals exuded. These were no tame pets, taught to take sugar cubes from a little girl's open palm. These horses lived in the open, survived the harsh winds of winter and the tearing storms of spring, foraging for food along the island's shores.

"You're beautiful."

Logan's quiet voice startled Jessica from her reverie. She glanced up to find him staring at her, rather than the view. The open appreciation in his dark blue eyes sent a wash of pleasure drenching through her body.

He'd complimented her before, with a wink and a smirk or a cheerfully leering grin, and she'd easily brushed it off. This felt different. Honest. Real, in a way that should have been terrifying, but wasn't.

"Thank you."

She'd been right to bring them here, where magic sparkled in the sea air and rode the hot rays of golden summer sunlight. Jessica could feel her heart, the heart she'd carefully encased in layers of ice years before, beginning to melt as she watched a gangly young colt kick up its spindly legs as it gamboled through the meadow, annoying its mother.

And with every breath, she was deeply, achingly aware of the man at her side. She didn't need to look at him to feel the moment when he lifted his hand to smooth a lock of red hair torn loose from her ponytail by the wind off the water.

The skim of his fingertips over the shell of her ear stole her breath, and everything low in her body tightened as if he'd plucked a string. Desire, the sharp, dangerous kind she'd forsaken a long time ago, heated her from the inside out. Reckless with it, drunk on the salt spray and the freedom of the wild horses, Jessica said, "I'm ready to answer your question now."

Logan felt the way Jessica's pulse fluttered under the sensitive pads of his fingers. From their closeness? Or from her obviously deep-seated fear of showing him anything personal about herself?

Deciding it didn't matter—they had a deal—Logan ruthlessly squashed any potential guilt and said, "I've been thinking about this a lot. The first question. And I've decided to dive right in, because that's how I roll."

Her heart kicked again, although her finely sculpted features remained impassive. Fascinated by the dichotomy, Logan dropped his hand to the side of her neck where he'd be best able to track the data of her heart rate. *Human lie detector,* he thought absently, although he didn't truly expect Jessica to lie. She might not be thrilled to share her history, but there was a rock-solid core of honor to Jessica that he knew would keep her from welching on their deal.

"Well?" Her voice was firm, even bored, but the tickle of her pulse against his fingers told another story.

"So eager," Logan murmured, low and heated,

just to see if her heart rate would jump. But instead it seemed to smooth out into a steady, slow rhythm. He frowned, and a smile curved Jessica's perfect lips.

"Yes, sir." She was the picture of demure professionalism, blinking wide green eyes up at him.

Dropping his hand with a muttered curse, Logan stepped back. "Balls. I can't do the seduction thing when you remind me that you're technically my subordinate."

Her smile faded. "I know."

Logan jammed his hands into the pockets of the track pants. "The way you boss me around, I forget sometimes."

"You sometimes forget to pay attention to anything that isn't related to the company or your gadgets." Jessica shrugged, wandering over to perch on a fallen tree trunk by the side of the path. "Someone needs to look out for you."

"It took me a while to realize that's why you're so damn bossy." Logan ran his fingers through his hair. "How many times did I fire you that first week? And since? But you never go."

He didn't mention the glow of warmth it gave him now, every time he pushed her away and Jessica pushed right back. In Logan's experience, people left. They couldn't freaking wait to leave, which was why he preferred to spend his time with the fascinating puzzles in his lab rather than socializing.

Jessica was different. She never courted his interest, never tried to intrigue—and yet, effortlessly and inevitably, the enigma of Jessica Bell had captured Logan's attention.

"I don't go because you have no power to fire me," she reminded him with relish. Man, she loved to hold that over his head.

"And apparently, even at my most deliberately obnoxious, I don't have the power to make your life miserable enough to quit." Once it had sunk in that he couldn't fire Jessica and make it stick, he'd pranked her mercilessly for a week.

He'd rigged her desk drawers to stick, then pop open at irregular intervals. He'd fiddled with her ergonomic office chair so that whenever she sat down, the seat sank to the lowest position. He'd reprogrammed the calendar application on her tablet to randomize the date and time of every event she entered. And when none of that fazed her, Logan got really creative.

"Remember when you convinced the entire security staff that I was a stalker and should be barred from Harrington Tower?" Jessica sighed reminiscently. "Good times."

"That was one of my favorites. I spent hours doctoring the security feed to show you sneaking into my private lab after hours. First time I ever missed a deadline for Miles."

Miles Harrington, in his capacity as CEO and president of Harrington International, had not been pleased when Logan failed to appear at the quarterly meeting of the shareholders. In his capacity as the eldest Harrington brother, Miles seemed to enjoy pointing out how much Logan's pranks looked like the pigtail pulling of grade school romance, to the untrained eye.

"That was the last of the pranks, come to think of it," Jessica realized.

"And it was the start of your campaign to transform me into a healthy, well-adjusted human being."

"Not that you make it easy."

With an evil grin, Logan flopped down in the grass, careless of staining the new workout gear. "Why would I make it easy for you to turn me into Miles when it's so much more fun to be me?"

He tilted his head back to catch the unfamiliar warmth of the sun on his face, and caught Jessica's troubled gaze.

"You know I don't actually want to change who you are, right? I want you to take better care of yourself. There's a big difference."

Equal parts uncomfortable with and delighted by her show of concern, Logan stretched his long legs out in the grass until his sneakered foot nudged hers. "And you're so dedicated to my health that you've agreed to answer whatever question I pose, no holds barred. So here it is."

She crossed her legs as elegantly as if she were wearing a couture gown instead of spandex pants and a sweatshirt. Without his human lie detector trick, there was not a single crack in her poised, professional façade. "Hit me."

Suddenly, all Logan wanted in the world was to shatter that mask of calm indifference. To make Jessica Bell react with passion. So he ditched the softball question he'd planned to ask about her parents, and went straight for the throat.

"Why are you so determined to keep me at arm's length?"

She froze for an instant, only a heartbeat, before opening her mouth. Too quickly.

Logan shook his head. "And don't give me that canned stuff about professionalism. I want the real answer. Because we'd be explosive together, Tink, and you know it."

The hot red flush that bloomed along her cheekbones set off a battery of triumphant fireworks in Logan's chest. Passion!

Of course, when she spoke, her voice was precise and calm, edged with enough acid to sting. "What I know is that you're spoiled. You're a wealthy, uncommonly intelligent man entirely too used to getting what you want. Maybe I turn you down just to help you get accustomed to hearing the word *no*."

Logan blinked, genuinely taken aback. "What makes you think I get everything I want? And I noticed your little evasion there, by the way. Don't expect me to let that slide. I want a real answer."

"To which question?" Jessica asked tightly.

"Both! All!" Logan clenched his hands into fists to stop himself from reaching for her. "I don't see how you can consider me spoiled when I've lost everyone that ever mattered to me. Just because I have the sense to read the pattern and limit my desires to those that are attainable—like casual sex, alcohol and my work—that doesn't make me spoiled. That makes me a realist."

Jessica fell out of her prim pose on the log, her lithe limbs going loose and appealingly awkward as her laser focus zoomed in on his face. "Logan."

It was all she said, his name, but it felt brand new, as if she'd never said it before. Or never so intimately. Heat constricted Logan's chest, threatening to spread downward to his groin.

Hastily drawing his legs up to rest his arms on his knees, he said, "But this isn't about me. I'm pretty sure deflecting the question onto me and my inner workings violates the spirit of our agreement. So unless you want to call for a helicopter to come pick me up from this godforsaken rock . . ."

Jessica narrowed a glare at him, her breath coming sharp and fast. Tension strung out between them, taut as a wire. Greedy for more of the real Jessica Bell, the passionate woman instead of the perfect assistant, Logan did what he'd do with any experiment that began to show signs of success. He pushed it further.

"I know you have the company's chopper pilot on speed dial," Logan taunted, standing up and dusting himself off as if he were on the point of heading back to the cottage to pack. "We could be landing at the Wall Street heliport before nightfall."

Jessica sprang to her feet, going toe to toe with him. "We're not leaving Sanctuary!"

"Then answer the question!"

Something flickered in her gaze, a lightning flash that ratcheted the tension even higher. Logan wanted to taste the sneer that twisted her gorgeous lips. "It's a ridiculous question. Have you honestly

Chapter Four

The imprint of Logan's strong fingers branded Jessica's back with heat, his arms like ropes of fire binding her to him. She gasped, but not in surprise.

She should be surprised, she understood dimly through the maelstrom of desire his lips and tongue stoked in her body, but she wasn't. They'd been heading toward this kiss ever since they first met. The only surprise was how long they'd held out.

Logan kissed the way he did everything else: with an intensity of focus and dedication to skill that made Jessica feel like the only woman in existence who'd ever gone weak in the knees at the taste of his mouth.

Of course, that wasn't anything like the truth. The memory of exactly how diligently Logan had practiced his kissing technique was enough to stiffen her melting spine. She pushed out of his arms, shuddering at the brush of her clothes against overheated, sensitized skin. "That's enough."

Logan's eyes darkened to cobalt blue, his blown pupils tracking her every move like a hawk hunting a field mouse. "No. One kiss is nowhere close to enough."

Every sharp breath in was thick with the scent of him, male and aroused, and Jessica swallowed against the temptation to slip back into his arms and finish what he'd started.

Dismayed, she snapped herself upright. She was dangerously, terrifyingly close to breaking her cardinal rule of never mixing business and pleasure. She had to remember what was at stake if she succumbed to Logan's seduction. And in case that wasn't enough, maybe she could kill two birds with one stone.

If she answered his question as fully and honestly as he seemed to want, Logan would finally understand why she would never, could never allow any intimacy with him. He'd see how hopeless it was, and that he was better off sticking to his one-night stands back in the city.

The thought gave her an odd pang in the region of her heart, but she ignored it.

"One kiss is certainly enough to prove the hypothesis," Jessica said, taking refuge in the dry, bland scientific language.

Logan arched a brow. "Or disprove it. You're not going to argue that lack of sexual compatibility is your reason, after kissing me like that."

You kissed me, she wanted to say, but the mischievous quirk at the corner of his mouth told her that was exactly what he wanted. Rather than argue about who kissed whom and how passionate it had been, Jessica forged ahead. "You're right, it would be pointless to claim I'm not attracted to you."

Desire flared sharply across his gorgeous face, his eyes never leaving hers.

Before he could take more than a step toward her, Jessica held up a hand. She needed to preserve her distance if she had any hope of getting through this awful, humiliating story. "The fact that my body reacts to yours does not obligate me to act on that attraction."

Throwing himself down to sit on the log she'd vacated, Logan was the picture of irritated frustration. "You know it'll be good between us. Why don't you just give in? It's what we both want."

Taking a deep breath, she let it out slowly. "Because what we want isn't always good for us, Logan. For instance, office romance. I know—from bitter experience—exactly how badly an office romance can go."

"That sounds like an interesting story." His eyes sparkled with curiosity. "A story that just might answer my question and fulfill your requirement for yesterday."

Jessica nodded, her mouth suddenly uncomfortably dry.

"Okay then. Story time with Tink." Without further ado, Logan reclined on the log more fully, twisting his back like a bear scratching an itch as he found a comfortable position. "Lay it on me."

He looked oddly like the stereotype of a patient in a therapist's office, fingers laced together and resting on his chest. She watched them rise and fall with the steady cadence of his breath, the expansion of his rib cage drawing her eyes to the lean, mouthwatering V of his torso, and bit back a smile.

Nervous as she was at what she was about to reveal, she couldn't help being amused at the typical Harrington male way Logan took up every available inch of space. Even in the great outdoors, with the vastness of the ocean rolling out into the distant horizon, Logan Harrington was larger than life.

But he wasn't the only man she'd ever known who sucked all the oxygen out of a room, simply by entering it.

Any urge to smile faded, and Jessica was abruptly glad Logan had taken over the seat. She needed to move around while she told this story, rather than feel stuck in one place. Trapped.

"Once upon a time," she began, pacing beside the length of the fallen tree, down to the torn-up roots and back again, "there was a very young, very naïve Midwestern girl whose first job out of college was personal assistant to the CEO of a hotel chain in New York City."

Jessica sneaked a glance at Logan's face as she passed where he'd propped his head on a knot in the tree bark, but his eyes were closed. The fact that he wasn't looking at her made it easier for Jessica to go on. "When the young girl met her new boss, she knew she'd gotten lucky. He was kind, considerate and handsome. He spent time with her one-on-one, every day, mentoring her. At least, that's what she thought at first."

But she was getting ahead of herself. Forcing her breath to slow and her hands to stop twisting the fabric at the hem of her sweatshirt, Jessica hesitated.

Without opening his eyes, Logan murmured, "What was the boss's name?"

Heart pounding, Jessica felt a sick wash of shame as she spoke the name she hadn't uttered in five years. "Russ. Russell Owens."

Saying it out loud broke the numbing, distancing magic of treating this story like a fairy tale. Not that it was headed for a fairy tale ending. *Stop being a child about this,* she lectured herself silently. *Just get it over with.*

"I worked for Russ for three years, but it only took him three months to talk me into bed. He was good at talking me into things. He hated my apartment—a tiny studio walk-up on the fifth floor of a building in Astoria that probably ought to have been condemned—and Russell refused to stay over there. So he found me an apartment on the Upper West Side, a nice one-bedroom I saw for the first time when he gave me the key and told me it was already furnished and the rent paid up for the entire year. He bought me clothes for work, and when I tried to refuse, he hinted gently that my professional wardrobe reflected on him and his office, so I didn't really have a choice."

She had to pause, to get control of the unacceptable shake in her voice. "I know what you're thinking. He doesn't sound like a monster, does he? In fact, I'm the one who doesn't come off so great in this story, letting this man pay my bills and help me professionally in return for sex. I know exactly how that sounds."

"I promise you," Logan said, with his eyes still closed though his voice was taut with suppressed emotion. "You have no idea what I'm thinking."

Jessica laughed to break the tension, but it came out a little choked and raw. "Right, of course. You're a genius—how could I know what's going on in that giant brain of yours?"

He sat up in a controlled rush, planting his feet widely on the ground and clenching his fingers on the rough wooden bark at his hips. "What I'm thinking is that Russell Owens is a dead man, if I ever meet him."

Shock dried Jessica's mouth. No one she'd ever told had reacted this way, including her own mother. "What?"

"He systematically took control of your entire life," Logan snarled. "Let me guess at the next part of the story. He also monopolized your off-work hours so that you lost touch with your friends. Of course, you had to keep your relationship a secret at work, and I'd lay good money on him giving you some reason why you couldn't discuss it with anyone else, either."

Jessica swayed in the ocean breeze. A higher wind would have knocked her off her feet. "I didn't have any friends in the city, actually. I moved there after college and got the job at Crown Hotels almost immediately. And the reason he asked me not to talk about our relationship with my parents was . . ."

She nearly gagged on the shame of it, the unbearable sense of having been stupid and weak, led astray from what she knew to be right, but this was the worst of it. Once she got this out, it was nearly over, and Logan would know everything.

The fact that he seemed to know, or to have intuited most of it already didn't make it easier to force the words out.

"When I met Russ, he wore a wedding band." Jessica wrapped her arms around her rib cage and held on for dear life. "The minute he saw that I'd noticed it, he gave me this sad smile and told me all about his marriage and how he and his wife were separated, in the process of getting divorced."

"And if you mentioned your affair to anyone, it might complicate and delay the proceedings," Logan guessed.

Miserable, Jessica nodded as she averted her gaze to stare blindly out to the horizon. "I never questioned it. He spent every evening at my apartment! Well, the apartment he'd paid for. He didn't sleep over, but that was because he had a long-standing arrangement with the company to send a car to pick him up from his house, and if he asked them to pick him up from my place instead—God. He had an answer for everything, so smooth and plausible and reasonable. Eventually I stopped asking questions."

"And then," Logan prompted gently when she broke off.

Wearily, she lanced the rest of the wound and drained the last drop of poison out onto the ground between them. "And then, after three years of buying me earrings and bracelets to distract me from the fact that it was never the engagement ring he kept promising, I found out that he was still married. Not separated, not nearing the end of a long, drawn-out divorce. It was all a lie—and a clichéd, predictable lie, at that."

Logan made a rough noise behind her, but she couldn't bring herself to turn and face the pity or condemnation on his handsome, familiar features.

"I should have known better," she said painfully. "Deep down, I *did* know better. I think that's what hurts most of all. I compromised myself and my ethics. I bought into an elaborate but ultimately formulaic and obvious fiction, because I wanted to believe. I wanted to believe that this smart, charismatic, wealthy man could fall in love with a nobody from Normal, Illinois. I thought I could have it all."

Forcing herself to meet Logan's gaze was one of the hardest things she'd ever done, but this was important. He needed to understand.

Storm clouds scudded over the blue of his eyes, darkening them with something that looked more like understanding than pity. Jessica swallowed.

"When it was all over, I had nothing. No friends, no job, no place to live. My parents—they're very decent people, very religious. They certainly didn't raise me to have a tawdry affair with a married man. In fact, they were so disappointed in me, they sent enough money for another apartment instead of letting me come back home to live with them. We don't talk much, other than holidays and birthdays."

"That's . . . horribly sad," Logan said, his voice oddly ragged. Or maybe it wasn't so odd. He'd lost his parents when he was very young, Jessica remembered, and his relationships with his brothers weren't exactly close. So maybe he did get it. But she hadn't completely finished answering his question.

"I will never be that girl again," Jessica told him, as starkly and strongly as she could. "I never want to be that naïve, that silly or easy to take advantage of. I never want to wake up in the morning aching with regrets. So that's why I hold you at arm's length, Logan. Because I am tempted . . . but if I were to give in to the fantasy of being with you, I'm smart enough now to know that I'd be giving something up in return. And I'm not willing to sacrifice my self-respect and my career for a moment's passion."

No matter how much the sight of his lean strength silhouetted against the ocean view made the blood throb in her veins.

Chapter Five

"Satisfied?" Jessica asked, her voice seductively hoarse from having talked for so long.

Not even close, beautiful.

Logan held himself still as he studied her, scrutinizing her tale from every angle like a multifaceted 3-D puzzle. "You've made your position very clear, and I accept it."

The slim line of her shoulders relaxed infinitesimally, as if she'd been unsure he'd get the message. He almost hated to make her tense up again, but a deep, primal part of him couldn't let this go without at least trying to address her concerns.

"But I feel I have to point out," he continued gently, "that your position rests on faulty logic."

Surprise widened her pretty green eyes. Pushing a strand of strawberry-blond hair out of her face, Jessica put her hands on her hips the way he loved, and stared him down. "Oh?"

Deliberately relaxing his posture to seem as unthreatening as possible, Logan assumed his driest, most professorial tone. "Yes. In fact, I spotted numerous irrationalities in the conclusions you drew from your past experiences. And while I don't doubt that those experiences were traumatic . . ." He paused to breathe through the resurgence of his intense desire to track down one Russell Owens and take him apart, systematically, until there was nothing left.

"I'm not traumatized," Jessica protested with a scathing curl of her lip. Good, he liked it when she got fiery. Anything was better than the resigned slump of her shoulders, the deadened tone of her voice, as she recited her litany of regrets. "I learned from my past mistakes. I *grew up*. Something you could stand to look into, yourself. Sir."

Logan fought the reflexive scowl. He wouldn't be derailed by her attempt to push him away and return to more formal footing—not when he could still taste the sharp honeyed sweetness of her kiss every time he licked his lips. "As I was saying. What happened to you sucked. Fair to say?"

She nodded shortly, and he went on. "But the lesson you seem to have learned is that you can't have everything. That allowing yourself to feel desire means you risk losing the job you worked so hard for. That won't happen. For one thing, I can't fire you, whether we sleep together or not."

"It's not that I won't allow myself to feel desire." Jessica gave him an acid look. "I simply won't act on it."

"Because you wouldn't be able to look yourself in the mirror the morning after," Logan said dramatically, swooning backward to lean his hands on the far edge of the log.

Mottled pink tinged her cheeks, and her knuckles went white where she was digging her fingers into her hips. "Don't make fun of me. Just because you have no conscience or morals to speak of . . ."

Logan grimaced, sitting up again. "No, sorry. I don't mean to make fun, it's just . . ." He spread his hands out to his sides in a helpless gesture of don't-hate-me-because-I'm-trying-my-best-not-to-say-the-wrong-thing-and-failing-epically.

Her lips twitched, and he could tell she wanted to laugh. Or at least snort a little. Satisfied, he doggedly returned to his argument. "Look, I refuse to believe that you can't have it all. You're one of the most intelligent people I know. Honestly, you should be running a division at the company, not babysitting me."

Jessica gasped soundlessly, betrayal showing in her narrowed gaze and thin lips. "I'm not interested in an unearned promotion. And I certainly have no intention of earning said promotion in bed."

Logan almost fell off the log in his haste to stand up. "What? I take it back, you're not intelligent, you're a blithering idiot like all the rest of them. I'm not offering to promote you in exchange for sex! How did you get that from what I just said?"

Her shoulders were coiled tight with tension under his hands, but she didn't shake off his touch. Logan was counting it as a win.

"I . . . sorry. Maybe I am a little traumatized." Jessica's attempt at a smile was the saddest thing Logan had ever seen. "Russ used to talk about how I was 'going places' in the company. 'Stick with me, sweetness, and you'll go right to the top.'"

Logan couldn't decipher whether the disgust in her tone was aimed at herself or at the King of All Douche Bags, Russell Owens. "Don't apologize. Seriously. I'm the one who should be sorry. I didn't think about how it could sound. And anyway, you're missing the point."

"Oh?" She lifted her chin enough to get him thinking about how close their lips were, and if he tilted his head to the perfect forty-five degree angle, he could . . .

"Your point, Logan?" A bare hint of a smirk had one corner of her mouth dimpling distractingly.

Logan tightened his hands on her shoulders for an instant, savoring the warmth of her flesh through the thin, clingy material of her workout top. "The main point, and your most egregious failure of logic, is simply this. Russell Owens was—probably is, there's no evidence he's changed—a textbook sexual predator. He targeted an innocent, unworldly woman in a subordinate position, isolated you from anyone who could talk sense into you, established complete control over every aspect of your life and lied to you about his intentions. He knowingly, de- liberately preyed on your desire to trust and your dreams for the future."

A cynical twist replaced the smirk on Jessica's lips, but her eyes were soft. "That assessment lets me off the hook too much, but okay. I certainly grant your premise that Russ was an exceptionally awful person. So what?"

"So . . . I'm not Russell Owens. I'm nothing like him." Logan tilted the corner of his lips in a maddeningly sexy smirk. "In fact, I'm not like anyone you've ever known. So perhaps you should take this opportunity to get to know me a little better."

She licked her lips, drawing his gaze. "I already know you quite well, thank you."

Logan leaned in. "Then you know I'm used to getting what I want, one way or another. And what I want is you, for the duration of this forced vacation to Boredom Island."

Tensing under his hands, Jessica never dropped her eyes. "And if I say no? What happens when we get back to New York?"

He shrugged. "The same thing that happens if you say yes. We resume functioning as normal, with you as my assistant and me ignoring your attempts to make me work less. No emotional entanglements inside the office."

"Very convincing." She grimaced. "But sex always leads to emotional entanglements. For me, anyway."

In that vein, Logan made himself drop his hands and take a step back. No undue persuasion or influence. "If your final decision is no, then I respect that. But before you make that choice, just keep in mind that you're no longer a naïve college girl. And I'm not a manipulative liar. I won't buy you an apartment or jewelry. I won't ask you to marry me. I won't throw a tantrum when this thing between us inevitably runs its course and fizzles out—and I won't hold a grudge or retaliate professionally if you choose not to pursue it."

"So it's completely up to me," Jessica clarified, color high in her cheeks. "My choice whether to sleep with you—temporarily—or not?"

"Completely your choice," Logan agreed with a magnanimous smile that morphed into a sharp, predatory grin as he leaned in to catch the ripe, sun-warmed scent of her skin. "But I'm giving you fair warning now. I intend to devote every bit of my considerable intelligence to convincing you to take full advantage of the extraordinary compatibility of our bodies."

"You're right," Jessica breathed, swaying toward him. "You're nothing like him." Nothing like the man who taught her that love was a pretty story for fools and children. Her heart would be safe with Logan Harrington, because he'd never touch it. He had no interest in it. He was skilled in the arts of no-strings-attached sex and avoiding emotional entanglements.

Maybe she'd live a happier, more independent life if she followed his lead.

All he was interested in was sex. He admitted it up front, without embarrassment or apology. That might sound unappealing to some women, but those women hadn't met Logan Harrington.

His eyes went heavy lidded and hot. "Does that mean you want to head back to the cottage and climb up into the loft with me?"

Heart skittering in her chest—was she really doing this?—Jessica refused to let her nerves show. "Nope."

Disappointment, surprisingly strong, flashed across his handsome face. But instead of sulking, he gave her a smile. "Okay. No pressure. However, I reserve the right to keep tempting you to change your mind."

That reaction gave Jessica the guts to say, "We're not going up to the loft because beds are for sleeping. That's one of the first rules of treating insomnia. So . . ."

She paused to control her voice, then thought, *what the hell?* And let it drop into the husky lower register that would take this conversation from suggestive to downright seductive. "We're going to have to get creative."

"Mmm." Logan's blue eyes lit up like the sun coming out from behind the clouds. Stepping forward, he put his hands back on her shoulders and let his thumbs caress shivery circles into the sides of her neck. Jessica felt as if the weight of his touch was all that kept her from floating up off the ground. "I can do creative."

A gull winged by overhead, soaring out over the marsh toward the sparkling ocean. Jessica sucked in a breath of salty air and let the new sense of freedom and possibility wash through her.

It had been a while, but she hadn't forgotten how to flirt with her eyes. Cocking her head at enough of an angle to brush her cheek against the side of Logan's right hand, she let her lips part in a slow smile. "The loft is off-limits, but that leaves the rest of the cottage up for grabs. Or, if you're feeling extra adventurous . . ."

Nearly vibrating with excitement and nerves, Jessica brought up her hand to tug down the zipper at the neck of her gym sweatshirt. Not the best outfit for a seduction, she mused wryly, but she was a born problem solver.

And judging by the hungry way Logan's gaze followed the path of that little zipper until it stopped right above her breasts, he wasn't suffering from her lack of sexy lingerie. She hadn't bothered with a sports bra, since they were only walking, and the work-out shirt had enough built-in support. So when Logan's long fingers dipped from her neck, over her collarbone, and drew a line down the sliver of her breastbone revealed by the open zipper, Jessica knew her instinctive shiver would reveal her bra-less state in no uncertain terms.

Logan's breathing changed, went deep and harsh in his chest, and the way his strong jaw clenched as he stared down at her made Jessica's breasts feel warm and heavy. Her nipples tightened even more beneath his hot stare, and the moment stretched tight between them.

Until Logan broke the tension with a single, guttural sound, and swept her up into his arms.

Jessica's last giddy thought before pleasure consumed her completely was, *This might be a mistake, but it's a mistake worth making.*

Chapter Six

That first morning of lovemaking, with the sun and the wind and the ocean all around them, stretched into an afternoon of strolling down to the beach and wading through the foamy white surf. The only other living beings they encountered were sandpipers hopping along the edge of the water, trying to catch the periwinkles before they dug down into the wet sand with a flash of sunlight glinting off their shiny shells. The band of wild horses was long gone— "Probably scared away by all the noise you were making," Logan noted smugly.

Jessica didn't have the energy to retaliate with more than a halfhearted glare and a determined snatch at his hand. Lacing their fingers together, she arched a brow that dared him to comment on her desire to hold his hand, but Logan mimed zipping his lips closed.

That didn't last long, of course. They turned to

head back to the cottage so Jessica could force-feed Logan something disgustingly healthy in retaliation for how thoroughly she'd answered his first intrusive personal question. She decided on a protein shake with apples and kale, to make it green and gloppy.

But before he agreed to drink it, he shot her a narrow glance. "If you want me to swallow that nasty concoction, it better earn me a bonus question."

Jessica nearly fumbled the glass in her surprise. "You want to keep going with the questions?"

She'd been under the impression he'd already asked the one he cared about—and since it had led directly to the result he wanted, Jessica naked and writhing in his arms like a woman who hadn't been touched in far too long, she didn't see why he needed to ask more.

But Logan only smiled, his mischievous grin setting Jessica's pulse pounding in delighted anticipation. "Oh, definitely. I haven't come close to plumbing the depths of you yet."

She felt the heat rise to her cheeks, but decided to ignore it in favor of rolling her eyes at his ridiculous innuendo. "Drink your smoothie. I'm going to shower—I have sand and dried saltwater in some very uncomfortable places. And when I get back . . . you can plumb my depths to your heart's content. So long as that glass is empty, and your phone stays dark, silent and in your pocket. In fact, hand over the phone now. I'll take charge of that until we leave the island. Consider it one of my rules for helping to rebuild your health."

A brief spasm of irritated, reluctant respect crossed his face. "Damn it, you know me too well."

He reached into his pocket with two dexterous fingers and withdrew the tiny, slim piece of high-tech gadgetry he was never without. It was his main link to the lab, and Jessica was well aware that if she left it in his possession, he wouldn't be able to resist checking in and attempting to remotely control and oversee the latest project. His team at the lab was good, but far too reliant on the fact that Logan lived, breathed and thought about nothing but work.

Well, not for the length of time they spent on Sanctuary Island. She'd get him to think about something other than work if it killed her.

"Gimme," she prompted when Logan clutched his fingers around the smartphone possessively.

"You're a hard woman, Tink," he said with a mournful look in his blue eyes. "Here. Promise you'll take good care of her."

"Her?"

How had she not known he thought of his phone as a woman?

"Sure." Logan leaned against the kitchen counter, all long, powerful lines. A Thoroughbred in repose. "I call her Wendy. She takes care of me, tells me stories, tells me what to do."

Jessica pocketed the phone smoothly. "If you're searching for a mother, Peter Pan, you're definitely better off looking to the phone than to me. Although I'm always happy to tell you what to do."

Old, remembered sadness darted through his

gaze, a silver-scaled fish appearing and disappearing through the currents of his blue eyes. She blinked and it was gone, replaced by the sardonic glint she knew so well. "Now Tink, don't be jealous of Wendy."

Shaking off the strangeness of the moment, Jessica paused in the bedroom doorway to throw a glance over her shoulder. "I'm not worried. After all, if Wendy were to invite you to join her in the shower, she'd be fried. Whereas if I were to ask if you wanted to clean up together . . . ?"

Never breaking eye contact, Logan tilted his head back and downed the protein shake in five huge, continuous gulps. He slammed the empty glass down on the counter without even a grimace at the taste and strode across the living room like a man on a mission.

Apparently, his mission was to back Jessica against the doorjamb, closing her into the circle of his arms braced on the wall, and nuzzle her neck.

They made it into the shower eventually.

After the emotional roller coaster of his first question, Logan decided to keep the second one light. He asked if she had any brothers or sisters, which led to a discussion of what it was like for Jessica to grow up as an only child with parents who didn't understand why she would want to leave their friendly Midwestern town to make a life for herself in New York.

"I always wished I had brothers and sisters. Preferably both older and younger," Jessica said, propping her chin on Logan's chest and tangling her fingers in his chest hair.

He winced, partly from the half-pleasurable sting of her distracted tugging, and partly because he knew better. "No, you don't. Being in the middle is like being the last kid on your team in dodgeball—you get it from every angle, but you're totally on your own."

Jessica melted against him sympathetically, brushing her cheek over his chest and watching him with wide, soft eyes. "Did Dylan and Miles always fight a lot?"

From his position stretched out on the living room couch with Jessica blanketing him, Logan contemplated the cottage ceiling. "I guess. But they were close, too. Dylan is the youngest by a bit, a late baby, so there's ten years between him and Miles. That kid tagged around after Miles everywhere he went, and Miles loved it."

"And you? Where were you in all this?"

He shrugged to get his shoulders into a more comfortable position against the arm of the sofa. "Too busy learning how to code new programming languages. I didn't have a lot of time for playing games and making friends. Even then, I wasn't much of a joiner."

"Weren't you in the chemistry club? Or chess club? Come on, you're stomping all over my nerd stereotypes."

Logan let his lip curl slightly. "We may have gone to the most exclusive private academy in the northeast, but the chemistry club was a joke. At least to me. They were decades behind me, even though I'd skipped a few grades and was the youngest in my year by far."

Jessica tilted her head to rest her cheek over his heart again, and Logan crunched up to get a look at her face.

He loved the freshly kissed plumpness of her mouth, the hectic pink still fading from her cheeks. But it was the gleam of moisture in her extraordinarily green eyes that sent his heart racing.

Of the many things he appreciated about Jessica Bell, the one that was simultaneously useful and problematic was her perceptiveness. She'd made it her business to learn all the ins and outs of Logan's occasionally twisted psyche. She knew him better than anyone left alive on the planet.

Which meant that Jessica, of all people, was liable to be able to hear and interpret the vague sadness that left a lump in his throat and a rasp in his voice.

"Sounds lonely," she murmured gently, and he dropped his head back onto the arm of the sofa with a thunk.

"Don't read too much into this stuff, Tink." Logan stared up at the loft where he'd gotten his first good night's sleep in months. "I'm not complaining. I've had more opportunities than most people can dream of."

"But it required sacrifices, didn't it? Being born into such a powerful family, and having the intelligence to make the business stronger," Jessica argued.

"Never felt that way to me. I preferred to spend

time in the labs working on my own projects. And hey, I was on the swim team."

Swimming, one of the few team sports in which athletes competed individually. Logan had enjoyed the aspect of competing essentially against himself, trying to top his own best time.

"Of course!" Jessica's face lit up. "Your membership at the Chelsea Piers gym makes so much more sense now. I always wondered if you only went there to pick up women, or if you were studying the trajectory of golf balls on their driving range or something."

"Nope. Sometimes when I can't sleep, I head over there and swim laps until my arms are too tired to pull me out of the pool."

"Does it help?"

Logan considered. "The whole place is deserted in the middle of the night. I like the privacy, the quiet. Swimming is one of the few things that can get my brain to shut down for minutes at a time." Running a hand down the length of her spine to make her shiver, Logan grinned. "That's another way. But if you're asking whether the swimming helps me get to sleep afterward, the answer is no."

"I'm not surprised," Jessica said with a slightly breathless undertone to her usual brisk, business-like voice. "I've been researching insomnia, and one of the things doctors agree on is that exercise is good—but early in the day. Exercising at night throws off the body's rhythms, and it can actually wake you up instead of tiring you out."

"Hmm." Logan hitched his legs apart so that

Jessica's hips settled more securely against the part of him that was becoming aware that the most gorgeous woman Logan knew was still pressed naked and yielding along the length of him. "So you're saying that since it's getting late, we definitely shouldn't have sex again?"

"Not if you want to sleep through the night." Jessica gasped, her thighs falling open almost unconsciously as she arched her back.

"Sleep is overrated."

Damn it. That made Jessica freeze up in his arms, her eyes narrowing to emerald slits.

"No," she said firmly, pressing up on her hands to hover over him. "It really isn't. You're sleeping another full night tonight, Logan. If that means we sleep separately to avoid temptation, that's what we'll do."

"Unacceptable."

Logan paused, startled. Jessica stared down at him, equally surprised.

"But . . . you don't sleep with other people," she said slowly. "I mean, you sleep with women—nobody knows that better than I do, but when you're done, you usually wander back down to your lab and nap at your desk."

"Or go back to work." Logan raised his brows. "Not to correct you, as the foremost expert on my mating habits. Should I be flattered that you paid such close attention?"

"It's my job to pay attention to you," she reminded him repressively. "You don't like to have strangers in your personal space."

"I bring women to my apartment all the time," he protested.

Jessica gave him the slightly pitying glance she used when he was being particularly oblivious. "Sweetie. Your apartment is where you store your clothes and other stuff. The lab is where you live."

Sucking in air to keep arguing, Logan stopped with his mouth open. He didn't actually have an argument to make. Jessica was right, on a fundamental level. "Hmm. That doesn't seem healthy."

"You think?" She quirked her brows. "So . . . maybe I had a point about this sojourn to Sanctuary Island?"

Unwilling to concede that yet, Logan returned doggedly to the main issue. She might be right about this island, but when it came to the question of sleeping arrangements, she was dead wrong.

"I want you in my personal space," he stated with rock-solid certainty. "In my bed. Even if all we do is sleep."

Jessica tried to hide the smile that tugged at her full lips, but she wasn't entirely successful. "I suppose I don't really qualify as a stranger. No point running from me to avoid intimacy. I've picked up your dry cleaning and taken care of your personal grooming for the last three years. We're already intimate."

Relieved that she'd identified the variable that made this equation come out differently from every other time he'd had sex with a woman, Logan traced the tip of one finger down the center line of her face.

"I like sleeping beside you," he mused, rummaging through his feelings to figure out why. "Maybe because I trust you to have my back, to wake me up if something happens."

That adorable crinkle appeared between Jessica's auburn brows. "What could happen? Logan?"

He realized she must be able to feel the way his heart suddenly kicked in his chest, and the way his body stiffened until it probably felt as if she were lying on a wooden plank. Making a conscious effort to relax, Logan twitched his shoulders against the sofa cushions and forced an analytical tone.

"There's no big mystery about it. Sleep has been difficult for me since my parents died—I'm sure you figured out the connection there. But what you probably don't know is that their accident . . ."

He paused, horrified at the break in his voice and the burning sting behind his eyes.

"Oh, Logan," Jessica said, as if the weight of unspoken memory was crushing her, too, and to get both of them out from under it, he made himself keep going.

"They were on their way home from a charity benefit. It was late. Statistically, there shouldn't have been anyone else on the road, they should have been fine—but the one other driver they encountered happened to be drunk. He ran a red light and plowed his SUV into their car. The drunk driver walked away without a scratch. My parents didn't."

In spite of the lingering rigidity of his limbs, Jessica melted around him. She tucked her face into the side of his neck. The smell of her hair was indescribably comforting.

"So one night, you went to sleep," Jessica murmured, "and when you woke up, your whole world had changed."

A faint smile tugged at Logan's mouth. "Not exactly a mystery where my insomnia comes from, is it? Unfortunately, knowing the rational cause of the problem has not helped me to solve it. Until . . ."

Jessica raised her head, meeting his gaze. "Until?"

"Until you." Logan struggled with the words for a moment, fighting the sensation of stripping himself bare. "The evidence doesn't lie. I sleep better when you're around. You make me feel like it's safe to close my eyes. Because I know you'll be there when I wake up."

With a shuddery breath, Jessica surged up to press her mouth to his. Logan locked his arms around her shoulders and rolled her beneath him, needy hunger rising like fire in his blood.

Logan squeezed his eyes shut and lost himself in the warmth and closeness of her body's soft, supple welcome—and tried to forget that Jessica had made no promises to stay with him forever.

Chapter Seven

Over the next week, Jessica only caught Logan trying to hack into her phone to check his e-mail once, and it seemed like more of a reflex than anything else. To her surprise, he mostly entered into the spirit of the island and did his best to relax. The frequent, athletic lovemaking probably helped with that.

Also, Logan asked Jessica a new question every day. From her first time—high school boyfriend after prom, sweet and fun, if not earth-shattering—to her dreams for the future. Apparently, he'd never quite understood what someone as smart, dedicated and ambitious as Jessica Bell was doing working as a personal assistant.

She was glad to be able to tell him his instincts weren't wrong. When Miles hired her, he'd basically promised that if she put in her time learning the R&D division's workings from the unique vantage point of Logan's lab, she'd be on track to run the entire division one day.

"Not that I'm in a rush," she'd told Logan on day five, breathless and still glowing from the aftereffects of yet another of his devastating assaults on her senses. "Working with you has been surprisingly rewarding."

Looking smug, Logan stretched luxuriously until his vertebrae popped. "Of course it has. I told you we'd be explosive together."

Jessica only smiled at him with what she knew was a ridiculous amount of fondness. She was tempted to take him down a peg about his sexual prowess, even if she'd be lying. But she didn't want to risk putting any distance between them, even with playful teasing. She sensed that Logan was connecting with her more deeply than he had with anyone in a long time.

He'd learned early on to turn inward, to retreat from the world and the expectations of the people around him, into his own head. He'd even retreated from his family. And now here she was spending every waking moment growing closer to him.

Since that first day on the island, they'd barely left the cottage. Jessica felt guilty about it—she ought to be encouraging Logan into the fresh air, playing on his love of swimming to get him down to the beach for some exercise. But every morning she woke to find Logan propped up on one arm, watching and waiting impatiently for the moment he could drag her out of the bed—at least she'd managed to stick to that rule—and pounce.

So it's not like we aren't getting any exercise at all, Jessica consoled herself as she seeded bell peppers and chopped cucumbers for a salad on the evening of their seventh day on the island.

The rules she'd implemented to combat Logan's insomnia actually seemed to be working. He slept less than she did, but he reported an unprecedented string of nights filled with uninterrupted sleep. She was cautiously optimistic about that, and every time she remembered Logan's confession of how much better he slept when she was around, a warm glow filled her chest.

All in all, apart from the surprise addition of their shockingly good sexual relationship, this trip to Sanctuary was going exactly according to her original plan.

Except for one thing.

Perking up when she heard Logan pad barefoot into the kitchen behind her, Jessica kept her gaze on the steady motion of her knife over the cutting board. "Dylan came down to the cottage while you were in the shower."

"Hmm," Logan said, sliding his arms around her waist and hooking his chin over her left shoulder to press a hot, open-mouthed kiss to her jaw.

Jessica shuddered, her unruly body immediately pushing back into the circle of his embrace, desperate for more of what it had gotten so alarmingly accustomed to in only a few short days. Struggling to maintain her focus on both her objective and the sharp knife in her hand, Jessica stiffened her spine. "Yes. He invited us up to the big house for dessert."

"I've got all the dessert I need right here." With unerring accuracy, Logan nipped the soft, sensitive spot beneath her ear to make her jump, then soothed the sweet sting with his tongue. Jessica bit back a moan and laid the knife down before she cut off one of her fingers.

"I told him we'd be there," she said, and immediately felt the way Logan tensed before dropping his arms. He moved casually to grab a glass from the cabinet beside the sink, and Jessica watched him go to the fridge and fill it from the jar of green, vegetable-laden protein smoothie he'd become hilariously addicted to.

"And if I don't feel like socializing?" Logan finally faced her, kicking the refrigerator door shut behind him.

Logan never felt like socializing. At least, not with his brother or the nice new family Dylan appeared to have stumbled into.

"Dylan said he had something important to tell us," Jessica pressed, determined not to let it go, or to let Logan sidetrack her, this time. "It's only dessert. When was the last time you sat down with your brother—either of them—for long enough to catch up?"

"Catch up?" Logan sneered and sipped at his drink. "Are we in a race now?"

"Catch up on what's happening in each other's lives!" Jessica pressed her lips together, trying not to let her frustration show through in her tone. "We're here. Dylan's here, along with a woman and teenaged boy who have become very important to him.

I don't understand why you don't want to spend time with Dylan. You seemed to get along fine the day we arrived, when you were giving him advice about how to go after the woman he loves."

"It's not that Dylan and I don't get along . . ." Logan put his glass down without finishing it and crossed his arms over his broad chest. "I prefer not to get in too deep with personal relationships. I'm better with theory, abstract problems and mechanical puzzles. You know that."

Jessica kept her tone even with an effort. "So when you go to bars and pick up your one-night stands, that's okay."

Logan shrugged, a cynical twist to his mouth. "Sure. Nothing about that is especially deep. Or personal."

"But it takes people skills. You can't simply grunt while pointing at your groin, and expect women to follow you to your car."

With a sardonic twist to his mouth, Logan drawled, "Not exactly, but if I grunt and point at the *car,* and the car is a chauffeured Bentley . . ."

"That is pathetic," Jessica told him bluntly. "I'm embarrassed and ashamed for you, and for every empty-headed, shallow woman who slept with you for a ride in a limo."

"A Bentley is not a limo. It's a work of art, a precision piece of automotive engineering—"

"I don't care about your car!" Jessica realized her voice had risen an octave, but she couldn't seem to bring it back down into normal range. "Why are we fighting about this?"

"We're clearing up confusion," Logan told her. "You seem to think I'm incapable of social inter-action, as if I suffered from Asperger's syndrome or crippling shyness. That's not the case at all. I'm perfectly capable of interpersonal relationships. I simply choose not to indulge."

Ignoring the dart of pain his calm, cool state-ment sent through her chest, Jessica pulled back her shoulders and stared him down. "Understood. But it changes nothing. Your brother has something important to tell you. We're going. Or I revoke your question for the day."

"That violates our agreement." His face dark-ened. "You want to get me out into the world—to be healthier and more well-adjusted, yet you want me to start with a man who has every cause to hate and resent me."

Shocked at the depth of angry despair in his voice, Jessica choked out, "What? Why would Dylan hate you? You're family."

"Exactly. Whose cuts slice deeper than your family's? When your parents rejected you after they found out about your affair, did it hurt more or less than the rejection you faced at work?"

Sucking in a breath, Jessica straightened. "My parents did not reject me. We may not be as close as we once were, but that doesn't mean—"

"You said you asked them for help," Logan went on, relentless as the tide. "You asked to go home. They refused to take you in."

"They did help me." Jessica swallowed, hating

how thin and plaintive she sounded. In her heart, she knew Logan was right. Her parents' reaction to her mistakes had been a kick to the ribs when she was already down. It had opened up a dark chasm between Jessica and her family that no amount of polite chitchat on Thanksgiving and Christmas could bridge. But that didn't answer her original question.

"We're not talking about my relationship with my parents," she said, proud of the steadiness of her tone. "We're talking about you and your brothers. What happened, Logan? What makes you think Dylan hates you?"

The emotion in his eyes was so raw, so visceral, Jessica almost took a step back. But she forced herself to hold her ground as Logan ground out, "Because Dylan was eight when our parents died. Miles was already gone, in college. Our grandparents, the ones who owned the vacation house here on the island, offered to take Dylan in. He begged me to come with him, but instead . . ."

Logan broke off, his hoarse voice grinding to a halt as he turned his back and braced his hands on the kitchen table. Jessica had to curl her fingers under the edge of the counter to stop herself from going to him.

She wanted nothing more in the world than to wrap Logan up in her arms and shield him from this pain—but the pain was inside him already, and he had to get it out. Terrified that if she moved, she'd shatter this rare confessional moment, Jessica held her breath.

"Instead," Logan said, low and hoarse, "I tested out of my senior year of high school and escaped to college a year early. I abandoned my grief-stricken eight-year-old brother to life in a new city with grandparents he hardly knew, buried myself in school and work and research, and I never looked back. Of course Dylan hates me."

Jessica's throat ached with tears she wouldn't shed. Logan hated tears, mostly because he was bewildered by them and didn't know how to react, she'd learned. So she wouldn't cry for this proud, lonely, regret-ridden man, no matter how badly she wanted to.

Instead, she finally pushed away from the counter and took the few steps that would allow her to slide her arms around his lean waist and press her hot face to his back. Logan's muscles were granite under her touch, but she didn't let go.

"It sounds to me," she murmured urgently, "like Dylan isn't the one who hates you for leaving him. It sounds like you hate yourself. But Logan—your parents had just died, tragically and suddenly, and your world was spinning off its axis. You handled it the only way you knew how. Please, please don't hate yourself for that."

"Dylan was only a kid. He needed me, and I could've stayed. I chose to leave, I chose college over taking care of my baby brother."

"You were a kid, too." Jessica snuggled up as close to Logan as she could, until she couldn't tell her own heartbeat from his. "So young. What were you, sixteen?"

Logan cleared his throat. "Fourteen. I'd already skipped a couple grades."

Squeezing her eyes shut against the burn of tears, Jessica mouthed a quick, fervent kiss against the body-warm cotton of his T-shirt. "Only a baby yourself. Logan—"

"I should have stayed. But what could I have done? I don't know the first thing about comforting someone else, or making them feel better. All I knew was that I was in raw, screaming pain, and I had to escape it any way I could—which was by throwing myself completely into my work."

"That's not true." She tightened her arms around him. "That you're bad at comforting people. No matter what we talk about, or how emotional I get, you always make me feel like it's okay. You listen. That's all anyone can do."

He slumped another inch over the table, hanging his shaggy head between his stiff arms. "So I should have stayed and listened to Dylan have nightmares and cry for Mom and Dad."

"That's not what I'm saying. You did what you needed to at the time, to cope with your own grief." Although she was starting to suspect that he hadn't coped with that grief at all; instead, he'd grabbed onto the challenges of college at fourteen years old to avoid facing it. How had he put it? That he escaped completely into his work.

But no one could outrun a loss like that forever. Jessica was very much afraid that Logan could never truly be healthy and well-adjusted until he dealt with the pain of the past.

"I should have listened to him," Logan repeated, like a looped recording, and Jessica let out a shaky breath.

"It's too late to help your eight-year-old brother," she said, as firmly and gently as she could. "You can't go back in time. You have to let it go . . . and realize that you've been blessed with a second chance."

"What do you mean?" His wrecked voice came from deep inside his chest.

"You can listen to Dylan now." She kissed him once between his shoulder blades, then again because she couldn't help herself, before glancing at the digital clock on the stove. "Come on. Let's go wild and skip dinner, head straight for dessert. Last one up the garden path to the big house has to wash the dishes."

Logan straightened slowly, as if his bones ached, but when she finally got a look at his face, there was a small smile curving his mouth. "Dessert for dinner? Doesn't sound very healthy to me."

"It's okay to let yourself enjoy life sometimes," Jessica said, brushing a tentative hand over his jaw.

He turned his head to plant a kiss that left her palm tingling. Meeting her gaze directly, he admitted, "That's not the easiest thing for me. But I'll try. I want to do better."

Joy lifted Jessica's heart into her throat. She'd never felt closer to anyone than she did to Logan in that moment. "That's good. Because you're a Harrington—and what you boys want, you usually get."

But as they left the summer cottage and walked up the winding path through the twilight garden, Jessica's happiness was tempered by the fact that if Logan was truly improving so quickly, then their time on Sanctuary Island was drawing to a close.

And once they left this magical little hideaway and returned to the real world . . . she and Logan would never be this close again.

Chapter Eight

Logan sort of wanted to hold hands with Jessica on the way to the house—it was a garden, there were flowers all around and the setting sun was flaming the sky with pinks and purples overhead. A textbook definition of a romantic setting probably called for something sappy like hand-holding.

To his surprise, he found he didn't mind the idea all that much, although it was something he usually avoided like malware and spam. Everything was different with Jessica. Take cuddling in bed, for example. He hated cuddling—the clinginess of a woman he barely knew expecting him to keep in contact long after the sex was over? Made no sense, was sweaty and awkward, and he just . . . didn't enjoy it. So he didn't do it.

But with Jessica and her crazy rules about not having sex in bed, there was nothing to do except lie close together, their heads on one pillow, and breathe each other's breath. Sometimes they talked, sometimes he watched her sleep until the steady rhythm of her soft breathing closed his lids and pulled him under.

He didn't mind it. Same with the hand-holding, as long as it was with Jessica—except at the moment, his palms were too clammy and itchy with nerves to inflict on anyone else.

Don't be stupid, he told himself. *This isn't going to be some huge emotional revelation. You've already met your quota for those today.*

Dylan just wanted his brother to meet the woman he was seeing for more than a thirty-second introduction in which Logan had inadvertently outed Dylan as a member of the Harrington family. Which Penny hadn't been aware of previously.

Jessica led them confidently up the back steps and rapped smartly on the window-paned door, giving Logan flashbacks of arriving at the house a week ago.

Only then, they'd waited on the front porch, and he'd felt like a reanimated corpse after weeks of nonstop work. Now that his brain no longer resembled a cracked-out hamster trapped in an exercise ball, Logan could appreciate the storybook feel of his family's old vacation home.

Most of the Victorian gingerbreading was festooned over the façade in front, but even from the back, the house was appealing. Three stories, gables, wooden shutters, the whole nine yards. There was even a bay window overlooking the garden; probably a nice spot to settle in and read a book.

Still, as footsteps sounded from inside and Logan braced himself for whatever was about to happen, he acknowledged silently that he was glad Jessica had maneuvered them out of the main house and down to stay in the cozy summer cottage across the garden.

In the cottage, they had privacy and peace, and no . . . teenagers.

A lanky kid opened the back door and grinned at them from under a shock of dirty-blond hair.

"Ha! Dylan, you owe me five bucks," he shouted over his shoulder before pushing the door wide and ushering them in. The kid studied them with open curiosity, his wide hazel eyes lingering on Jessica in a way that made Logan suddenly, intensely aware of how extraordinarily beautiful she looked. Dressed more casually than he was used to in a linen button-down shirt over a pair of jeans, Jessica took his breath away.

"You're very lovely tonight," Logan told her immediately. He should have said it before. He should be saying it constantly. "Well, objectively, you're lovely all the time, but tonight you look especially beautiful."

The blush that suffused her cheeks in no way detracted from her beauty, he noticed with interest.

"Thank you. That's very sweet—and awkward—of you." Reaching past Logan, she put out her hand to shake the kid's. "Hi, I'm Jessica Bell. This is Logan Harrington."

"Dylan's brother." The kid nodded in that know-it-all-way common to teenagers. "I told him you'd show. I'm Matt Little. Come on in, my mom already sliced the pie but she said we had to wait for you."

At the word *pie,* Logan shot Jessica a glance and saw her biting her lip against a smile. They followed Matt through the open, airy kitchen, past a round table that showed the obvious marks of frequent use and into a formal dining room.

Dylan sat at the head of a large oval table, his elbows resting comfortably on the polished mahogany surface, one hand extended across the table to clasp the hand of a smallish brunette with a beaming smile. Penny Little, Logan remembered through the haze of exhaustion and confusion that had dimmed his vision when he met her.

The moment before they became aware of the presence of guests, Logan caught a glimpse of something he dimly recognized, an invisible spark that flew between them and tied Dylan and Penny together as they smiled into each other's eyes. Dylan lifted their entwined fingers to his mouth and kissed Penny's knuckles so tenderly, Logan felt his own cheeks heat uncomfortably. Feeling as if he was intruding on an unbearably intimate moment, he froze in the dining room doorway, unable to make his feet move forward.

Clearly unburdened by any feelings of being an intruder, Matt breezed past him. "I told you they'd come," he said confidently, grabbing a dessert plate and a fork before retreating in a rush of big feet and lanky limbs. "No one can resist Mom's famous buttermilk pie. I'm taking this up to my room so y'all can have boring grown-up time."

Dylan jerked, clearly startled, and as he started to get up to greet them, Logan's gaze caught on something sparkly in his brother's grasp.

It was a ring. A diamond ring, on Penny Little's left hand, and its facets winked in the light when Dylan pulled her to her feet beside him.

"Logan. You're looking much better than the last time I saw you. I was worried you'd starved to death down in the cottage."

"Jessica would never let that happen," Logan retorted automatically.

"No, sure," Dylan said, darting a quick glance at Penny. "Of course not."

Logan swallowed. He'd been right, this was awful. Stilted and weird, too formal and polite. Nothing like the conversation they'd had a week ago, when Logan had told his brother to believe in himself, that he was more than the Bad Boy Billionaire the tabloids made him out to be, that he deserved to find love.

He stared at the ring on Penny Little's left hand. Looked like Dylan had taken that advice and run with it.

"So you're engaged," Logan said abruptly, aware that his tone was brusque, almost cold, but not sure how to fix it.

"Logan!" Jessica hissed, poking him in the side, but he twitched away irritably and kept his gaze on his brother's face.

Instead of looking sheepish or caught out, the way he had when he was six years old and dragged every pot and pan out of the lower cabinets and piled them up to try and climb the counter to get to the cookie jar, Dylan seemed perfectly at ease. When he smiled and rolled his eyes, contentment radiated from every pore.

"I should have known you'd notice it the minute you walked in." Lifting Penny's hand for another one of those fairy-tale kisses, Dylan said, "I asked Penny to marry me. And she said yes!"

"Congratulations," Jessica said into the brief silence that followed Dylan's jubilant announcement. "What a wonderful surprise!"

Some of the light in Penny's pretty face had dimmed, and Logan noted the way her eyes flicked worriedly from him to her fiancé. But she smiled and held out her hand when Jessica asked to see the ring.

"My boss and coworkers at the Firefly Café want to throw us an engagement breakfast at the restaurant tomorrow morning," Penny said. "I hope you can both be there."

"Of course! We wouldn't miss it," Jessica assured her, stepping sideways to tread on Logan's toes in an obvious effort to make him contribute to the conversation.

But Logan was at a loss. This wasn't Dylan's first engagement. His previous fiancée had been working an angle, looking for a soft landing with a rich husband—or a heavy payoff for leaving him alone, which was the route their eldest brother had taken to get rid of her.

Logan knew he was the last person on the planet that Dylan would—or should—take romantic advice from, but he couldn't help being concerned.

"You've known each other for three weeks," he pointed out abruptly, killing the conversation around him.

Dylan's face went hard, his eyes glittering with emotion. "Don't start. I already heard it from Miles. Yes, it's fast—but when it's right, you know it."

"So Miles is aware. Good." Logan seized on the pertinent information and ignored the rest, including the small pang at the knowledge that he was the last to hear about the engagement. So much for Jessica's theory that Dylan was reaching out to him.

"Yeah, I called him this afternoon." The downward curve of Dylan's mouth revealed that it had not been a happy conversation. Logan could only imagine Miles's reaction to the news that his reckless, directionless youngest brother was marrying a single mom who worked two jobs and lived on a tiny, backwater island off the coast of Virginia. "I'm starting to regret telling either of you. Damn it, Logan . . ."

Penny moved to Dylan's side and slid an arm around his waist, presenting them as a united front. She faced him with head held high, her eyes clear and body language open when she said, "I understand your concerns. I truly do. The world you live in—you have to be constantly on guard against people taking advantage, or wanting more from you than you're willing to give. But that's not my world. I love your brother, and he loves me. We want to make a life together, here on Sanctuary Island. We think we can make each other happy. That's my ulterior motive here. My happiness, Dylan's happiness and my son's happiness."

A small flame of respect kindled in Logan's chest at the proud, direct way Penny spoke. Her matter-of-fact words about love and happiness tugged at his heart in a way he didn't like. Unsure how to react, Logan looked to Jessica.

She gave him an encouraging smile, tilting her head as if to say, *Go ahead*.

Uncomfortable, Logan shrugged and shoved his hands in the pockets of his trousers. "Do what you're going to do. You hardly need my approval or my blessing."

"We don't need it," Dylan agreed, curling his arm around Penny's slender shoulders. "We're getting married, building a life and being happy, just as Penny said, whether you and Miles like it or not. But I guess I hoped you'd see that, for once, I know what I'm doing."

"Are you sure?" With Dylan's track record, Logan had to ask.

A slow smile spread across Dylan's face as he stared down into the upturned eyes of his fiancée. "I've never been more sure of anything in my life. Marriage is a big step, a real commitment . . . but I

Chapter Nine

Jessica was a pace behind Logan all the way back to the cottage, his long legs and quick, restless strides eating up the path.

The rest of the evening with Dylan and Penny had been ... well, "disaster" was probably too strong a word, but not by much. Logan had shut down completely after Dylan's heartfelt speech. He sat there at the table with an untouched piece of pie in front of him, mouth a thin, hard line and his eyes dark and shuttered.

Jessica did her best to keep conversation flowing by offering to help Penny set up for the engagement party and asking if they'd set a date yet, while the two brothers glared at each other across the table in silence.

Sighing as Logan slammed into the screened-in porch and flopped down on the glider, Jessica leaned against the doorway. The drone of cicadas rose and fell around the cottage, accompanied by the song of crickets and the rustle of a breeze through the magnolias. It was a beautiful night.

Too bad her plan to strengthen Logan and Dylan's relationship was a total bust.

"That could have gone better," she observed to the top of Logan's head as he leaned over his knees and fisted his hands in his hair.

"Where is my phone?" he asked abruptly, glaring up at her.

That startled her into straightening away from the doorjamb. "It's in a safe place, don't worry."

"Give it to me," he demanded.

Jessica crossed her arms over her chest as dismay trickled into her belly. "No. The rules haven't changed."

"*Everything* is changing." Standing in a controlled rush, Logan prowled the length of the porch. "Too fast."

Empathy tightened like a fist around Jessica's throat. Always an introvert, Logan had locked all his tumultuous emotions away in a box when his parents died, and then carefully constructed his life so he never had to deal with them in any way.

Until now. The lid was coming off that box, exposing him to feelings he hadn't ever learned to master, and no matter how hard he worked to suppress them, Jessica didn't think he'd be able to close that box up again. Not entirely.

The boy who'd learned that deep personal connection only led to pain and loss had grown into a man who did his best to hold people at arm's length. But in the last few days, Logan had gotten closer to his brother—and to her—than he'd been to anyone in a long time. It was no wonder he was freaking out.

"It's late," she tried. "Come to bed."

"I'm not tired."

Heart heavy with guilt, as if she were somehow responsible for the fact that Logan and his brothers couldn't seem to find common ground, Jessica attempted a smile. "I could tire you out."

His eyes gleamed briefly in the moonlight, but he shook his head. "You're right, it's late. You should get some rest. I'll follow the rules, have some hot milk, come to bed when I think I'll actually be able to sleep."

Jessica hesitated before agreeing. Those were the rules, suggested by sleep experts who alleged that spending time lying in bed unable to sleep would only begin a cycle of frustration that prevented a person from nodding off. Better, they said, to reset the brain by getting up and reading for a bit, then going back to bed to try again.

And Logan was used to spending most of his time alone. If he needed a few solitary hours to process the evening's events, that was certainly understandable.

Still, this felt like a step backward. He'd been doing so well, falling asleep every night in her arms, that tonight's nervous energy and restless pacing made her wary.

"Okay," she said slowly. "Wake me up when you come to bed?"

He nodded, crossing the porch to cradle her face in his large, warm hands. Her pulse fluttered like the wings of a moth, unable to resist the lure of the light.

Logan bent his head and brushed a kiss over her mouth. "Good night," he whispered against her lips.

"Wake me up, seriously," she reminded him again.

"I will," he promised.

But when Jessica startled awake hours later, as the silvery light of dawn filtered through the curtains, she was alone in the bed. The sheets on Logan's side were cool to the touch, the pillow undented.

Sliding from the bed, Jessica shivered and wrapped her blue silk robe around her shoulders. She padded from the bedroom out to the main room, her bare toes flinching from the cold hardwood floor. "Logan?"

There was no answer but a shuffling sound from above. Still half-asleep, Jessica looked up. Had he slept in the loft? Since they started sleeping together, the loft and its smaller, less comfortable bed hadn't seen much use beyond storing their empty suitcases.

Annoyed at herself for feeling a pang that Logan might be learning to sleep better on his own than with her, Jessica started for the built-in stepladder that reached up into the loft space.

She was on the third rung before she remembered what else was up in the loft, besides a low, narrow bed.

Hurrying up the ladder, heart in her throat, Jessica cleared the floor already knowing what she'd see.

And there he was. Logan crouched beside the bed with his confiscated cell phone clutched in his hand, thumb typing so furiously and intently, she knew he hadn't even heard her call his name.

This was why she'd taken the phone. When Logan got embroiled with work, he lost track of everything else. Nothing mattered but the problem in front of him.

Nothing and no one.

Gritting her teeth against the vulnerable girl inside who was hurt that she'd been forgotten in favor of a piece of technology, Jessica climbed the rest of the way into the loft and cinched her robe more tightly around her waist.

"All right, you checked in. Now hand it over," she demanded.

Without looking up from the backlit screen or ceasing his lightning-fast typing, Logan bit out, "There's an emergency at the lab. They need me back there. I'm catching the morning ferry back to New York."

Jessica closed her eyes and gathered her patience. This was exactly what she'd tried to avoid. "No, you're not. You're on vacation. Deal with it. The lab can deal with it—this so-called emergency is nothing more than a group of employees who have been spoiled by constant access to you, and who need to learn to self-direct and take responsibility for their jobs."

His head shot up, his bloodshot blue eyes lasering in on her face. "You knew about this?"

"I've kept up to date with the e-mails from the

lab, yes." The increasingly frantic e-mails, begging for more direction and next steps on the project Logan had handed them before he left. "I told you I'd monitor the situation, and I have. You left them with adequate instructions. They may not be geniuses like you, but they should be able to figure this out on their own, without bothering you."

Finally tossing the phone aside, Logan rounded the bed and dragged his suitcase out of the space by the wall. "I'm leaving. I need to get back to my lab, my work."

"You need to stay here and keep healing," Jessica said, reaching to take the suitcase from him, but Logan jerked away.

"I'm fine," he said in a rusty voice. His swift, shaky movements told another story, and Jessica noted all the familiar signs with a growing sense of alarm.

"You didn't sleep at all last night, did you? Logan, you have to see how bad for you this is."

"It's my job. I'd think you, of all people, would understand why that's important to me."

Rocking back on her heels, Jessica didn't have time to figure out why that felt like a slap. "Important enough to jeopardize your recovery?"

"I'm not jeopardizing anything." Dropping the suitcase over the side of the loft with a bang that made Jessica jump, Logan started down the ladder after it, clearly intent on packing.

A deep wellspring of panic bubbled up unexpectedly, goading Jessica to say, "So the fact that once we go back to Manhattan, this thing between us is over—that doesn't even factor into your decision."

She heard Logan pause halfway down the ladder, but mortification and an intense need to hear his response kept her from walking to the edge of the loft to catch sight of him.

When he replied, his voice had lost some of the frenetic distraction in favor of a coolness that sent shivers down her spine. "You still want to go back to the way we were, when we leave here."

"I mean—that's what we agreed." Surprise and confusion pushed her to the loft ledge to peek over. Logan stood with his legs braced apart, his head slightly bowed so that Jessica's gaze snagged on the vulnerable nape of his neck, the light brown tendrils of his overlong hair. From this angle, his shoulders were immense, wide and strong, before his torso tapered to the whipcord leanness of his waist.

As well as she now knew that body, and as hard as she'd worked to make herself an expert on the man inside, this trip to Sanctuary Island had shown her how much there still was to learn. She could spend a lifetime unraveling the complexities of a man like Logan Harrington, and never tire of the challenge.

On the teetering, dangerous point of throwing caution out the window and telling Logan she wanted to continue their relationship when they went back to New York, Jessica opened her mouth—only to be interrupted by Logan.

He tilted his head back, and it was as if he'd slammed an iron shield down behind his blue eyes, hiding everything he thought and felt. "You're right, we had an agreement. I won't go back on my word. So I guess it's over."

And that was it. The tender green shoot of hope that had taken root in Jessica's heart withered and died, killed by the frost of Logan's cool declaration. Dimly, she was aware of the irony—that she'd been the one to put these rules in place, trying to protect herself, and yet here she was with a yawning, aching emptiness cracking open her rib cage.

Desperate to hide her hurt, Jessica turned to descend the ladder in a flurry of blue satin.

"But you are going back on your word," she argued, hoping the hoarse breathlessness of her voice could be attributed to the effort of climbing down from the loft. "You said you'd stay here until you were well."

"No, I said I'd stay here one day for every question you answered honestly." Every distant, abstracted word flicked over her raw nerves like a whip. "I don't have any more questions, so I don't have to stay. And, by the way, I'm not a child. As much as you love to direct my life and organize my every movement, you are not actually the boss of me."

She reached the bottom of the ladder in time to catch the bleak irony of Logan's half smile. He was really leaving, without actually making a full recovery. How long would it be before he was right back where he'd been two weeks ago, in full-blown exhaustion, collapsing in his lab from stress and overwork?

Fear and hurt sharpened Jessica's voice to a pitch that shocked her. "You may technically be a full-grown man, but if I treat you like a child, it's because sometimes you act like one."

For the first time, a flicker of anger pierced the defenses he'd slammed into place over his expression. Good. Jessica preferred angry Logan to the robotic stranger he'd turned into.

"I see. So taking responsibility for my job, my department, that's childish behavior."

Holding her head up, Jessica firmed her jaw. "No. But running out on your brother's engagement breakfast, to avoid facing the emotions that brings up for you? That's childish."

With a sardonic twist to his mouth, Logan bent to retrieve the suitcase he'd tossed to the living room floor. "Well, to be fair, I never promised to change. I only promised awesome, temporary sex."

Jessica abruptly wished she'd taken the time to get dressed before going in search of Logan. She needed the armor of her professional wardrobe, her clean, classic suits and sensibly sexy heels. This satin robe didn't provide enough cover from Logan's sharp, searing glare.

And when he scored a direct hit like that, she couldn't help glancing down to see if the bloody wound was visible.

Playing her final card, Jessica reached out a hand and caught Logan's arm as he brushed past her toward the bedroom. "Logan. Please don't do this. Stay, for me."

He stiffened under her touch as if her fingers

carried an electric charge. "I've wasted enough time here," he growled.

Jessica stumbled back a step, pain rocketing straight through her chest.

Wasted time. The days and nights on Sanctuary Island that had been some of the most intimate, important hours of Jessica's life were no more than wasted time to Logan.

Cold and numb, Jessica wrapped her arms around her ribs and met Logan's impassive gaze. "Fine. But if you go back to New York today . . . I'm not coming with you."

Chapter Ten

Logan stared at Jessica, a volcano of emotion seething under his skin. He didn't understand his own feelings, the restlessness and need to fight against the shackles binding him to this island.

He had to get out of here.

But to leave without Jessica? Even though she intended to follow through with the end of their affair when they got back to New York, the very idea of leaving her behind made him pause—just as she must have known it would. She'd always known how to maneuver him. Well, he was through with that.

Narrowing his gaze against the rise of anger and betrayal, Logan kept it as chilled down as he could, even while striking back. "Now who's using a personal relationship to try to manipulate our professional lives?"

She drew back as if he'd raised a hand to her,

and Logan had to clench his fists against the urge to step forward and soothe the hurt he'd caused. This was madness, the chaotic welter of confused emotion she pulled out of him as effortlessly as breathing. He couldn't stand it, didn't know any way to weather it other than to run.

"Fine, go then." Jessica looked away, the bed-tousled strands of her red-gold hair like flames against the paleness of her cheeks. "I'll cover for you with Dylan and Penny when I go over to the café to help set up for the party."

Logan forced himself to shrug. "If you want, since you promised to help out. But I never actually promised them I'd be there."

Her lips thinned. "And you always keep your promises."

The scorn in her uneven voice caught him on the ragged edges of his nerves. "All except one," Logan snarled, his mouth running ahead of his brain for once. "I was actually fool enough to start to fall in love with you."

Every line of Jessica's body, lovingly outlined by her shiny, clinging blue robe, went still and tense. Eyes large and intent, she murmured, "And yet, you're still leaving?"

He nodded once, short and sharp, and she closed her eyes.

"You don't know what love is. Sir." And she turned and walked into the bedroom, closing the door behind her with an implacable, gentle click.

Logan stared at the blank expanse of white-painted wood, paralyzed for a long, agonizing moment before he realized she'd shut herself into the room that contained everything he'd intended to pack in his suitcase. Part of him wanted to storm into the bedroom, shake her by the shoulders and force her to admit that she felt something more for him than a week's worth of lust—and part of him only wanted to leave and never see her again.

The vibration of his phone in his hand, signaling an incoming text, jolted him out of the black cloud of indecision.

He had his phone. Everything else was replaceable. "To hell with it," he muttered, turning on his heel and throwing open the front door. Thanking God and GPS that the island was small and easily walkable, Logan jogged around the house and out to Island Road. He paused by the town square to key in the location of the wharf that docked the ferry.

Totally absorbed in his map app, it took Logan a few seconds to register the increase of wind gusting against his face and hair. Until suddenly his wrinkled button-down was flapping like a flag, and the air was split by the unmistakable rhythmic whir of helicopter blades.

Shading his eyes with the flat of his hand, Logan stared up in bewilderment. For one crazy moment, he wondered if he'd summoned the company chopper with the power of his brain and the intensity of his desire to get off this island.

He tracked the progress of the sleek bird as it touched down on the green grass of the town square, right next to the picturesque little bandstand at the center. The side door slid open, and his older brother, Miles, descended from the chopper with an enigmatic gesture at the pilot.

The only man Logan had ever seen exit a helicopter without crouching and scuttling away from the still-rotating blades, Miles strode across the town green as if he were crossing a corporate boardroom. He was all pressed lines and perfectly tailored three-piece suit, his light brown hair ruthlessly combed back and anchored in place.

That's what a healthy, well-adjusted human being looks like, Logan couldn't help thinking with a grimace. Maybe Miles was the Harrington brother Jessica ought to be with.

Even the merest suggestion of that idea caused a chain reaction of possessive denial and anger so strong, Logan was all but snarling by the time Miles reached him.

"Good, I didn't know if you got my text," Miles said without preamble.

"I didn't. But thanks for bringing the chopper to pick me up."

"Pick you up?" Miles raked him with an impassive look, then glanced over his shoulder. Logan followed his gaze to watch, wide-eyed with disbelief, as his perfect escape route lifted off the grass in a tornado rush of wind and scattering leaves.

"Damn it, Miles," Logan growled, clenching his fists until blood throbbed in his fingertips. "Call her back. I need to get out of here."

"You're not going anywhere. We have a situation."

"I know!" Logan ran his fingers through his hair. "The lab—"

"The lab is fine without you." Miles flicked his fingers dismissively over a nonexistent speck of dust on his charcoal-gray sleeve. "I checked in with them before I flew down, and empowered your second-in-command to take charge, to keep them from panicking."

Feeling the cage around him constrict, Logan scrubbed a hand over his prickly jaw. "Damn it, Miles."

"Focus." Miles snapped, sharp and loud, in front of Logan's face, as if he were an unruly puppy. It took everything Logan had not to bite at those fingers. "I'm talking about Dylan."

"What?" Confused, Logan whirled to stare across Island Road at the white-trimmed Victorian house. "Something happened to Dylan? I just saw him last night, he was fine."

Miles snorted. "For values of 'fine' that include 'being taken for a ride by yet another scheming gold digger,' sure."

"Oh, that." Logan frowned.

"Yes, that." Impatient, Miles started walking, as if assuming Logan would fall into step beside him. When Logan stayed put, Miles arched an imperious brow over his shoulder. "Well? Come on. We have work to do."

A headache screamed to life behind Logan's tired eyes. This was why he preferred the controlled conditions of his lab. The fierce rush of life in the outside world was too hard to keep pace with. "Work."

Miles paused on the curb to study his brother, a critical frown lowering his brows. "I thought you were supposed to spend this week resting. Damn it, Logan, you look worse than when you left. Where the hell is Jessica Bell?"

The sound of her name in Miles's stern, uncompromising voice sent an odd jolt through Logan. "Leave Jessica alone."

Miles's mouth went hard and flat. "I pay her—very well, in fact—to keep you functioning. She's obviously falling down on the job. But I'll deal with that afterward."

"After what?"

Smoothing a hand down his already perfectly smooth suit coat, Miles glanced up at their grandparents' vacation home. "After I break up Dylan's engagement, of course. Now let's go."

Logan, who had never in his life considered trying to stop Miles from doing something he was determined to do, hesitated. "Wait."

"What's the holdup?" Miles scowled. "Look, I know you usually leave this kind of thing to me, and that's fine. It's my responsibility to take care of the family. But this is crunch time. The way Dylan sounded on the phone . . . I think we need to present a united front about this."

For the most part, Logan was content to let Miles sweat the small stuff—and the big stuff—when it came to taking care of business. All Logan concerned himself with was the scientific end of things, both developing and then creating the cutting-edge technology that would take their company into the future. But a kernel of shame lodged beneath Logan's breastbone at the realization that he'd let Miles also bear the full burden of holding together what was left of their family.

And as he stared at his older brother now, he noticed for the first time that there was a thin layer of frazzled worry under his normal, unruffled façade.

This wasn't just another problem to solve, for Miles. He was genuinely concerned about Dylan—which meant he'd be even harder to dissuade from the course of action he'd set. Miles would save Dylan from another gold-digging fiancée, or die trying.

However, Logan wasn't a hundred percent sure in this case that Dylan needed saving.

His phone buzzed with another incoming e-mail, and his fingers itched to check for more flailing and freaking out from his lab rats.

Miles sighed, and Logan looked up to see a spasm of something tighten his older brother's mouth before Miles said, with his usual calm composure, "Never mind. You won't be happy until you're in your lab, overseeing everything. It's fine, I'll call back the helicopter, then go deal with Dylan myself."

He reached into an inner pocket of his suit jacket for his phone, and Logan's breath hitched. Escape was so close, he could almost taste it . . .

A vision of Jessica's face as he'd last seen it rose up before him. Pale as milk, but blank. Expressionless.

Except for her eyes—they'd burned with a green fire that threatened to reduce him to ashes.

You don't know what love is.

Her parting shot echoed in his mind, and Logan filled his lungs with clean, clear, salt-scented air. She was wrong. He knew exactly what love was. That's why it terrified him.

But all his fear and all his defenses hadn't stopped love from slipping into his heart and setting up a home. And what did all that fear boil down to, in essence? What was he afraid of?

The pain of loss. The very same pain that was currently squeezing his lungs and boring holes in his heart—because the worst had already happened. He'd lost Jessica.

And yeah, it hurt. A lot. But he was still alive, and so was she. Something his mother used to say, an old-fashioned sentiment he hadn't thought of in years, echoed in his ears.

Where there's life, there's hope.

"No, don't call the helicopter," Logan said, surprised by how calm he sounded as his long-held fears sloughed off him like a snake shedding its skin. He stood tall and proud, steadier than he'd been in years. "I'll stay and talk to Dylan with you. It's time we faced things as a family."

One look into Jessica's gorgeous green eyes would be enough to tell if Logan should keep that hope alive—or bury it forever, along with his heart.

Chapter Eleven

"Who on earth can that be?"

Greta Hackley, who'd proudly informed Jessica that her family had owned the hardware store on Sanctuary Island for generations, was kneeling in a booth and staring out the picture window at the front of the Firefly Café with wide dark eyes.

Jessica joined Penny's maid of honor to peer through the glass. "Oh no. Damage control time."

As if reluctant to take her eyes off the spectacle of two incredibly handsome, tall, broad-shouldered men striding up to the restaurant, Greta turned her head slowly to study Jessica. "There, now there's a little color in those cheeks. When you first walked in here to help, I thought we were going to end up picking you off the floor. But you're a hard worker, even when you're feeling poorly."

"Poorly," Jessica murmured, most of her attention

on the approach of the elder Harrington brothers. "That's one way to put it."

Another way would have been "heartbroken." But that was ridiculous, she chastised herself. Of all women, Jessica, who'd been through this before, who'd cleaned up after Logan's endless string of one-night stands, should know better. She *did* know better.

So why did the sight of Logan, still on the island and walking toward her with a determined edge to his jaw, make her heart race?

Probably adrenaline, she told herself as her attention finally shifted to the man who paid her salary, Miles Harrington. From what hints Penny had dropped, with many a concerned glance at her fiancé, Miles had been coldly furious to hear about Penny and Dylan's whirlwind romance.

His presence at the engagement breakfast might signal a change of heart—or it could mean he was here to lay down the law and forbid the marriage, like some soap opera patriarch come to life.

Checking behind her, Jessica saw Dylan taking advantage of a brief moment of quiet before the party really started to draw his bride-to-be around a corner and steal a kiss. Happiness shot through with shards of loss tightened Jessica's throat.

By God, someone in this whole drama deserved a happy ending.

Pushing away from the booth, she jerked her head in the direction of the oblivious couple. "Keep the lovebirds occupied in here," she told Greta. "I'll take care of those guys."

Greta arched a dark blond brow and flicked her long braid over her flannel-shirted shoulder. "If you need help, you know where to find me."

Smiling, Jessica thanked her. But as she moved swiftly to the door to head off the invasion of the Harrington brothers, she thought bleakly that she was probably the only person on Sanctuary Island who stood a chance of making Miles Harrington listen to reason.

And even then, it wasn't a very good chance. Miles was famous for making up his mind and sticking to his guns.

Jessica had braced herself for the emotional charge of coming face-to-face with Logan after their recent fight, but nothing could have prepared her for the reality of staring up into his stern, hard-planed face and seeing his ice-blue eyes fire with open, obvious desire.

Faltering, heart stuttering, Jessica darted a nervous glance at her boss. She'd already lost Logan—she couldn't lose her job, too.

Miles's gaze narrowed on her face, his expression as cold and implacable as granite. She felt the piercing force of his stare as if he could peer into her mind and see that she'd made the colossal, ridiculous mistake of falling for one of the Harrington brothers.

Jessica dug deep and unearthed a reserve of strength she hadn't known she possessed. It was enough to straighten her shoulders and pull her spine taut. Enough to enable her to face her boss as calmly as if she were wearing her favorite red wool suit and heels, rather than a white T-shirt and a pair of jeans that were dusty from climbing a ladder to hang streamers.

"Mr. Harrington," she said coolly, extending a hand before belatedly realizing it was smeared with a bit of buttercream frosting from the cake she'd helped set up on the café counter. Withdrawing it, she wiped it smoothly on her pants. "What a surprise. We weren't expecting you."

Her gaze slid sideways to Logan before she could stop it. "Either of you," she finished, as impassively as she could manage.

The light in Logan's eyes dimmed as if she'd snuffed it out like a candle. His abrupt shift to slide his hands in his pockets made her wonder if he'd been about to reach out to her.

Jessica flinched away from the urge to hope like a person with vertigo on the edge of a cliff. Logan wasn't ready to change who he was, wasn't ready for a real emotional commitment. He might never be. And in the meantime, she couldn't wait around, wishing and hoping for more.

It would hurt too much.

Forcing herself to look away from Logan, Jessica faced her boss. A muscle ticked in Miles's stony jaw. "Ms. Bell. Here you are."

"Here I am." She projected a light professionalism she didn't really feel. "I promised Dylan and Penny I'd help set up for the party."

Miles frowned. "Yes, so Logan mentioned. Not exactly in your job description, Ms. Bell. Unlike accompanying Logan when he travels. That *is* part of your job, as I remember explaining it."

Jessica suppressed a wince. Miles could smell fear, like blood in the water. But before she could make the excuse that she'd told Logan not to travel anywhere—and Miles would see it as an excuse, he didn't accept any rationalization of failure—Logan said, "It's fine. I told her to stay here, and that I'd see her back in New York on Monday."

His voice was quiet, a little tired around the edges, but the fact that he was trying to cover for her made emotion rise up to clog Jessica's throat.

She couldn't stop herself from meeting his gaze, and the weary defeat in his blue eyes nearly exploded the ball of emotion into a storm of tears. But Logan smiled at her, a small, private smile that looked as if it intended to be reassuring. "Bright and early, Monday morning, back to the real world. Everything just as it was before we left."

The world screeched to a halt around Jessica's ears at the subtle message Logan was sending, like a whisper only she could hear. Back to normal, exactly as they'd agreed.

He was telling her she could have what she'd negotiated for up front—a week of bliss, of fun and discovery in his arms, and on Monday, they'd pick up where they left off, as colleagues. It was everything she'd thought she wanted, especially since it was all she believed she could have after he stormed out of the summer cottage.

As Logan handed her what she'd asked for, free

and easy as a gift, Jessica realized the truth. She wanted more.

She wanted it all. And for the first time in years, Jessica seriously wondered if it might be possible.

Jessica didn't even appear to register the way Miles was complaining that everything better not be back to the way it was, because he couldn't have Logan dropping dead of a heart attack before the age of forty due to stress and exhaustion.

That was fine. Logan was ignoring him, too. But then, he usually ignored Miles, while Jessica usually hung on the man's every word. Miles was her boss, after all, and her job was the most important thing to her—which she'd proved by acting like there was nothing between her and Logan, the minute Miles showed up.

But now she was staring at Logan in a daze, as if he'd somehow shocked the sense out of her by trying to finally give her what she'd asked for.

Which didn't make Logan feel too good, especially when combined with the fact that he was here now, with Miles, to try to start standing together as a family. Tuning the big man out probably wasn't the best way to go about it.

Logan tuned back in with a vengeance when the front door of the café pushed open, and Dylan stomped down the steps to confront them. He went right up to Miles, toe to toe with their older brother, and it gave Logan a jolt to notice as if for the first time how alike they looked. Not merely their blue eyes, light-brown hair, and tall, athletic frames, but in their identical stubborn expressions.

Maybe he should read up on genetics—clearly a fascinating field of scientific study.

A tall woman Logan didn't know hovered in the restaurant doorway behind Dylan, watching with definite interest.

"Great job keeping him distracted," Jessica muttered, and the woman grimaced.

"Sorry, he's a force of nature when he's going after something."

"Family trait," Jessica replied tersely, causing the young woman to grin and flick a sideways glance at Miles.

Ignoring all the byplay, Dylan divided his glower equally between both of his older brothers as if unsure whose ass should be at the top of his to-be-kicked list. "If you're here to try and stop me from marrying Penny, you may as well head back to the city."

Miles stepped up, as usual, raising his smoothly shaved chin to stare down his long, straight nose. "Don't cast me as the villain in this drama. I'm only here to make sure no one is taking advantage of you."

Dylan snorted as if he didn't buy it for a second, but Logan saw the way the lines at the corners of Miles's eyes deepened and his frozen mask chilled down another few degrees.

This was the kind of fraught, intensely emotional confrontation Logan hated. Everyone here believed he was right, utterly and completely, and no one was ever going to back down. Usually he stayed out of it, knowing the chaos would eventually resolve itself.

"And I suppose the fact that I love Penny and she loves me," Dylan argued, "that means nothing to you."

It was Miles's turn to register complete disbelief, although he was too controlled to snort. "Dylan. You've known each other for less than a month."

"So? Grandma told me once that Dad asked Mom to marry him on their third date."

The mention of their parents shut Miles up as nothing else could. Turning his hard-jawed face away to stare out at the ocean vista that provided a backdrop to the Firefly Café, he muttered to Logan, "Reason with him. I can't deal with him when he's like this."

A tiny intake of breath to his right had Logan looking back in time to see Jessica subtly stepping closer to Dylan, aligning herself with him. She stared at Logan, her whole heart in her eyes, and he read the plea there as clearly as if she'd written it on the air between them.

She didn't want him to systematically take the whole concept of love apart, to reduce it to pieces and parts, components scattered across a lab table for dissection. That's all Jessica thought he'd know to do with love.

Maybe that was true, before Sanctuary Island. But now . . . Logan took a deep breath and faced his younger brother—although his words were meant for the older brother.

Once again, Logan was in the middle, tugged in opposite directions. But this time, he was sure enough of his own footing to keep from budging. Jessica had given him that. So he paid her back the only way he knew how.

"Miles wants me to tell you that love is nothing more than chemicals in the brain, a means to promote the propagation of the species. Maybe he thinks the fact that there's a biological basis for the experience of loving another human being means it's not real. But I'm a scientist, and a man, and I know that love is real . . . that it's something more than an evolutionary imperative."

Miles swung around, hell in his eyes, but before he could blast Logan, Jessica said, "You wanted him to talk. So let him talk."

A little thrown by the novel experience of Jessica defending him against Miles—usually, the two of them ganged up on Logan to bug him into working less and eating more—Logan had to refocus on Dylan's set, uncertain face to keep going.

"Love is not an equation," Logan told him. He told Miles, and Jessica, and himself, the truth revealing itself to him as he spoke, unfolding from deep inside him. "You can't plug in a given set of values and solve for x. Two virtual strangers might look at each other across a crowded room and know . . . while for others, it might take years as coworkers—friends—to understand the truth."

Keeping his gaze steadily locked on his brother, heart hammering at even the thought of glancing at Jessica, Logan saw the moment Dylan realized that he had at least one brother's support. The gratitude and relief on his face was almost enough to knock Logan off his feet.

But he managed to keep his balance—until he had an armful of warm, soft, trembling woman.

Staring down at Jessica in stunned surprise, Logan murmured, "What are you doing?"

"For a genius, sometimes you're kind of slow on the uptake," she said, a beaming smile breaking through the tears rolling down her pink cheeks. "Kiss me, Logan."

"But what about—mmmf . . ." Logan broke off his question about Miles with a happy groan, wrapping his arms around Jessica tightly enough to pull her fully against him.

If she didn't care that she was kissing Logan directly in front of her boss, Logan wasn't going to be the one to remind her. Not when he had the taste of her in his mouth, the sweet smell of her in his lungs, and the lush curves of her body in his hands.

And when the kiss finally broke, purely for lack of oxygen, Logan looked up to see Dylan giving him a wink as he steered their shocked oldest brother down the path to the deck at the back of the restaurant to finish their conversation there.

"Looks like your impassioned speech about love didn't manage to completely convince Miles," Jessica observed.

Logan adored the breathless tone of her voice, the way she could sound so serene and amused even as her body tried to mold itself to his.

"As long as it convinced you," he said roughly.

A note of uncertainty threaded through as she replied, "You convinced me that I was wrong—you do know what love is. But if you wanted to be completely explicit about what you think is happening here between you and me, I wouldn't complain."

Which was her wordy, professional way of asking what the hell Logan intended. In response, Logan dropped a kiss on her uptilted nose.

"What I think is happening is that I love you. And you love me. And maybe we're both still figuring out what that means for us, and how to make it work—but I know I want to try. If you're willing to take a chance on trying to have it all, I want to be the man who shares it with you."

Misty moisture clouded her green eyes, and she did that bewildering laughing-while-crying thing again, but Logan didn't let it bother him. Because she was also nodding, and kissing every inch of his face and neck that she could reach, and as the sun of Sanctuary Island beat down on their bare heads and gulls wheeled overhead and his lab sat empty hundreds of miles away, Logan had never been happier.

Yep, he thought smugly as he dipped Jessica to make her laugh and nipped at the tender side of her neck to make her shiver. *I am definitely a genius.*

Island Road

Chapter One

Miles Harrington stared at his two younger brothers and wondered where the hell he went wrong.

Although, come to think of it, Miles knew the exact spot where his family had collectively lost its mind.

Sanctuary Island.

What made two grown men with access to the best lifestyles a staggering amount of money could buy decide to chuck Manhattan in favor of romance on a tiny, backwater island off the coast of Virginia?

Deliberately smoothing his frustrated frown, Miles strove for a reasonable, logical tone. "This is simply unacceptable. You're both coming back to New York with me, and that's final."

Okay, perhaps a little less reasonable than he'd planned, Miles acknowledged silently as his youngest brother, Dylan, threw up his hands.

"Miles, I just got engaged! To a woman who

lives on this island and loves it here. And by the way, not that it matters to you, but I love it here, too. I think I could make a real home here, the kind of home we haven't had since . . ."

Dylan broke off to stare out over the ocean, his throat working visibly. A tiny chink cracked open the shell of ice Miles used to numb down his heart, and he had to work hard not to finish his brother's sentence.

The kind of home we haven't had since Mom and Dad died.

Refusing to allow the tragic loss they'd all suffered so many years ago to derail him, Miles slammed a patch over the crack in his armor and forged ahead. "Logan, help me talk some sense into him."

But Logan, the brother Miles could usually count on for cold logic and emotionless rationality, merely shook his head, his light brown hair blowing in the breeze off the water.

"You probably don't want my help," Logan mused, narrowed blue eyes searching the restaurant behind Miles. Probably hoping for a glimpse of the personal assistant Miles had hired to take care of his brilliant middle brother.

Miles's blood chilled enough to make him shiver even in the humid summer heat. "Wait. You're telling me you don't plan to come back to New York, either?"

"Not just yet." Logan met Miles's gaze squarely, with none of his usual abstract disregard for human interaction. "I like it here, too. And Jessica thinks I need more time to rest, so . . ."

Logan shrugged, and Miles fought the urge to pull at his own perfectly combed hair until it matched Logan's windblown style. The family resemblance was strong enough already.

All three Harrington brothers had blue eyes and brown hair, but where his younger brothers favored a casual bad boy look, in Dylan's case, and an I-dressed-in-the-dark look, in Logan's, Miles Harrington took care with his appearance. An impeccable three-piece suit, well-groomed hair, and a close shave—that was Miles's daily uniform.

As with everything he did, he was viscerally aware of the connection between his image and the image of the family company he lived for.

Familiar frustration coursed through him, tightening his jaw until his molars ground down painfully. "Fine, Logan. Do what you need to do to get better. God knows, I don't want you collapsing in any more board meetings. But as for you, Dylan, if you think I'm going to give you my blessing for this giant mistake of an engagement to a woman you've known for less than a month, you're sadly mistaken."

With a furious huff, Dylan turned on his heel and stalked up the steps that led to the back door of the Firefly Café, and slammed it behind him.

The two older Harrington brothers watched him go. Amusement touched Logan's mouth as he stuck his hands in his pockets. "Thanks for the permission to stay on the island, Miles, but I didn't actually ask for it."

"Don't start," Miles snarled, pacing over to the

low wall that separated the patio from the sandy slope down to the beach. "I don't enjoy being cast in the role of the bad guy, here, when all I'm trying to do is protect my family."

A warm hand landed on Miles's shoulder, startling him. He glanced over to see Logan regarding him with unusually soft eyes. Miles blinked. He couldn't remember the last time his remote, cerebral brother had reached out to him.

"That's all you're ever trying to do, isn't it?" Logan gave him an odd smile. "Protect what's left of our family."

The sudden lump of aching emotion in his throat shocked Miles to the core. "It's my responsibility."

"And we don't make it easy for you." Shaking his head, Logan dropped his hand and stared out over the ocean. "Sorry about that. I'll try to do better. But Miles, you've got to lay off of Dylan or you're going to lose him."

"I lost him a long time ago," Miles said bleakly, swallowing the grief and regret down into the depths of his gut. "The best I can hope for now is to control the damage and keep him from getting hurt by yet another woman who only wants him for his money."

"I don't think that is what's going on here."

Miles gave him the look he usually reserved for incompetent middle managers. "Right. Because your instincts about interpersonal relations are always spot on."

Logan shrugged. "Point. Although Jessica says I'm getting better."

Jessica says.

Miles ground his back teeth again. "About that—Logan, please consider the potential fallout from an affair with a Harrington International employee. The company is in the midst of some delicate negotiations right now. I'd rather not deal with a lawsuit."

Any hint of softness disappeared from Logan's eyes. "Don't go there. You're not firing Jessica, and I'm not giving her up."

With that, Logan strode away, following Dylan back into the café.

Pinching at the headache building in his temples, Miles groaned. "What the hell kind of insanity-inducing drug is in the water around here?"

"Judging by what's happened with your brothers since they arrived," a woman's voice said from behind him, "it must be a love potion. Maybe you should be careful what you drink, Mr. Harrington."

He whirled to see a tall woman in dark jeans and a heather-gray tank top leaning against the stone wall at the side entrance to the patio, long legs stretched out in front of her. From the hint of a smile pulling up one corner of her pale pink lips, she'd been there long enough to catch the tail end of Miles's fight with Logan.

Affronted embarrassment drew his shoulders straight and stiff. Aware that he sounded like a pompous ass, but unable to soften his tone, Miles said, "I'm afraid we haven't been introduced, Ms. . . . ."

Her smile widened a bit, exposing a dimple in her tanned cheek. "Hackley. Greta Hackley."

Her voice was naturally husky, pitched slightly low like a woman who'd just woken up after a night of passion, and it sent rough shivers down Miles's back. Ignoring the hot surge of desire in the pit of his stomach, Miles peered down his nose at her. "Ms. Hackley. Is it an island custom to eavesdrop on private conversations?"

"Is it a Harrington family custom to hold private conversations in public spaces?" she shot back, jumping to her feet.

Standing, Greta Hackley was only a few inches shorter than Miles's six-foot-two, and she wasn't getting much extra height from the lug-soled work boots she wore. This close, he could see the fine-grained texture of her skin. A scattering of light freckles dusted the bridge of her nose, and when she narrowed eyes the color of dark chocolate, he noticed that her long lashes were tipped the same golden blond as her hair.

He realized he'd been staring at her, unblinking, for an awkwardly long moment. Shaking himself loose, Miles summoned all his considerable dignity to say, "You're right, of course. We are in public. It was my mistake to believe anyone who happened by would have the manners to leave us alone."

A darker red than any achieved by blush suffused her cheeks, but she didn't back down. If anything, her strong chin tilted higher. "I'll happily leave you alone, as soon as you tell me you're heading back to New York City."

"So anxious to get rid of me." Miles quirked a

brow. "And I'd always heard such glowing praise of Southern hospitality."

"Anyone who shows up on Sanctuary Island with an open mind and an open heart will find plenty of hospitality," Greta declared. "But I'm not wasting any on the man who's all set to ruin the happiness of my very best friend."

Miles allowed a frown to lower his brows. "Your best friend. Remind me, again . . ."

From the ticking of a muscle in her jaw, Miles thought it was probably Greta's turn to grind her teeth. "Maybe I should have mentioned when I introduced myself. I'm Greta Hackley—Penny Little's best friend and maid of honor. It's my job to make sure every step of her fairy tale, from engagement to honeymoon, is perfect. And that means no disapproving soon-to-be in-laws allowed."

Miles didn't have an excess of time for taking women out, but he never had trouble finding a date for the various charity benefits and gala dinners that formed a necessary part of his life as CEO of a major international corporation.

The women he tended to bring to those parties and dinners were interchangeably beautiful, poised, and focused on their own careers. Miles took care never to date anyone who might see more in him than an evening of mutually beneficial networking, possibly followed by a night of satisfying, no-strings sex.

One glance at Greta Hackley, with her velvety dark eyes and strong-boned face, and Miles knew she was nothing like his usual women.

Greta Hackley was a true romantic.

The question was, could Miles figure out a way to use that to his advantage, to find out the truth about Greta's best friend, the woman his brother was all set to marry?

Chapter Two

Sometimes life really wasn't fair.

After twenty-seven years stuck on Sanctuary Island with the same guys she went all the way from kindergarten to high school with, every man Greta Hackley knew thought of her as the little sister he never had.

She loved her hometown, but it was an extremely limited dating pool full of fish who were friends with her brothers, and who knew every detail of her childhood. The combination ensured that Greta spent a lot of lonely Saturday nights watching TV with her mother.

Now, a trio of gorgeous, wealthy men had turned up out of the blue . . . and one fell for her best friend, one was already dead gone over his personal assistant, and the third? The handsome eldest brother with the razor-sharp creases in his gray wool trousers and the subtle, spicy cologne that smelled like the most expensive of woods?

Miles Harrington turned out to be a proud, stuffy, arrogant jerk who was determined to ruin Greta's best friend's life.

Well, good thing for Penny that Greta was here. She wasn't about to let Mr. Billionaire CEO swoop in and mess things up.

"You might as well head back to your penthouse on Park Avenue," she told him, projecting as much confidence as she could manage. Men like Miles Harrington responded to confidence. "You've made your objections to the marriage clear—and thanks very much, by the way, for the attempt to derail the engagement party I stayed up all night arranging—but no one here cares what you think."

He didn't like that much, she saw with satisfaction. Those chiseled lips of his went flat and hard. "I'm not sure what you hope to gain from supporting this alliance. I have every intention of stopping it, but you can believe me when I say that even if Dylan marries this best friend of yours, she won't be getting her hands on a single cent of my family's money."

Incandescent rage filled Greta like helium in a party balloon. "Listen here. You might be a big man back in New York, but on Sanctuary Island, you're nothing but a bully with an inflated sense of his own importance."

She took a step back before she could give in to the urge to take a swing at his perfectly smooth jaw, but from the gleam in his shockingly blue eyes, Miles took it as a retreat. "Oh, now, Ms. Hackley. That's not fair. We only just met. I promise when you get to know me better, you'll realize there's nothing inflated about me."

The low, caressing tone of his silky voice made Greta shiver unwillingly. Suddenly uncaring of whether he thought she was retreating or not, she took another step back. All that mattered was getting a little distance between their bodies.

"You know what? I feel sorry for you," she said. "Going through life always believing the worst of people, that the only reason anyone could be interested in you or your brothers is your money. That's awfully sad."

He shrugged, a negligent motion that made her very aware of the strength in his broad shoulders. "Based on past experiences, I can only assume I'm right. But maybe you're here to teach me how wrong I am, that there are people out there who care nothing for the billions of dollars and incalculable power my family wields in the business world. Right here, on Sanctuary Island, my brothers have been lucky enough to find real love, true love, unsullied by thoughts of money and influence. Is that right?"

"Don't mistake sympathy for weakness," Greta snapped. "I'm not here for you at all. The only reason I'm wasting breath talking to you is to warn you that nothing is going to stand in the way of Penny marrying the man of her dreams."

At least one of us will have a happily ever after, Greta vowed silently. *And no one deserves it more than Penny.*

Shoving down her own soft, silly tendency to wonder if the man of her dreams was out there somewhere, Greta turned on her heel to stalk away, confident she'd made her point.

A big, warm hand closing around her bare wrist stopped her in her tracks. Electricity shot up her arm and raised every hair on her body. Breathless, she tugged against Miles's grip, but he pulled her gently, inexorably closer until the tips of her breasts brushed his chest through layers of fabric.

Sparing a brief instant to be grateful that the man was walking around a tiny island town dressed for a formal business meeting in shirt, vest, and suit coat, Greta ignored the tight, tingling points of contact. "I have nothing more to say to you, Mr. Harrington."

She was surprised to see a flicker of chagrin in his cool blue eyes. But even that didn't prepare her for the shock of hearing him say smoothly, "I apologize. This is . . . an emotional time for my family, and if I offended you, I'm sorry. I appreciate your position, and the fact that you gave me fair warning of your intentions. I was all set to head back to New York this afternoon . . ."

Hope flickered in Greta's chest. "Whatever your concerns are with Penny, forget them. Your brother is lucky to have found her. She may not have a fancy diploma from an Ivy League school or a cushy trust fund, but she's a truly good person."

The way he studied her made Greta feel naked, as if he had the ability to strip away not just her clothes, but every layer of invisible protection she'd wrapped around herself after her surgery. She licked her lips nervously, and his gaze dropped to her mouth.

Heat surged between them, sudden and shocking. Dipping his head slightly, until Greta's heart pounded with a jittery will-he-or-won't-he anticipation, Miles said, "Maybe I should stick around a little longer, try to understand what's really going on between my brother and his fiancée. Approach the situation with an open mind, as you suggested."

Greta sucked in a deep breath, sparking a flash of lightning behind her eyes as the tips of her breasts pressed into his jacketed chest. "An open mind. You mean you might be willing to give the marriage your blessing?"

Penny and Dylan were adults, independent and sure of what they wanted—they didn't technically need Miles's blessing. But as someone with an intensely close bond with her family, Greta understood that Dylan might hope for Miles's approval, just the same.

"That depends," Miles murmured, bending his head until the words puffed out against her lips.

"On what?" she breathed.

"On you." A slow, predatory smile spread Miles's perfect lips. Open, frank appreciation warmed his ice-blue eyes to the color of the summer sky. "I'll agree to keep an open mind about my brother's fly-by-night engagement if you agree to show me around the island that appears to have captivated my entire family. Show me what's so special about this place, that Dylan and Logan would get addicted to it after a matter of weeks."

A frisson of danger skittered down Greta's spine. It would mean spending more time in Miles's company. Touring him around Sanctuary, just the two of them and the long sunny days and hot humid nights . . .

As many romance novels as she'd read, Greta could recognize the clear signs of masculine desire in every line of the hard body pressed against hers. Miles Harrington wasn't shy about letting her know he wanted her . . . but a man like him wanted only one thing from a woman like Greta.

She might not have much hands-on experience with men, but she wasn't a fool. There was no way Mr. Billionaire CEO was going to give up the reins of his company to move to Sanctuary Island and run Hackley's Hardware with her.

And Greta could never leave the island behind, no matter how much she sometimes yearned after the endless mysteries beyond the horizon of her small world. But Miles Harrington wasn't her fantasy Prince Charming, here to sweep her away to a life of adventure and faraway lands. So what was the point?

The point, she realized, was that this was her chance to make Miles see that Penny had no designs on anything other than Dylan's heart.

Even though every self-preservational instinct she possessed was clamoring for Greta to get away from Miles Harrington as quickly as possible, she knew she couldn't pass up the opportunity to help

Penny. After everything her best friend had been through with her ex-husband, Penny had more than earned a fairy tale ending.

The fact that it wasn't in the cards for Greta only made her more determined to see her friend settled happily. Even if it meant spending time with the first man in years to both tempt her and infuriate her in the space of a single conversation.

With a sense of sealing her own fate, Greta said, "Fine. I'll be your tour guide to the wonders of Sanctuary Island. And you'll see that no one here cares about your money or whatever power you think you have."

Something flared deep in Miles's eyes, and he finally let go of her captured wrist only to wrap both muscular arms around her. "I have one more condition. You think you don't like me—but sweetheart, chemistry like this doesn't happen every day."

Gasping at the searing heat of all the muscle he concealed under his perfectly tailored suit, Greta said, "I don't know what you're talking about."

"No?"

Her only warning was the gleam of challenge in his seductive smile before he pressed those lips to hers. Greta opened her mouth to . . . she didn't know what, to protest? To moan? But she didn't have a chance to do either, because Miles immediately pressed his advantage and took her mouth in a deep, searing kiss that wiped every thought of protest from Greta's mind.

She melted against him automatically, reveling in the fact that he was actually taller than she was so that their bodies lined up perfectly, but Miles drew back.

Staring down at her with wide, almost surprised eyes, he blinked once—and then the expression was gone, buried under a smooth, practiced smile. "I'll keep an open mind about your friend and my brother," he purred. "If you keep an open mind about me."

Greta drew in a shuddery breath. "Okay," she said, blushing at the hoarse rasp of her own voice. "I'll try."

Miles Harrington was judgmental, controlling, full of himself—he was no Prince Charming. But as Greta touched a fingertip to her lips, still buzzing with pleasure and plump from his kiss, she realized that even though she had no future with him . . . she had the present. And, as Miles pointed out, they had chemistry.

An exploding high school lab experiment's worth of chemistry. Yowza.

Could she really afford to let this opportunity pass her by, on the off chance that Prince Charming might show up one day and wish she'd waited? Especially when she was uncomfortably aware of exactly how big a fantasy that was, anyway.

Maybe it was time to take a break from dreaming and live, even if only for a little while.

Chapter Three

Maybe some people would find it awkward to spend the night as a guest in the house of a woman they had all but accused of being a gold digger. Luckily, Miles was made of sterner stuff.

He was a pragmatist, at heart, and there was no suitable alternative to staying at the house on Island Road—which belonged to his family, incidentally, so Miles refused to give in to the awkwardness. In fact, before there was ever a town called Sanctuary, the entire island was owned by Silas Harrington, Miles's however-many-greats great grandfather, who founded the company that eventually became the legacy Miles had dedicated his life to continuing.

But the Harringtons no longer owned any part of the island but the property on Island Road, and whoever was running things now hadn't seen fit to establish a single hotel or inn. There wasn't even a crappy motel or a kitschy bed-and-breakfast.

And Logan, damn him, was happily ensconced in the summer cottage with Jessica Bell.

That was a problem for another day, Miles told himself as he straightened his tie in the antique silver-framed mirror hanging over the porcelain pedestal sink in the guest bathroom. For now, he needed to focus on his plan to get the full story on Penny Little and her motives for marrying his youngest brother.

A plan that was going fairly well, if he could force himself to focus a bit more tightly on the goal. That kiss, yesterday . . .

Miles's fingers paused in the act of checking his collar stays. Staring at himself in the mirror, all he could see was an image of Greta Hackley's unpracticed, questing mouth, the unconscious sensuality of her body as she abandoned herself to the pleasure of the moment.

Caught up in his own seductive web, Miles admitted to himself that he'd taken it further than necessary to test the waters of Greta's attraction to him. Greta Hackley, with her tomboyish, casual clothes and messy golden-blond braid, was surprisingly tempting.

Well, he'd have to resist the temptation. That was all there was to it. He was willing to seduce her a little, in order to get her softened up to the point of telling him the truth about her best friend, but there was a line Miles certainly wouldn't cross.

He stared into his own blue eyes in the mirror and swallowed the knowledge that the line had already shifted a couple of inches.

After a breakfast of stilted conversation during which Miles made no attempt to probe Penny's background while Dylan hovered over her, growling like a suspicious pit bull, Miles chose to wait on the front porch for his tour guide.

According to the weather app on his smartphone, it was going to be yet another hot, cloyingly humid day in paradise. It was barely nine o'clock, and he already regretted the tie. Loosening the knot with absent fingers, Miles sauntered over to the love seat swing hanging at the end of the wraparound porch and dropped into it.

He'd braced slightly for the motion of the swing, but when the chain attaching it to the porch ceiling gave way with a loud crack, Miles shouted in surprise as he crashed to the floorboards.

Sitting in the wreckage of the swing, Miles winced and shifted. The thin seat cushion hadn't been enough to protect him from bruising. Drawing his knees up, he rested his elbows on them and stared contemplatively up at the jagged hole in the porch ceiling where the swing's hook used to be anchored.

"Need a little help?"

Miles closed his eyes briefly. "Your timing is amazing. How do you always manage to show up when I'm in the midst of making an idiot of myself?"

"Just lucky, I guess," Greta said. He could hear the smile in her voice before she vaulted up the porch steps to give him a hand.

"I promise you, it's an unusual occurrence back in New York." Miles accepted her help, a little surprised by how easily she set her weight against his to pull him to his feet. "My assistant would never believe this."

"So you've got everyone who works for you fooled into thinking you walk on water, make no mistakes?"

Tensing against the implication that he considered himself godlike, Miles said, "What happened to you keeping an open mind about me? Already going back on our deal?"

Eyes widening, Greta's mouth twisted into a rueful smile. "Sorry, and no. I was actually thinking that it sounded like a hard way to live."

"What do you mean?"

She shrugged, the motion apparently making her aware that she was still clasping Miles's much larger hand between her palms. Dropping her hands with a sweet flush, Greta said, "Oh, you know. The expectation level you live with—it must be brutal. To be expected never to make a silly mistake? You're only human."

Miles tilted his head, amused, as he straightened his suit. "It comes with the territory. When you're responsible for hundreds of people's livelihoods, their careers and their futures, you learn never to show fear. Never show weakness. Your employees take their cues from you, everything flows from the top down. Be confident and competent, and they'll strive for that in their roles, as well."

"I wish I'd brought a notebook so I could record all these pearls of wisdom."

Casting her an irritated glance, Miles gave in to

the heat and unknotted his tie completely. Sliding it free of his collar, he rolled it up and stuffed it in his pocket. The temperature seemed to have risen ten degrees in the last few minutes. "You know, plenty of people would think this is a great opportunity to pick the brain of a successful CEO."

She snorted. "Oh sure, for when I try to take the hardware store public and turn it into a Fortune 500 company."

"Hardware store?"

Miles recognized family pride in the straight set of Greta's shoulders, the way she held her head. "Hackley's Hardware, founded by my great grand-parents when they first settled on Sanctuary Island in the forties. I run the store itself, now that Mama has gone down to part time. My brothers mostly work the side business, consulting on local build-ing and maintenance projects."

The green bite of envy scraped across Miles's consciousness. "A true family business, hmm? It must be nice to have that support."

Shrugging, Greta shaded her eyes and peered out into the bright sunlit front yard. "Sometimes. Other times, it feels like since I'm the only one in the store most of the time, and that's still the core part of our business, that it's all on my shoulders."

Miles was startled by the sense of kinship he felt with this woman, whose day-to-day life probably didn't resemble his constant whirl of high-intensity meetings and power lunches, but who clearly un-derstood something about the demands of carrying on a family tradition.

Somehow uncomfortable with using that in his campaign of seduction, Miles gestured vaguely at the flower-lined paving stones that led through the front yard out to Island Road. "I hate to ask you to go into work on what I'm guessing is a pretty rare day off, but it appears we need to make a trip to a hardware store if we're going to fix this porch swing."

Laughing, Greta put her hands on her slim hips, drawing him to notice exactly how low those denim cutoffs hung from her trim waist. "I make plans to show you all the beauties this gorgeous hidden jewel of an island has to offer—and you want to see the hardware store, so you can get to work on a repair? Something tells me I'm not the only one who isn't used to taking time off."

"Guilty." Miles grinned and spread his hands. "Although I have to admit, I'm partly motivated by a desire to see this family business of yours."

She blushed, and Miles tried not to be charmed by her. That wasn't the way this was supposed to go.

"Really?" Greta shook her head hard enough to swing the long tail of her dark gold braid over one shoulder to trail enticingly between the curves of her small, high breasts. "It's nothing fancy, you know. It's not a big box store or one of those renovation depots that's stocked with a ton of crap you never knew you always needed. Hackley's is a homey little place where you can get the basics to take care of your property."

Surveying the sad, crumpled swing, Miles gave Greta a wry half smile. "Well, technically this house is my property. And I haven't done much to take care of it since my grandparents died. Maybe it's time I started."

"This house has been taken care of," Greta argued staunchly. "You hired Penny as caretaker, and she's done a great job."

"Sure. If you don't count the front porch swing collapsing under me without warning."

"You probably sat in it wrong. Don't have a lot of front porch swings up there in the Big Apple, do they?"

"Maybe not, but we have chairs," Miles retorted. "I'm the head of a multibillion-dollar international corporation with interests ranging from security and national defense contracts to the challenges of sustainable energy. I think I can handle the tricky procedure of *sitting*."

Greta's dark eyes narrowed. "Obviously not."

Without being aware of moving, Miles was suddenly toe to toe with the exasperating woman. "Are you going to take me to your hardware store, or do I need to find it myself?"

She huffed out a sigh that tickled against the underside of Miles's jaw, reminding him he hadn't been able to shave that morning. At some point today, he was going to need to find a way to outfit himself for a longer stay than originally planned.

"You're not used to anyone standing up to you," Greta observed.

He would have found it more annoying, if it weren't for the catch in her breath, and the way her gaze dropped unconsciously to his mouth. That was all the reminder he needed to force himself to back down.

Sliding his hands into his pants pockets, Miles rocked back on his heels. "Not really," he agreed. "Although it's not as if I'm careful to surround myself with yes men, either. I appreciate a good debate as much as the next CEO. But when it comes down to it, the buck stops with me. My company turns on my decisions. I can't afford to waffle or to argue every point with the people I trust to carry out my commands. You must face some of the same issues, running your business."

The appeal to what they had in common had the desired effect. Greta smiled, a little reluctantly, but he'd take it. "Not exactly. My mother is still in charge when it comes to the big decisions."

Miles frowned. "Even though you're the one who puts in the time, working the store?"

"It's complicated." A distant expression stole into the velvety depths of Greta's brown eyes. "My mother is . . . well. You can meet her for yourself. She's covering for me at the store today."

Meeting the parents. That was a step Miles had thus far managed to avoid taking with any woman he'd dated. Still, desperate times and all that. "I look forward to it," he said, aiming for polite enthusiasm, but falling short, if Greta's smirk was anything to go by.

She looked him over from head to toe, the sly grin deepening. "If you're planning to actually help me rehang that porch swing, we're going to have to get you something else to wear."

Glad to lighten the mood, Miles flicked open the top button of his shirt and raised a brow. "You don't approve of the suit?"

Humor mixed with desire hooded her eyes as her gaze traveled over him. "Oh, I approve. But I wouldn't want it to get messed up. Especially since I bet it cost more than my truck."

Privately admitting that might be true, Miles glanced back toward the house. "I can probably borrow something from my brothers."

Greta marched over to the front door and opened it, as casually as if she lived there. "Why don't you go change? I don't mind waiting."

"Now? But . . ."

"When I said Hackley's was homey," Greta informed him, "that was code for 'dusty and a little disorganized.' You'd hate to snag that fine Italian wool on a stray pitchfork or something, wouldn't you?"

She twanged out the word *eye-tally-en* with a slow, exaggerated drawl, and Miles caught himself grinning. She really was the most disarming woman. It was a problem.

"Fine," Miles agreed, smoothing down his slightly rumpled jacket. "But only because I like the idea of clean clothes. I haven't worn the same shirt two days in a row since college."

"Great, I'll just slip through and chat with Penny until you're done," she said brightly.

Miles watched her walk down the hall toward the kitchen, the tanned length of her forever-long legs glowing golden in the dim light. He never would have thought the sight of a woman in ragged-edged cutoffs and thick-soled, tan work boots would do it for him, but Greta wore them as if they were her second skin, as comfortable and confident in her body as any socialite or female executive he'd ever known.

Focus, he reminded himself again, shoving down the inconvenient swell of lust. *You're not flirting with this woman because you like her or intend to start something you'll never finish. You need an in, a source of good intel. Focus on that.*

And whatever happens, don't drink the water.

"I'm not the best-friend ethics police, or anything," Penny said, wide-eyed over the rim of her coffee cup, "but I believe I'm going to have to cite you for a violation."

"No way," Greta protested. "I deserve a medal! The keys to the best friend city! Maybe a tiara and a sash—I am the queen of best friends!"

"You kissed the enemy." Penny—the woman who used to be able to hold a grudge until kingdom come—broke and giggled into her coffee. "I think we're going to need a judge's ruling on this."

"He's not the enemy. Or at least, he doesn't have to be." Greta shivered even in the warmth of the kitchen, remembering the banded steel of his arms around her, the hard lines of his shockingly muscular body. *He must get up at the crack of dawn and put in a couple of hours at the gym before hitting the office,* she mused dreamily.

Penny's soft laughter dragged Greta out of her

contemplation of what Miles might look like with his perfect hair mussed and sweaty, his impressive chest heaving with the effort of pumping iron.

"Oh, honey," Penny said, all sympathy. "Be careful. From what I can tell, the Harrington brothers are all dangerous."

"Please, I grew up with four older brothers. I can handle myself."

"I don't mean physically dangerous." Penny set down her coffee cup, the better to give Greta her Serious Mom expression. "Except in the sense of, well . . . I know you've always intended to wait. Until you found Mr. Right."

Ignoring the breathless edge to her own laughter, Greta propped her elbows on the scarred pine tabletop. "I don't need the birds-and-the-bees speech, Penny. Four older brothers, remember? I doubt there's anything that goes on between a man and a woman that I haven't heard a million dirty jokes about."

"Okay, fine." Penny sat back, looking a little relieved. "But that wasn't what I was getting at anyway. The Harrington brothers are . . . well. The word 'irresistible' has been used."

Butterflies swarmed around Greta's insides. Tracing a decades-old water ring stained into the wooden table, she whispered, "But what if I don't want to resist?"

Penny's brows went up. She knew more than most people did about Greta's situation, but she didn't scoff. Instead, she stretched her arm across the corner of the table to lightly clasp Greta's strong wrist in her slim, sturdy fingers. "Protect your heart, sweetie. That's all I'm saying. I don't know that you can trust Miles with it."

"Trust me with what?"

The deep, smooth voice had both women popping up straight in their chairs and turning toward the doorway.

Lounging against the doorjamb like something out of a magazine Mrs. Gooch would insist on selling wrapped in brown paper down at the general store, Miles Harrington hooked his thumbs in the belt loops of his sinfully tight, borrowed jeans and smiled a cool, inquisitive smile.

The jeans obviously came from Logan's suitcase, since the two elder brothers were about the same height, but Logan was built slightly leaner than Miles's powerful bulk. Greta swallowed hard.

Miles's T-shirt, on the other hand . . . That was all Dylan. Tight enough in the sleeves to strain against biceps Miles sure as hell didn't acquire from typing away on a computer, the clinging black cotton showed every slab of muscle banding Miles's chest, every line corrugating his abs. And when he breathed in, the hem rose above the waist of the dark denim, baring a strip of tanned belly and the enticing shadows of two divots on either side of his hips.

"No one had a T-shirt that would fit you, huh?" Greta knew she sounded odd, her voice hoarse and thick, but hell, she was proud of herself for being able to string a full sentence together.

Miles tugged briefly at the hem of the shirt, then

shrugged, exposing another brief flash of washboard abs. "All of Logan's were even tighter. Plus, they had nerdy slogans on them. This one might be short, but at least it's plain. What's this about not trusting me?"

Casting Penny a furious, shushing glance, Greta leapt out of her chair and herded Miles down the front hallway and out the door. "Nothing! We weren't even talking about you. Not every conversation two women have is about you, Harrington."

"Mmm," Miles hummed, obviously unconvinced, but thankfully he let it go. "Dylan mentioned he'd been into your store and bought a full tool kit when he first arrived on the island. We should check the shed in the backyard, but he didn't think we had the right kind of screws to support the weight of the swing. And there might be issues in the ceiling structure, so we should grab the ladder and check that out before we head to the store."

Relieved to have a clear set of tasks—and ones Greta could perform in her sleep, after growing up hearing her mother advise their customers on home repairs—she hurried down the porch steps and around the side of the house.

The heady perfume of rosebushes in full bloom filled her lungs, and the steady beat of the sun made her glad to slip into the darkness of the tiny shed.

"It's already hot out there," she remarked, then felt stupid. The weather—what a fascinating conversationalist she'd turned out to be!

"The heat feels different here than it does in New York," Miles replied, ducking down to rummage through the clutter piled against the shed's walls. "Softer, wetter, saltier—but somehow cleaner."

His words caused an answering heat to beat through Greta's bloodstream. Clearing her throat, she said, "At least I remembered to slather on the daily moisturizer Mama's always after me to wear. The one with sunscreen in it." Greta rubbed a self-conscious finger over the bridge of her nose. "I don't need any more freckles. I already look like a ragamuffin as it is."

Miles leaned across her in the small space, the breadth of his warm chest blocking the light from the open shed door for a moment so that Greta felt utterly surrounded by him. Heaving the stepladder up off the floor and over his shoulder with a soft grunt of effort, Miles said, "I don't know what a ragamuffin is—if I check my phone, will I find it in Webster's dictionary?—but I like your freckles. They're like specks of cinnamon in cream."

"I'll cream you," Greta said nonsensically, then cringed. "Sorry. Autopilot response drilled into me by years of dealing with brothers."

Even in the darkness of the shed, she could see the way his eyes lit with laughter, tinged with a bit of wistfulness. "You have brothers, too? Sounds like you're close."

Close in a way Miles clearly wished he could be, with Dylan and Logan. Heart squeezing in empathy, Greta helped him carry the stepladder and the other supplies they'd gathered around the house to the front porch.

But as she followed the tall, wide-backed, lean-hipped form and watch the play of muscles under that sexy black T-shirt when he twisted his torso to deposit the heavy metal ladder on the porch, Greta had to take a moment to remember her friend's words of wisdom.

Protect your heart.

No matter what else she yielded to Miles Harrington in her quest to live a little, for however long it lasted—she had to defend the one part of her he definitely didn't want, and wouldn't know how to care for.

Chapter Four

Being right usually felt more satisfying.

Miles browsed through the shelves of Hackley's Hardware and contemplated the leaden weight that had descended on his gut when he'd walked in on Penny Little cautioning Greta about trusting him.

Penny obviously had something to hide. Something Greta knew, and hadn't told him.

Yet, he promised himself, picking a bottle of grill cleaner off the shelf at random. He stared blindly at the label for a moment before setting it back down next to a stack of gardening gloves.

She hadn't told him yet. But she would when he stepped up the intensity on this seduction campaign.

If she ever comes back out here. He sent an impatient glance toward the back of the store, where she'd disappeared behind the counter and into an interior office as soon as they walked into the empty shop.

In the five minutes Greta had been gone, no one else came into the cramped rabbit warren of Hackley's Hardware. Old wooden shelving units stretched up to the ceiling, forming narrow aisles broken up by the occasional item that was too large to fit on a shelf. He wandered closer to the front of the store to peer out the large display window at the bustling small-town street, and found himself gazing straight into the curious stares of the old men who'd been playing checkers out front when Greta and Miles arrived.

The skinny, whiskery one in flannel scowled, almost as if he were warning Miles off, but the jolly-looking guy wearing the battered gold-painted crown gave him a jaunty wave.

Waving back bemusedly, Miles didn't hear Greta come up behind him until she was close enough to put a light hand against the small of his back. Her fingers slipped below the hem of the slightly too short shirt, and brushed hot, sensitive skin.

Accidental slip? he wondered with a pleasurable shiver. He hoped not. He hoped Greta was as into this as he was.

"Are they your store mascots?" he asked, gesturing at the unabashedly interested old men.

Greta laughed. "Pretty much. King and Pete set up their checkerboard out there most every day during the summer, until it gets too hot. They do more gossiping than playing, though. They know everything that happens on this island, and they spread news better than the *Sanctuary Gazette*."

"Nothing much to see in here—we're the only customers."

Greta opened her mouth to reply, but before she could say a word, a soft voice drawled from the rear of the shop. "Bless your heart. Aren't you funny? Why, surely you know that your sudden arrival by helicopter yesterday is the biggest thing to happen on little old Sanctuary Island in years."

Miles turned to see the petite, trim figure of an older woman with Greta's velvety brown eyes behind the pitted wooden counter. When she hoisted herself onto the stool situated by the cash register and smiled at him, the expression made her look exactly like her daughter.

Because who else could this be, but Mother Hackley?

Rushing forward with hands outstretched, as if to help with balance or support, Greta confirmed it by saying, "Mama, wait, let me . . ."

"Pssh." Mrs. Hackley waved her away gently. "I'm fine. The day I need help climbing up onto my throne, here, is the day you can put me out to pasture. Until then, remember your manners and introduce me to your friend."

Glancing over her shoulder as if unsure the term "friend" truly applied, or wondering if Miles would be offended by it somehow, Greta said, "Sure. Um, Mama, this is Miles Harrington. Miles, this is my mother, Esther Hackley."

Sparing a fleeting wish for the comfortable armor of his three-piece bespoke suit and perfectly broken-in wing tips, Miles put on the smile he used on the wives and family members of his board of directors.

"Mrs. Hackley," he said, stepping forward to envelop her papery-skinned hand in both of his. "I'm glad to meet you. Your daughter has been so hospitable, showing me around the island."

Mrs. Hackley fluffed her silvery blond curls and tilted her chin up proudly. "Of course, any tour of Sanctuary Island would have to include this place. It's one of the oldest businesses on the square, been in our family for generations."

"Mama," Greta cut in, her voice slightly muffled with embarrassment. "Miles already knows all about Hackley's, I told him on the way over. Don't fuss."

"Don't fuss?" Esther spread her thin arms wide to encompass the store. "This place is your history and your future, Greta. You should be proud."

"I am." Darting him a glance, Greta hooked her arm through Miles's elbow and started tugging him toward the front of the shop. "You know that. But Miles and I have a lot to see and a few errands to run, so we'll just grab a couple of eye bolts and be on our way."

Because he was watching the interaction with interest, on the principle that any information he learned about Greta Hackley could be useful in his plan, Miles saw the way Esther's gaze sharpened. Hopping off the stool, Esther rounded the back counter and barreled straight over to them.

"What sort of errands?" she demanded, crossing

her arms over her chest and staring her daughter down, like a military general in a pink, fuzzy cardigan. "And what do you need the hooks for?"

"Don't worry, Mrs. Hackley." Miles studied the woman's tense face. "We're just rehanging the porch swing at my family's house on Island Road. Nothing nefarious."

"Esther," she snapped, without even glancing at him. All her attention was focused on the stubborn set of Greta's jaw. "Tell me, Mr. Harrington. Will this repair require my daughter to climb around on a ladder?"

Feeling as if he was missing something, which was an unfamiliar and uncomfortable sensation, Miles glanced back and forth between mother and daughter. Locked in a silent battle of wills, neither woman seemed to remember he was even in the store with them.

Sticking out a careful feeler, Miles said, "Not necessarily. I could be the one up the ladder, with Greta directing from below."

That surprised a look from Greta, her wide brown gaze snapping to his face. "You'd take direction from me? I would've thought you'd be a macho, arrogant know-it-all."

"Greta." Esther's shocked voice made her daughter wince. Finally looking away from Greta, Esther said, "I apologize for my daughter, Mr. Harrington. I'm the one she's angry with. She shouldn't be taking it out on you. And she shouldn't be angry with me, either, I might add—since all I want is what any mother wants. To keep her safe."

"Mama, nothing is going to happen to me." The pleading note in Greta's voice surprised Miles, but he was by no means an expert on parent-child relationships. Was it normal for an adult daughter to still be subject to so much worry?

Esther was shaking her head. "I never would have agreed to mind the store today if I knew you planned to spend your time off recklessly climbing up ladders and attempting repairs you have no business making." Brightening, she turned to Miles. "Why don't you call one of my boys, Mr. Harrington? They'd be much better suited to helping you with your porch swing."

Aware that he'd somehow stumbled directly into the middle of a long-standing mother-daughter battle, Miles held up his hands to remind them both that he was an unarmed combatant.

"That won't be necessary, Mrs. Ha—Esther." Miles corrected himself at the glint of swift annoyance in the older woman's frown. He wasn't here to make enemies. And even though he didn't fully understand the subtextual ramifications of this conversation, he was a CEO. Smoothing over personnel problems and getting people on the same page was basically his entire job. So he smiled blandly and said, "I'll take care of the repair myself."

"I'm not a child," Greta gritted through clenched teeth. "And I'm not suggesting that I help him roof his house, followed by a rousing game of tackle football. I'll be fine."

"Don't you minimize my completely valid

concerns, young lady." Esther put her hands on her round hips and stared at her daughter as if calculating whether Greta was too tall to fit over her knee for a good spanking. "You know you have to be careful. If I can't trust you to take care of yourself . . ."

Greta went pale, her bloodless lips an unhappy curve, and Miles didn't even stop to wonder why he hated the sight so much. He simply rushed into the fray. "I have an idea, Esther. What if you hand over the care and safety of your daughter to me, just for one day? I promise not to let her fall from any ladders, and make sure she enjoys her day off in a completely safe, responsible manner. You have my word."

The look Esther gave him let Miles know she wasn't at all sure his word was worth the oxygen he'd used to form the sentence, but before she could turn him down, Greta huffed out a shuddery breath and stalked out of the store.

Miles started after her at once, but the light touch of Esther's hand on his shoulder made him pause. He glanced back to find her offering him a handful of large silver hooks ending in long screws, and a sad smile. "Here, on the house. You're going to have your hands full with my daughter."

"You'll trust me with her for the day?" Miles accepted the hooks with a sense that he was signing off on a contract he hadn't read.

"I'm trusting that Greta has been reminded that she needs to take care of herself. She's not like everyone else, Mr. Harrington. There are things she can't do, ways that she needs to be careful, but she hates to admit it. Even to herself."

In the short pause that followed, Miles was torn between the urge to demand Esther be more specific, and the intense need to follow Greta. In the end, the invisible tether connecting his rib cage to Greta Hackley pulled taut, and he started for the door.

"Thank you for the hooks," he said over his shoulder. And even though he had no idea what Esther thought could happen to her daughter on this sleepy little island, he said, "I promise I'll keep her safe."

"Just bring her back to me in one piece," Esther called. "I'll take it from there."

Miles didn't have time to question why the thought of handing Greta back over to her mother released adrenaline to tighten his muscles. Greta was halfway down the block already, and he had to catch up with her.

Wrestling his phone from the back pocket of his borrowed jeans, Miles swiped open the lock and scrolled through his recent contacts for the number he wanted.

He had plans to make.

Chapter Five

Anger fizzed and bubbled through Greta's veins like anesthesia, numbing her to every other emotion.

Except, of course, embarrassment.

You'd think she'd be used to the way her mother wanted to cocoon her in endless layers of bubble wrap, but somehow, it had felt different to be told how helpless and fragile she was in front of Miles Harrington.

But since she couldn't bring herself to get mad at her mother, Miles was the one who got the brunt of Greta's embarrassed rage when his long, loping strides caught up to her at the corner of Main Street and Island Road.

"I don't appreciate you ganging up on me with my mother," she snapped out, whirling to face him. "And I certainly don't need you to take care of me."

"Of course you don't," he agreed.

But Greta was on a roll. "And if you think I'm too delicate or weak to help get that swing rehung—"

"Here," Miles interrupted, grabbing her flailing hand and dropping a couple of heavy metal hooks into her palm. "Peace offering to prove I don't think you're weak. Please don't take a shot at me with those in your fist. I like my nose the way it is."

Closing her fingers over the cold metal, Greta deflated. "Sorry. My mother knows me too well. I *am* taking it out on you. I apologize, and I promise your nose is safe."

Of course that led to Greta thinking about the other things her mother might be right about, and the surge of frustration at her body's limitations was almost comforting.

She'd been dealing with it ever since she could remember, in one form or another. And no matter how strong she felt or how she pushed herself to gain the strength others took for granted, Greta could always count on her mother to slap her in the face with reality.

She glanced up to see Miles studying her expression, head cocked inquisitively to one side like a panther trying to understand the nonsensical flailing of its prey. "There's no ticking clock on that repair back at the house," he said slowly. "Let's take our time, see a little more of the island."

Sighing, Greta said, "You mean my prison? Sure, great."

"Prison." Miles frowned. With the light growth of beard after one day without shaving shadowing his hard-edged jaw, he looked piratical. Dangerous, like Penny said.

Greta shook her head, ignoring the tingle of desire. "Forget about it. My mother turns me into a crazy person. So!" She gestured expansively at the wide, flat swath of green grass dotted with flowering tulip poplars and dogwoods.

While they were in Hackley's Hardware, the sky had clouded over with dark, forbidding gray. The humidity, always intense in the summer, had thickened until every breath felt like a gulp of tepid water.

"This is the town square. That's the pavilion. All the core businesses on the island have storefronts along Main Street on this side, and all the big, old houses are along Island Road on that side of the park."

"Interesting," Miles said, never taking his eyes off her face.

Greta fought the urge to squirm under the laser intensity of his scrutiny. "The high school marching band plays concerts on the steps of the pavilion sometimes," she said breathlessly.

Grabbing her hand, Miles turned and pulled her into the park. "Great. Let's see this pavilion up close."

The heat of his rough fingers on hers sent chills up her arms, even in the moist thickness of the still noonday air. "It's nothing special," Greta tried to tell him, almost tripping over her own booted feet in her hurry to keep up with his ground-eating strides.

"I'll be the judge of that."

The pavilion squatted in the center of the town square, paved pathways leading out from it like rays of light from a star. Miles hustled them up the steps and into the hexagonal, open-sided building just as the sky opened up and poured rain down on the island.

Gasping, Greta leaned on the white wooden railing and stuck her hand out to feel the cooling sting of fat raindrops on her bare skin. "How did you know it was about to start raining?"

"I didn't."

He sounded genuinely aggravated, as if he hated admitting that he didn't have perfect foreknowledge of everything that would happen.

Greta laughed over her shoulder at him, then turned to prop her hips on the low railing and stretch her legs out in front of her. "Well, we're stuck here now until the rain lets up. Shouldn't be too long. These summer storms blow over in a heartbeat."

Another sheet of rain fountained over the gazebo's roof, loud enough to drown out her last few words. The rain formed an impenetrable veil around the pavilion, enclosing Greta and Miles in their own private world made of white noise and fine mist.

Absently wringing water from the sodden hem of her tank top, Greta felt her breath catch at the soft, rough sound that rumbled from deep in Miles's chest. She dropped her hands, tugging the shirt down self-consciously, but it was too late.

Miles had already seen it.

Without even meaning to, Greta pressed her hand defensively over the short scar that curved over her left hip. No longer than three inches, pale with age, she knew intellectually that it wasn't a hideous, deforming mark.

But try telling that to the weak, scared, seventeen-year-old who still lived somewhere inside Greta.

She tensed against the inevitable question. All through high school, and after, if she ever encountered the rare person on Sanctuary Island who didn't already know everything that happened to Greta Hackley when she was a kid, one look at her scar was all it took for that person to feel they had a right to ask.

Sometimes people would reach out and touch it, almost unconsciously, as if the fact that there was visible proof of her past pain made it public property.

But Miles didn't move one inch closer to her. Instead, he lowered himself to sit on the bench that ran along the back of the gazebo, hooking his elbows over the railing. He said not a word, asked no questions, didn't imply in any way that she was obligated to spill her entire life history to explain the scar on her abdomen.

The very fact that he didn't push made her want to tell him. And why not? It wasn't some horrible secret. Everyone on the island already knew, anyway. What was one more person who looked at her and saw an invalid, a victim, a weakling to protect?

If Miles Harrington was going to look at her that way, with that horrid, soft pity she hated so much . . . better to find out now.

"I was sick a lot, as a kid." Greta pitched her voice to be heard over the rain, but it still came out low and private. Clearing her throat, she pressed on. "In and out of the hospital, lots of different doctors. They finally figured out it was chronic kidney disease, which would have meant lifelong dialysis just to manage the symptoms—but my mom gave me one of her kidneys when I was seventeen. And now we're both fine."

For a long moment, there was no sound but the incessant roar of raindrops hitting the gazebo roof. Greta searched Miles's expression for any change, any hint of pity, but other than a slight tightening of his jaw, he didn't react at all.

"I see. Thank you for telling me. It explains a lot."

Greta bristled, straightening up from her slouch against the railing. "What do you mean? What does it explain?"

Apparently oblivious to Greta's rising tension, Miles tipped his head back until droplets of rain misted his hairline. "That disagreement with your mother, about how careful you need to be."

Even though he hadn't actually criticized her mother, Greta found herself leaping to Esther's defense. "She can be a little overprotective, but it comes from a place of love."

"Of course." Miles shook water from his hair like a dog surfacing from a lake, blinking furiously.

"I would never dream of implying otherwise. I can only imagine how it felt to come so close to losing you."

Perversely, Miles's easy acceptance of her mother's struggle made Greta want to argue the other side. Stomach in knots from the roller coaster of her emotions, she pressed a fist to her belly button. "It was hard for her, I know. My dad died when I was a baby, so it was just Mama on her own, with this passel of boys and me. The lone, sickly girl. The whole island helped out, babysitting and holding pancake breakfasts to raise money for treatments, but still—I know she felt very alone."

But does that justify the way she keeps me close to her, never wants to let me far enough out of her sight to actually live my life?

Her voice dried up around the words, too disloyal to think, much less to say. But from the barely leashed power of Miles's body as he surged to his feet and paced across the pavilion toward her, Greta had the insane feeling that he could read her mind.

His words, spoken softly against her cheek as he lifted his fingers to burrow into the damp tendrils of hair behind her ear, confirmed it. "Have you ever been off this island, Greta?"

The ache of longing that rose up her throat stole her voice for a moment. Swallowing it down, Greta looked away, out into the rain. "Sure. I was such a frequent visitor to Harbor General, the big hospital on the mainland, that the nurses joked about naming a room after me."

A strange tone came into his voice. "And that's it. You've never been farther from home than the podunk town at the other end of Sanctuary Island's ferry line."

"Hey, don't knock Winter Harbor! That's the metropolis to us. They have a grocery store there that sells packs of sushi in the deli department!"

"Well, if you can get grocery store sushi, what more do you need from life?" Miles paced the confines of the gazebo, the motorcycle boots he must have borrowed from Dylan striking hard and loud against the wooden boards. Then he sat down. "There's a whole world out there, Greta. You must have wanted to see it. What about college?"

"Mama . . . I mean, I decided it was better to take courses online through the EVCC. Eastern Virginia Community College."

"Right, you decided."

The skepticism in his heavy-lidded blue eyes got Greta's back up. Tilting her chin, she glared at him. "Yes, I decided. My brothers all left the island for school, and there was no one else to help Mama with the store. She needed me. And after everything she's done for me, the sacrifices she's made—how could I do anything else? So yeah, I stuck around. And for the most part, I have no regrets. It was the right thing to do."

"Doing the right thing for your family." Understanding smoothed the ragged edges of Miles's tone. He shook his head, and the light brown hair he usually swept back fell forward over his forehead to give him a sudden boyishness that made her want to hug him. "It's amazing how little comfort that is, at times."

Greta licked her lips, tasting clean, fresh rain. Drawn like a magnet to her true north, she moved to sit sideways on the bench beside him, drawing her feet up to rest on the seat by his hips. She leaned back against one of the pillars holding up the pavilion roof and watched Miles. "You get it. I know you do. I've seen the way you are with your brothers."

Sighing, Miles settled deeper into the bench. He didn't turn his head to face her, and the stark lines of his profile stood out against the silvery air like a marble statue. "According to Dylan and Logan, how I am with my brothers is domineering, overbearing, demanding, hypercritical."

"Some people might say that about my mother," Greta pointed out. "From the outside, she may seem that way. But that's not her at all. She wants what's best for me. She loves me, and she wants me to be safe. She was willing to let a doctor practically break her in half to rip out a vital organ, so she could give it to me. I'm alive right now only because of her."

A muscle clenched visibly behind Miles's jaw. He dropped his insouciant, lounging pose, bringing his arms down from the railing to rest in his lap. His right hand landed on the bench right beside her foot, and in the next breath, Miles had wrapped that hot hand around her bare, chilled ankle.

"Don't say that," he rasped, his eyes a wild, chaotic blue that almost glowed in the stormy light. "I hate the idea that I might never have met you, that the world could have missed out on you. That we came so close to never . . ."

He broke off, his fingers tightening until she felt the imprint of his fingerprints on her anklebone.

"But we did meet," Greta said, her heart beating like the wings of a hummingbird. She felt as if they were poised at the top of Wanderer's Point, on the edge of the cliff staring down at the churning waves and fixing to jump.

"And we have the chance to get to know each other," Greta went on. "All because you're as protective of your family as my mother is. Personally, I don't think it's a fault. I have to admit, I actually admire the way you look out for your brothers. It's how you show love; I get that."

Going still as an ice sculpture, Miles darted a probing stare to her face. "So you're saying I'm right to be concerned about Dylan? Penny Little is after his money."

Chapter Six

"What? Oh, my God. No." Greta pulled her legs out of his grasp and planted her boots on the floor. "Way to ruin the moment."

Miles flexed his suddenly stiff fingers, tightening them into fists to keep from reaching for her. He'd jumped the gun badly, he realized while cursing himself silently. But this conversation, this entire scheme to get Greta to trust him and turn on her friend—it was getting completely out of hand.

He needed to move things along, or he was going to find himself falling for his own stratagem.

Rubbing a hand over his face, he grimaced at the bristle of whiskers to hide the instinctive flinch of remembering how it had felt to hear Greta Hackley—a woman he barely knew—describe how close she'd come to death as a child.

The raw, instinctive rasp of terror over his nerves, the urge to spring to his feet to do battle with whatever threatened her—Miles was out of his depth and sinking fast.

After years of burying his emotions under the drive to succeed, the need to keep the family company going as a tribute to his dead parents and a way to be sure his younger brothers were always provided for, Miles was way, way out of practice at handling conversations like this.

"I'm sorry." His throat clicked when he swallowed, dry and tight. "Forget I said that."

"I can't just forget," Greta protested, pushing to her feet as if she needed some distance. "Is that what you've been thinking about, this whole time?"

He ought to let her go, he knew. Tactically, it was the right move—not to push, to let Greta come to him.

Screw tactics, Miles decided, standing and wrapping his arms around Greta from behind in one swift motion.

If she struggled at all, he told himself he'd release her . . . but she didn't. Though her tall, willowy body was rigid in his embrace, she didn't shove him away. Instead, she breathed through her nose for a taut, unending moment, then softened against him as if she couldn't help herself.

When her head tipped back to his shoulder and she turned her face into his neck, a dark surge of triumph flared to life inside Miles. "To be completely honest, I had forgotten about my brother and your friend until that moment. And I *am* sorry," he growled, truth in every syllable.

He deeply regretted letting his impatience get

the better of him—even though it freaked him right the hell out that the first part of his confession was true, too.

That he'd allowed himself to forget, even for a moment, that he was only here with Greta to keep his brother from making a painful mistake . . . that was terrifying.

Miles held the solution to his brother's problems in his arms and struggled against the bone-deep yearning to let the rest of the world go to hell.

"Okay. I believe you." The words were almost a sigh, a kiss of warm breath to the side of his neck, and Miles went hard in a violent rush.

He savored the feel of Greta in his arms and let the sturdy strength of her long limbs and lean muscles help him beat back the darkness of knowing exactly how quickly and easily her life could be snuffed out. Miles held himself inflexibly still and breathed in the maddening, rain-washed scent of her hair.

He needed a distraction, for both of them, in the worst possible way. Something to get Greta to forget his poorly timed question about her friend's motives, and something to keep Miles from taking them both down to the floor of the pavilion and chasing every stray raindrop over her skin with his tongue.

The steady drip, drip, drip that filtered through the drumbeat of blood rushing south told Miles the shower had finally slowed to a drizzle. He opened eyes he hadn't even been aware of closing and stopped nuzzling Greta's temple long enough to

confirm that the brief summer storm had blown itself out.

Just as the sun pierced the clouds to bring the
sparkling, wet leaves and grass into brilliant green
relief, Miles heard the unmistakable sound of the
best distraction he could ever have devised.

And to think, he hadn't even realized how brilliant this next move was when he planned it. Confidence restored and mood leveling out, Miles
maneuvered Greta over to the gazebo steps while
managing to keep her close.

"Oh, look, the rain stopped. Where are we going?" she asked.

Miles didn't bother to reply, merely tucked his
fingers under her chin and directed her gaze sky-
ward. Her eyes went round with shock. Over the
loud whirring hum of rotating blades, Miles said
into her ear, "You showed me your family's legacy.
Let me show you mine."

Turning in his arms, Greta pushed up on her
toes like an overexcited child. "You mean . . ."

"We're getting on that helicopter, and I'm taking
you to New York. Right now."

"But." She blinked hard, as if the emerging sunlight glinting off the white sides of the helicopter
had struck her blind. "That's insane. I can't run off
to New York City on a whim."

"Why not?" Miles trailed his fingers down her
arm and took her hand in his. Lifting it to his mouth
in the smooth, practiced gesture that regularly
made rival CEO's wives titter and blush, he pressed
a kiss to the back of her knuckles and gave her a

slow smile from under his lashes. "You're an adult, taking a bit of rare time off from an all-consuming job. You deserve a break."

"This is more than a break." Greta stared at him, her fingers stiff in his grasp. "This is like something out of a fairy tale, the handsome prince swooping in to carry me off on his white steed, to his castle in the clouds."

"Only in this case, the steed is a Eurocopter EC135 with interior design by Hermès, and the castle in the clouds is my penthouse on Central Park South. But basically, yes."

"This can't be happening for real." Greta's eyes were round and dark as she watched the branches whip sparkling fans of rainwater in all directions as the wind from the rotor shook them.

Alert to any signs of disbelief, Miles was quick to say, "Greta. Have you ever been farther away from Sanctuary Island than the transplant hospital in Winter Harbor?"

She shook her head mutely, terrible longing and nervous excitement sending a flush to her face.

"There's a big world out there. And the thought that you've never experienced any of it—let me have that first experience with you. Please."

Reaching up a hand to touch one of those hot, fever-bright cheeks, Miles tilted her head to the perfect angle for a kiss. *Just to seal the deal,* he promised himself.

But from the first touch of his lips to hers, he was lost. When she kissed him back, her mouth opening under his and meeting him hunger for hunger,

Miles's brain was washed clean of everything but Greta.

His last clear thought before the whir of the helicopter and the overwhelming pleasure of the kiss obliterated sanity was, *This is a dangerous game we're playing.*

And for the first time in a long time, Miles wasn't sure he even knew what winning would look like.

Riding in a helicopter was everything Greta had always imagined it would be. Partly because even her wildest imaginings could never have dreamed up a helicopter as comfortable and luxurious as the spacious four-seater cabin of Miles's EC135, with its buttery leather seats and burled-wood accents.

It was too noisy to talk, and Miles spent most of the three-hour flight working on the laptop the pilot had produced when they boarded, along with a bottle of chilled champagne and a pair of flutes.

Greta had never been more sorry to have to turn down alcohol in her life. Sinking back into the deep cushions of her seat and staring around at the opulence of the interior, she said, "Kidney transplant, remember? I try to stay away from anything that puts stress on my body."

Miles frowned a little at the reminder as he waved the black-uniformed pilot back up to the cockpit with the champagne. "Sorry, I gave instructions for the helicopter's return trip before I knew about your medical situation."

"It's really not that big a deal," Greta said, buckling up with fingers that shook from the thrill of doing something she knew would cause her mother to have a total meltdown. "The transplant changed my life, made me healthy in a way I'd never been before. I'm fine now. I can do almost anything a quote-unquote normal person can do."

"If you believe that," Miles said slowly, "then why is this your first real trip away from home?"

Greta was spared from having to come up with a quick response by the helicopter lifting off. The sudden intensification of sound and vibration from the engine and the propellers made conversation impossible.

But as the small aircraft soared up and over the flowering trees and backcountry roads spiraling out from the heart of Sanctuary Island, Greta thought about it. She tried to reconcile the pure, elated joy she felt at this moment, impulsively running away from home to have an adventure with a handsome stranger, with the nagging coil of guilt at leaving her mother behind without a word.

Miles had already promised they'd be back before the shop opened the next day, and reminded her that he'd told Esther he'd take care of her. He'd offered to have the pilot wait while Greta called her mother, if she wanted to explain where she was going, but Greta had refused. It was one thing to buck her mother's authority and climb onto a helicopter, but it was another to tell her mother all about it and hear the naked fear and worry in her voice.

Resolving to put negative thoughts out of her mind and simply enjoy the madcap craziness of this spontaneous adventure, Greta focused her attention out the window for the entire three-hour flight. When the vast stretch of rippling blue ocean gave way to the towering gray skyscrapers of the Manhattan skyline, Miles closed his laptop and leaned over her.

"There's the Statue of Liberty."

Greta followed his pointed finger, craning her neck to see. Breath caught in her chest. The regal magnificence of the familiar form rose up, torch raised to the sky, and Greta felt tears spring to her eyes.

Slanting Miles a sideways glance, she refused to wipe the tears away. She wasn't ashamed. "You're probably going to regret bringing me to New York. All I want is to do all the horrendously touristy stuff you've probably done a thousand times," she yelled cheerfully over the noise of the helicopter.

Miles made a face before pressing his mouth to her ear. "Like Times Square? I haven't voluntarily set foot on Forty-Second Street in years."

Figuring she could afford to be generous, Greta shrugged. "We don't have to do Times Square. It's probably too late to get tickets to a Broadway show tonight, anyway."

But Miles only smiled, that enigmatic quirk of the lips that didn't so much as hint at the man she'd started to see underneath his polished exterior, and pulled out his phone to send a few quick texts.

The helicopter glided over the East River and over the tops of tall buildings gleaming with glass and chrome. Peering as far forward as she could,

Greta clutched at her armrests as she realized they were passing the Empire State Building. The city looked exactly the way it did in movies, huge and overwhelming. She could feel the energy of the streets below, the hustle and bustle of millions of people going about their daily lives.

The skyline passed in a blur of concrete and steel, and before Greta knew it, the helicopter was angling toward a swanky, tall building with a flat roof marked out as a landing pad.

Just as the helicopter centered itself and began to lower for touchdown, a gust of wind shot through the canyon created by the rows of sky-scrapers. The helicopter fishtailed wildly, and Greta instinctively clutched for Miles's hand.

He wrapped strong, reassuring fingers around her wrist, tight enough that she could feel her pulse throbbing to the double-time drumbeat of her heart.

"We're okay," Miles said into her ear. "Landing can be a little tricky here, but Arturo has never let me fall, yet."

Greta nodded, her face and toes oddly numb. She didn't get her voice or her breath back until the pilot had righted the helicopter and landed. Tumbling out as soon as Miles slid open the door in the side of the aircraft, Greta resisted the urge to kiss the dirty concrete of the landing pad, but it was a close call.

She ducked away from the minitornado caused by the swirling blades, heading for the relative shelter of a glassed-in structure on the far side of the roof. After a brief conference with the pilot, Miles followed her. And this time, Greta didn't even try to resist the urge—she threw her arms around him and held on tight, a complicated wave of emotion crashing through her.

"Hey," Miles said, finally able to speak without shouting as the helicopter powered down. "I told your mom I'd make sure you got back to her in one piece, and I meant it. I know, I know, you don't need anyone to take care of you, but . . ."

"But that's exactly it," Greta said. "That's what I'm afraid of."

She could hear the frown in Miles's deep voice. "I don't follow."

"The question you asked me before we left Sanctuary Island." Great paused, feeling broken open, like an egg shattered on the ground. "About why I've never traveled."

One of his big, warm hands came up to cradle the back of her head, and Greta let herself soak up the silent comfort.

"I tell myself—I tell everyone that I'm fine. Completely over all the crap from when I was a kid. But the kidney transplant could only do so much. It cured my body, but in my heart . . . I'm still afraid."

"That seems very natural to me." Miles petted at her hair as if he wasn't sure what else to do or say, and the hesitance in his normally assured voice made Greta smile through her turmoil.

"I don't want to be afraid." She pulled back enough to look up into Miles's concerned face. "I don't want to be someone who needs to be taken care of. But I spent so many years unable to do much of anything, always weak and sick, making everyone around me worry. And now I'm the one who worries, that even if I had the chance to do all the things I dream of . . . I don't have the guts to make it on my own."

Dragging his fingers through the wind-tangled mess of her hair, Miles palmed her cheek and tilted her chin up. He dropped a tender kiss on her up-turned lips, soft and brief enough to light Greta's nerves up like fireflies.

"I have no doubt that you've got the courage and strength to do whatever you set your mind to," Miles said, all hesitation erased from his voice. "But for now, you don't need to go it alone. I'm going to be right beside you, every step of the way."

Greta knew her smile was shaky, at best, so she pressed up on her tippy toes and kissed him to hide it. And to thank him, because he was trying so hard, and he made her remember how glad she was to be on this adventure with him.

For now.

Chapter Seven

It wasn't that Miles had previously been unaware of the benefits of being a billionaire. The benefits were obvious, many, and varied. From last-minute reservations at the best restaurants in town to having a chauffeur on staff to drive him through Manhattan's terrible traffic, Miles enjoyed the lifestyle he worked so hard to maintain.

But nothing he'd ever spent money on compared to the fun of splurging to give Greta Hackley the most lavish first trip to New York anyone could imagine.

One text to his assistant, Cleo, was all it took to get the whole day set up for them, from box seats at whatever sold-out show was hottest to a very special final stop that required Cleo to pull more than a few strings. But it was more than worth it for the look on Greta's face.

Watching her as she raced through his stylish

apartment with barely a glance at the expensive, modern Italian furnishings and priceless art on the walls, just so she could get downstairs and run straight across the street and into Central Park . . . Miles couldn't do anything but laugh and try to keep up.

He followed her as she plunged through the crowds of shoppers mobbing Fifth Avenue, fingers twined together like schoolkids. When he tried to get her to go into Bergdorf Goodman, already imagining her in a slinky couture cocktail dress, Greta refused in favor of studying each artful window display.

When they walked by a street musician playing a Bangles song from the eighties to the delight of the tourists bopping along to the beat, Greta mentioned that she'd always been fascinated by ancient Egypt. One more text to poor, beleaguered Cleo netted them a private tour through the Metropolitan Museum's famed Temple of Dendur exhibit.

The awe on her face as she peered into the dim recesses of the reconstructed temple left Miles with no choice. In response to his firm nod, the museum docent smiled slightly and backed out of the temple long enough to let Miles kiss Greta under the weight of centuries-old stone from a faraway land.

When Miles got confirmation that the tickets had come through for the hot show, which turned out to be a musical based on a comic book superhero, he gritted his teeth and pretended to be excited at the prospect of watching actors in tights sing and dance their way around a Broadway stage.

But once the curtain came up and Greta leaned forward, the motion making the sequins on the cocktail dress he'd had sent up to his penthouse catch the stage lights and sparkle, Miles couldn't have cared less that the show was nothing he would have chosen for himself. All he cared about was the delight in Greta's grin every time the guy playing the superhero was hoisted up to fly through the air, borne aloft on the magic of stagecraft. And the fact that she let him press her into the shadows at the back of their private box during intermission and kiss her against the red velvet that covered the walls.

She made everything feel new again.

After the show, Ira maneuvered the Bentley through the packed street at the side of the theater. Greta slid across the black leather seats with a noise that sounded like relief. Reaching down to rub at her arches, she gave him a rueful smile from beneath the dark gold hair curling loosely around her face. "I'm not used to three-inch heels. Steel-toed work boots are more my style."

"They wouldn't exactly go with that dress." Miles leaned down to pull her bare feet into his lap, carelessly tossing the black patent Louboutins to the floor.

Greta blushed and shoved the hem of her cocktail dress down before it could ride up and reveal too much of her creamy thighs, but Miles concentrated on her feet. He dug his thumbs into her arches, swept his knuckles around the ball of each foot, and smiled when Greta stopped squirming and just moaned. The low, guttural sound from deep in her chest vibrated down her legs and into Miles's lap, making him go hard and thick against the press of her feet.

"That's miraculous." Greta laid her head back against the tinted side window, careless of messing up her hair. "This whole day has been miraculous."

"It doesn't have to be over yet," Miles offered, keeping up the foot massage to see how much more he could melt her. "I had planned something special for after the show, but if you're too tired . . ."

Greta struggled to sit up straight, her eyelashes fluttering. "No! I want to see it all, do it all, whatever you have planned. Although I can't imagine what could top everything we've done so far."

With most women, Miles would take that as flirtation, a coy invitation for him to growl and roll her under him to show her exactly what they could do to cap off the perfect day. But despite Greta's adventurous spirit and the core of steel she'd developed over years of battling illness, there was an innocence to her that Miles never wanted to sully.

What do you call this scheme, then, a little voice asked inside Miles's head. *You're setting up the perfect seduction scenario, all in the hopes that Greta will be so overcome with lust for you that she'll betray her best friend.*

Lead sunk into Miles's stomach as he considered the full ramifications of his plan for the first time. He still wanted to protect Dylan—it was one of the guiding principles of Miles's life, that it was his job to hold his family together and keep his brothers safe from harm. But the more he got to know Greta, the less likely it seemed that she'd ever betray her friend.

Actually, what seemed unlikeliest of all was that straightforward, loyal Greta would be party to any sort of deception. If Penny Little was taking Dylan for a ride, Miles found it difficult to believe that Greta knew anything about it.

So what was he doing here?

"Miles? Is everything okay?"

Greta's tentative question jolted Miles from his thoughts. He realized his hands had fallen still, his fingers wrapped loosely around her wiggling toes. The warmth of her skin, the slip of silk between them, the slender turn of her ankle—Miles swallowed. He'd never been so tempted to chuck his moral code out the window and simply take what he wanted.

But he couldn't live with himself if he hurt this woman.

"Everything's fine." He smiled, hoping she wouldn't be able to see that it didn't reach his eyes. "But you're probably right, nothing could top the day we've had. I'll tell Ira to take us back to the penthouse, there's a guest room all ready for you, fully stocked with all the necessities."

Greta drew her feet away from him, curling her legs under her on the seat. Miles let her go with a pang of regret.

"Oh. I thought . . . never mind." The flashing multicolored lights of Times Square illuminated her disappointment for a bare instant before she shook it off. "Sure, let's go back to your apartment. Might as well get to bed early, since we'll have to get up at the crack of dawn to get me back to Sanctuary in time to open the shop."

It was true. Greta was right. And this was the right thing to do, Miles knew. But he could feel her pulling away from him in more ways than the physical, the bright light of her happiness dimming in front of him, and he couldn't stand it.

Meeting Ira's inquisitive gaze in the rearview mirror, Miles didn't even hesitate. He gave a slight shake of the head, knowing Ira would interpret it correctly after years of driving Miles around town.

Maybe it was masochistic of him to drag this thing out any longer, knowing he couldn't allow himself to give in to Greta's innocent temptation, but he'd be damned if he let her big New York adventure end on a sad note. He'd give her the best night of her life, no matter how much it might make him wish for what he could never have.

A guest room all ready for you.

Greta leaned her overwarm forehead against the cool glass of the car window and clamped down on the lump in her throat.

If someone had told her when she woke this morning that before the night was over she'd be close to tears over the fact that Miles Harrington—proud, stuffy, condescending jerk extraordinaire—clearly had no designs on her body after all, she would have laughed herself stupid.

She certainly didn't feel much like laughing now.

The car slid to a silent, elegant stop and Greta took care to hide her wince as she slid her aching feet back into the torturous high heels she'd been so excited about earlier. Telling herself she needed to shake off this let-down feeling and be grateful for the trouble Miles had gone to—even if it hadn't been a prelude to seduction, as she'd assumed with a giddy tingle all day long—Greta looked up from wrestling with the strappy heels to see that Miles had already gotten out of the car.

He held out a hand to help her, and as she steeled herself against the sensual excitement of his touch, Greta's feet hit the sidewalk and she looked up with a determinedly bright smile plastered to her face.

She looked up . . . and up . . . and up, all the breath leaving her lungs in a whoosh. Clutching Miles's hand in an iron grip, Greta stared at the building spearing straight into the night sky, brilliantly lit and beautiful as only an architectural icon could be.

"That's not your apartment," Greta said, feeling as disoriented as if she were waking up from anesthesia.

"Nope."

The anticipation in his voice was the only thing that could have dragged her attention off the building. Miles was watching her avidly, his intense blue eyes soaking up her every reaction, and Greta let him have it.

With a smile so wide her cheeks ached with it, Greta said, "You brought me to the Empire State Building."

"You said you wanted to do the whole tourist routine. This place is on every tour of the city—although we'll be seeing it a little differently from most tourists."

"What do you mean, because it's nighttime?"

Miles shook his head, clearly enjoying the mystery. "Actually, the Empire State Building is open every single day of the year, rain or shine, until late at night."

"Then what?"

Tilting his chin toward the doors, Miles said, "You'll have to go in to find out."

Excitement and adrenaline flooded Greta's bloodstream, a better wake-up call than a vat of coffee. Her tired feet forgotten, she bounded across the sidewalk and spun through the revolving door into the gorgeous art deco lobby.

Greta was so busy gawking up at the ornate silver-and-gold ceiling mural that she almost walked right into a trim, middle-aged black woman standing with an older man in the livery of an old-fashioned elevator operator.

"Oh! I'm so sorry," Greta said, wobbling on her stilettos.

The woman she'd bumped gave her a small, professional smile and held out a hand. "No worries. You must be Greta. It's lovely to meet you."

Greta shook the woman's hand just as she heard the click of Miles's dress shoes on the tiled lobby floor. "Greta, this is Cleo Packard, my right-hand woman. I'd be lost without her. She's the one who arranged everything we've done today."

"Including this outfit, I bet," Greta said, a little overwhelmed by the knowledge of how much work must have gone into today from behind the scenes. Impulsively, she threw her arms around Cleo and squeezed her into a brief, grateful hug.

"Thank you for everything," Greta whispered, pulling back. She knew from the rising heat in her cheeks that she was blushing, but she'd never meant anything more. "It's been the most amazing day of my life."

Cleo's wide, surprised eyes warmed. "I'm glad. And I'm even gladder Mr. Harrington invited me here to meet you."

"After everything I put Cleo through today," Miles explained, "I wanted to thank her."

Turning a fond, indulgent smile on her boss, Cleo shook her head. "I work for you, Mr. Harrington. The exorbitant salary you pay me is thanks enough. I've told him before," she said, shrugging in Greta's direction. "But it never seems to sink in."

"You do more for me than any amount of money could repay," Miles said firmly. "So come on. Your thank-you gift is at the top of the building."

Clearly reluctant, Cleo glanced back and forth between Miles and Greta. "Now Mr. Harrington, I don't know. Having met this young lady, I'm not sure I should intrude on your evening."

Greta didn't have a crystal-clear picture of exactly what was going on, but she knew enough to link her arm through Miles's elbow on one side, and Cleo's on the other.

"Nonsense. You've known Miles a lot longer

than I have, but even I am already completely aware of the fact that once he sets his heart on something, he gets it. You're coming upstairs with us!"

With a little laugh, Cleo allowed herself to be towed toward the elevator. "All right, but only for a minute. Mr. Harrington, I think you may have met your match with this one."

Ignoring the flutter of happiness that gave her, Greta bounced on her toes in anticipation as the silent old gentleman in the uniform called down the elevator. The metal doors engraved with a stylized deco outline of the iconic building's exterior slid apart with a muted ding.

"Going up," the uniformed man announced as they all trooped in.

Greta kept her gaze glued to the old-fashioned floor counter as the elevator zoomed upward. Her stomach fluttered as they climbed higher and higher, excitement sending chills over her skin.

They got off at the eighty-sixth floor, but instead of following the signs to the Observation Deck, the stony-faced elevator attendant ushered them across the hall to another elevator. "Wait, aren't we . . ." Greta broke off as the second elevator's doors whooshed closed. "Oh, my gosh."

And farther up they went. This elevator had a series of numbers beside the floors, and as they climbed ever higher, Greta realized that the second numbers were estimates of height in feet.

When the elevator wound to a stop at the one hundred and second floor, the number illuminated next to it was one thousand, two hundred and fifty.

As in, they were now one thousand, two hundred and fifty feet off the ground.

Greta's mind could hardly process what she was about to see when they stepped through those doors.

It was a much quieter observation gallery than the bustling deck below on eighty-six, and her heart raced at the views through the glass picture windows. But instead of giving her time to wander and stare out over the tops of buildings and the ocean of lights, Miles prodded her toward a door she hadn't even noticed.

Plain and unmarked, the door was entirely unassuming. For some reason, she expected it to be locked, but when Miles twisted the handle, it opened easily to reveal a narrow set of metal stairs going up.

"And . . . this is where I get off," Cleo said suddenly, hanging back.

Miles frowned. "But your thank-you gift!"

"I know." She cocked her head. "But now that I see those stairs . . . I think I'll just enjoy the view from here, thanks. You two go on ahead."

Greta's heart leapt into her throat as she contemplated the stairs. She completely understood Cleo's change of heart. They were so high already, the vast blackness of the night sky all around them and the city spread hundreds of feet below. Fear stalked her, the old familiar refrain of caution like her mother's voice in her head, but Greta stuffed it down. "I'm not going to make it in these heels."

"So take them off." Miles shrugged, a mischievous glint in his blue eyes. "Don't worry, I'll happily go up behind you and be ready to catch you if you stumble."

Greta snorted, some of the fear dissipating in the face of his flirtation. "My hero, willing to climb a ladder behind me while I'm wearing a short, tight dress."

Miles leaned in to murmur, "What if I promise I won't look?"

The mixed signals were giving Greta emotional whiplash. She arched her brow in a clear challenge. "Look all you want, Miles. I'm not shy."

It wasn't completely true—more than a decade of hiding her body, her scar, from the world had left Greta with a few hang-ups. But she wanted Miles Harrington. And maybe if she showed him clearly enough, he'd get over whatever was holding him back.

Right then and there, Greta decided she wasn't spending the night in any guest room. She'd either sleep in Miles's bed . . . or she'd find her own way back home to Sanctuary Island tonight.

"Are you ready?" he asked, gesturing at the steep stairs.

Slipping out of her heels, Greta filled her lungs with a deep, cleansing breath, and set her foot on the bottom step. "As ready as I'll ever be."

Chapter Eight

"Surprise," Miles said as they climbed. "These stairs lead to the private deck, at the base of the building's mooring mast. The highest point in New York not open to the general public, with three-hundred-and-sixty-degree views of the entire city on the other side of that door."

Ducking under the network of pipes at the top of the stairs, he watched Greta hesitate for a second at the exit to the outside.

Concerned, he said, "If you're nervous, we don't have to go out. We can head back down to the observation gallery, or even to the regular deck down on eighty-six with the rest of the tourists."

"I am nervous," she muttered. "We must be so high up now! But I made it this far. I have to see what's out there."

Miles took her hand, unsurprised to find her fingers chilled with fear. Bringing them to his mouth, he blew warmth over them. "You have nothing to prove to anyone, Greta. Whatever you want, it's all good."

But she shook her head, her fingers curling around his as she stared up at him earnestly. "Thank you. But you're wrong. I do have something to prove. To myself, more than anyone."

And with that, she stepped away from him and out onto the narrow balcony. Pride, respect, admiration for the sheer gutsiness of her, filled Miles's chest. Not wanting to miss a moment of her triumph over herself, he followed her.

Wind whipped across his face, and even this high in the clouds, it still carried the city scents of exhaust fumes and dirty-water hot dog carts. The secret deck up here was insanely narrow, no more than two feet of space between the exterior of the tower and the ludicrously short knee-high railing.

"Ever been up here before?" Greta called into the breeze as she inched her barefoot way around the ledge, back hugging the tower.

Miles shook his head. "I can't believe they let anyone up here. I guess this explains the waivers I had Cleo forge my signature on so we could get this confirmed."

Somehow, that loosened the taut line of Greta's creamy shoulders, bared by the spaghetti straps of her sparkly cocktail dress. "So I'm not the only one who thinks this is a little crazy? We could topple over the side here any second. If the wind were strong enough . . ."

Her fingers went white-knuckled as she clenched them for purchase against the wall, and Miles forgot to be nervous about the thousand-plus-foot drop straight down into Midtown traffic. Stepping quickly, he maneuvered himself next to her and slipped a steadying arm around her shoulders, relieved when she relaxed into his side at once.

"What did I tell you," he said. "You don't have to do this alone. Hell, you don't have to do it at all—but since you're determined, I'm right here with you. I'm not going anywhere."

"I want to look over the edge." Determination hummed in her low voice, threading steel through her limbs, and once again, Miles could only marvel at her.

Instead of arguing, the way he knew she half-expected him to, Miles silently nudged her forward and slid his body behind hers. Bracing his feet securely against the buffeting of the wind, he clasped his hands around her narrow waist.

"Go ahead," he told her. "I'll be your anchor."

Greta folded her hands over his, shooting him a smile full of nerves, thrill, and the incandescent joy of doing something crazy for once in her sheltered life. And then she leaned out, trusting him to hold her securely.

Miles was ready to pull her back against him the instant he felt her stiffen in fear or panic, but she didn't. She laughed. Wild and carefree, with her arms stretched out to the sides like wings that would catch the wind and let her soar off into the night, Greta laughed.

And Miles fell in love.

"I can't believe we're doing this!" she called over her shoulder, eyes glittering and hair flying in tendrils around her shoulders. "Look, you can see all the way to . . . gosh, there are three bridges all lit up. Is one of them the Brooklyn Bridge?"

"That one." Miles risked letting go of her with one hand just long enough to point.

"Beautiful." Her sigh was lost in the breeze, but he felt the way the breath pushed out of her rib cage. She leaned back against his chest, and Miles crossed his arms over her torso to hold her close.

"This is *my* island," he said into the delicate pink shell of her ear. "I'm glad you got to see it like this. Thank you for coming here with me."

"I'll never forget today, as long as I live. I'm the one who should be thanking you."

Guilt scoured out his insides with a merciless hand. "You don't owe me anything, Greta Hackley. Today was for me as much as for you. I've lived in this city my entire adult life, and I guess I take the sights and sounds and smells of it for granted. You brought them back to life for me."

He paused, everything he wanted to say getting stuck behind the giant ball of emotion in his throat. But this was too important, he had to get it out.

Dredging his voice up from deep in his chest, he rumbled, "You brought *me* back to life. I was dead inside, and didn't even know it."

Miles felt, more than heard, the broken noise Greta made before she turned to wrap her arms around his neck.

Right there, at the top of the world, Greta kissed him. And as Miles snugged her in tight and tried his best to breathe in her essence, he knew he had to do whatever it took to keep this woman in his life.

From here on out, Miles would be honest and open with her. He wanted a relationship, a future, a chance to make Greta fall in love with him for real. He'd started this campaign of seduction for all the wrong reasons, but that didn't mean it couldn't work. He'd just keep it up until Greta was as head over heels, crazy in love as he was.

And he'd make damn sure she never, ever found out the truth about how this all started.

Jittery anticipation made Greta fumble as she slipped off her heels and kicked them across the marble-floored foyer of Miles's penthouse. She caught herself against a sleek, glass-topped display case that held what looked like an ancient family Bible and several framed photos.

Greta nudged the spindly legged table back into place with a guilty glance over her shoulder at Miles, who was distracted by a phone call to check in with Cleo, who'd been gone by the time they came down from the secret deck.

The baritone hum of his low voice behind her sent pleasurable vibrations into her stomach and chest. Her heart rate, which had finally slowed to something resembling normal on the car ride uptown, ticked up again.

To distract herself while she waited for Miles,

Greta leaned down to study the pictures in the display case. Several were old, sepia-tinted shots of people staring straight at the camera without smiling, and there were a few soft-focus baby pictures.

But the one that caught her eye was of a bright, smiling woman with her head leaning on the broad shoulder of a tall, handsome man with Miles's stern jaw and electric blue eyes. Ranged in front of them was a toddler waving a wooden bulldozer and an older kid with a bored expression and a book clutched to his chest. A tall, teenaged boy stood beside his father, mimicking his straight-backed posture and the gleam of pride as he gazed at his family.

Eyes and nose stinging, Greta blinked quickly to stop any tears as Miles stepped up beside her. She pointed at the photo. "I love this one."

"It was taken a few years before our parents died. Car crash, very sudden," he said, sounding totally matter of fact. But the slow, tender way he took out his silk pocket square and wiped at the fingerprints she'd left on the glass told another story.

She'd seen it over and over in the short time she'd known Miles Harrington. From the outside, he appeared so buttoned up and focused, nothing but will, arrogance, and pride. But that wasn't who Miles was inside.

Greta believed the real Miles was the one who knew the name of every person who worked for him, and freely showed them his appreciation for all that they did. The real Miles was the man who invited his assistant along on their date as a thank-you, and then called to make sure she'd made it home safely.

The real Miles was the man who met a woman who'd always longed to see the world . . . and gave her a view of it that would be seared into her memory for the rest of her life.

"I never knew my father, and I still miss him," Greta said, feeling her way. "I can't even imagine what it must have been like for you, to lose both your parents so young."

Miles shrugged heavily, and Greta could almost see the weight that had dropped onto those shoulders along with that tragic loss. "It was worse for Dylan. Poor kid was on his own, had to go live with our grandparents. At least Logan and I could escape to school. I was almost done with college, and once I finished, I always planned to ask Dylan if he wanted to come live with me instead. But by then, he was settled with Nana and Gramps, and the board of directors was pressuring me to pick up the reins at Harrington International. I got my MBA at Columbia, working weekends and nights while trying to make sense of the chaos the company had fallen into without a Harrington at the helm. Dylan was better off where he was."

Greta swallowed, not sure what to say. "I'm sure Dylan was fine with your grandparents. But Miles, he would have been fine with you, too. You know that, don't you?"

He glanced away, into the dark interior of the spacious living room. "Maybe."

Grabbing for his hand to keep him from walking away, Greta insisted, "No maybe about it. I'm not saying you did the wrong thing by concentrating on the company—that's your family's legacy, it's important to all three of you. But if you've been thinking all along that you couldn't have taken care of Dylan when he was a teenager, I just have to tell you, I think you're completely wrong. I've never known anyone to take care of people the way you do, Miles. It's part of your nature, it's who you are. The way you treat the people who work for you, the things you've done for me—even how you fight with your brothers! All that tells me you have a whole lot of love to give. Don't ever think different, okay?"

Even in the muted golden glow of the backlit display case, Greta could see Miles's throat work silently for a long moment before he shuddered and reeled her in for a deep, drugging kiss. Greta's knees wobbled, and with a few short, sure steps he'd backed her against the foyer wall and pinned her there.

Need, hot and urgent, raced through Greta's body with every beat of her fast-pounding heart. She made a muffled moan, the noise trapped between their lips, and wrapped one leg as high as she could around Miles's lean hip. There was an achy emptiness at the core of her that made her restless and fretful, unable to simply dissolve into the kiss and let Miles set the pace.

Greta wanted him. And now she knew he wanted

her back, despite his earlier assurances of her own guest bedroom.

"Shh," he whispered against her lips when she whimpered again. "We need to slow down, sweetheart."

Clutching at his shoulders to feel the line of his hard muscle under the stiff structure of his suit jacket, Greta shook her head. "Don't want to go slow. Please. I know you've already given me everything I asked for today—but I'm greedy. I want this, too."

Groaning, Miles fell on her mouth again, licking into her voraciously. She could feel each separate imprint of his fingers where they shaped the curve of her waist. When he came up for air, shaking his head as if he were attempting to shake some sense into himself, Greta panicked.

Reaching for the concealed side zipper, she whisked it down and shrugged out of the black sequined dress before she had time to think it through or get nervous. The light was perfect, a low glow that gilded the skin and minimized the faded line scored above her hip. The look in Miles's wide, stunned eyes as he took in the sight of her small breasts cupped in black lace and the matching lacy undies, made Greta feel beautiful. Womanly and desirable, for the first time in her life.

"Come on, Miles." Her voice was a low, husky whisper in the darkness. "I want the whole fairy tale."

His eyes went hot and wild, but when he reached

for her, his touch was soft, tender, careful. He slid his hands into the tumbled mess of her hair so gently, his fingers never snagged on a tangle. Framing her face, Miles's thumbs drew lines of fire over the fragile skin below her eyes, the blood-warmed flush of her cheeks.

Greta stood there, stripped down to her underwear while Miles still wore his three-piece suit, and smiled. She ought to feel naked or embarrassed, she thought dimly—but instead, clothed in nothing but wisps of lace and the heat pouring off of Miles's big body, she'd never felt safer.

"Are you sure?" he asked, his gaze searching her face intently.

In answer, Greta stepped close enough to feel the brush of fine wool suit cloth over every inch of her bared skin. She pushed her hands into the open jacket and wound her arms around him until they were pressed heartbeat to heartbeat.

"I've never been more sure of anything in my life." The words were a throaty whisper against the salty delicious skin of his neck, and they had the exact effect Greta had been hoping for.

Miles groaned, then all of a sudden, bent at the knees to sweep Greta off her feet and up into his arms. "You want the fairy tale? You got it," he muttered as he carried her down the hall toward the sumptuous master bedroom.

Laughing into his shoulder, Greta hung on tightly and surrendered to the magic of the moment. Her last coherent thought before Miles laid her on his Egyptian cotton sheets and proceeded to slowly, tenderly take her apart with pure pleasure, was to send a fervent prayer of gratitude up to heaven.

After years of wondering what the fuss was all about, years of looking at herself in the mirror and wondering what was so wrong with her that no man on Sanctuary Island ever seemed to glance at her twice, Miles came along and made her glad she'd never caught those boys' eyes.

Thank you, she breathed silently as stars burst behind her closed eyelids. *I'm glad you made me wait.*

Miles Harrington was worth waiting for.

Chapter Nine

Greta pushed open the door to Hackley's Hardware, twitching her hips to the familiar tinkle of the entry bell, and flipped the sign from Closed to Open.

"Good morning," she called out, sashaying down the aisle toward the back. It was all she could do not to skip.

"Well, look what the cat dragged in." Esther poked her head out of the back office. From the ink smudges on her fingers, she'd been doing her morning crossword before settling in to checking inventory.

Brimming with affection for her hardworking mother, Greta rounded the counter and planted a loud, smacking kiss on Esther's powdered cheek. "Isn't it a glorious day? I don't know when I've ever seen Sanctuary looking prettier."

After a long night of passion, she'd slept through most of the predawn helicopter flight back home, but Miles had kissed her awake in time to appreciate the aerial view of the sun bursting over the horizon to shine down on Sanctuary Island.

Esther's silvery-blond brows climbed toward her hairline. "My, my. Someone's in a good mood."

Hiding a small, secret smile, Greta went to power up the cash register and flip through the change drawer to check if they needed to make a run to the bank. "I had a good night, is all."

"Oh? Care to share?"

Greta hesitated. She'd always told her mother everything, but this . . . she wanted to hug the memory of last night to herself for just a little longer. Plus, she decided, she wasn't at all in the mood to deal with Esther freaking out over the helicopter ride, and she could only imagine her mother's horrified reaction to the death-defying trip to the top of the Empire State Building.

So all she said was, "I spent some more time with Miles Harrington."

"Hmm." Esther sounded amused. "I figured."

With a sudden jolt, Greta wondered if she actually looked different today than she had yesterday. Could her mother tell she'd been with Miles?

But before she could spin out too wildly into embarrassment, Esther tugged lightly on Greta's sleeve. Pinching the fine Italian wool between two fingers, she smirked a little.

"Is this the billionaire CEO version of giving you his varsity letterman's jacket?" Esther asked.

Relief washed through Greta's body, the sudden relaxation of tensed muscles making her vividly aware of the unusual ways she'd strained and stressed those muscles the night before. "I forgot I was wearing it," she admitted, hunching her shoulders to inhale the complicated scent of Miles still clinging to the material of his suit jacket.

She wondered if she should tell him that the cologne he no doubt paid big bucks for smelled exactly like fresh cuts of the expensive cedar wood her brother bought to redesign their mother's closet as a birthday gift.

The smell made her mouth tingle as if she'd just been kissed. Greta hugged herself, bunching the extra fabric and probably wrinkling it horribly, but if Miles minded that, he wouldn't have draped it over her while she napped on the helicopter.

Something vibrated inside the inner jacket pocket. Startled, Greta fished out Miles's slim black smartphone. A missed call from Cleo showed on the locked screen.

"Uh oh. I bet he's already looking for this." Greta stroked the phone fondly, remembering how she'd teased Miles about having it permanently welded to his hand.

"I can mind the shop if you want to run out and give it to him," Esther offered.

"Nah." Greta smiled her thanks at her mother. "Miles is on a mission this morning."

"A mission that doesn't require a cell phone?"

"A mission I don't want to interrupt," Greta corrected her. She couldn't help smiling when she thought of Miles tipping up her chin and kissing her good-bye. For luck, he'd said.

He might need some luck. It was going to take more than a quick apology to mend fences with his brothers, but giving his blessing to Dylan and Penny's upcoming wedding was a good start.

Joy bubbled up from her chest like fresh spring water. Everything was happening so quickly, and coming together so perfectly! The happiness she'd found with Miles made her immensely grateful to have been able to play even a small part in helping Miles come to grips with his brother's engagement to Greta's best friend.

Greta wanted everyone she loved, everyone she knew, everyone she'd ever met to be as happy as she was at that moment.

The phone buzzed in her hand, and she absently glanced down to see a text message from Cleo lighting up the screen.

She didn't mean to read it, but the name "Penny Little" jumped out at her. Frowning, Greta looked more closely, confusion and dread tightening her stomach.

Got the PI report on Penny Little background check today, no obvious flags. I'm attaching in email, but she looks clean.

Greta breathed out, shaky and a little sick. Okay, that didn't necessarily mean anything. So Miles hired an investigator—probably when he first heard about the engagement—and hadn't called the guy off yet. No big . . .

The phone buzzed again. Greta tightened her

suddenly clammy fingers around it and told herself not to look. It was a private message, between Miles and his assistant, and it had nothing to do with her.

But it might have something to do with Penny. They were so close, all of them, to getting what they wanted; Dylan and Miles were about to make up, then Penny and Dylan would live happily ever after. It was meant to be.

Unable to stand the idea of anything messing with her best friend's perfect happy ending, Greta peeked at the phone's screen one more time . . . and felt the bottom drop out of her world.

"Thanks for agreeing to sit down with me." Miles spread his hands on the kitchen table, the same table his grandparents must have eaten at when this was their summer hideaway, and met the eyes of both people sitting opposite.

Dylan was guarded, his gaze shielded the way he'd learned after their parents died. Beside him, Penny cast her fiancé a worried glance, but when she faced Miles, her dainty jaw went hard with determination.

"I know the last time we spoke, I said some things . . ." Miles began, more hesitant then he liked as he searched for the right words.

Sitting up straight in her ladder-backed chair, Penny tilted her chin up defiantly. "You certainly did. And I, for one, am not interested in hearing anything from you other than an apology."

This was why Miles preferred to go into meetings already knowing what he intended to say. He hated losing control of the conversation.

"It's okay, Penny," Dylan said, probably reading the tension in the set of Miles's mouth. "Let him say whatever he's going to say. It doesn't matter."

Ouch. Knowing he'd earned the distance and distrust he saw in his brother's eyes didn't make it any easier to swallow. Still, he was here to apologize, anyway. Steeling himself, Miles looked Penny straight in the eye and said, "I'm sorry."

Her lips tightened into a tight line. "Not me," she hissed, the words *you dolt* heavy in her tone. "Apologize to Dylan."

A quick glance at his baby brother's raised brows showed Dylan didn't know what was going on, either. "Uh, sweetheart, not to belabor the point, but you're the one Miles called a gold digger."

"Exactly," Penny seethed, righteous indignation burning hot pink across her round cheeks. "He implied that the only reason a woman would want to marry you—his own brother!—isn't because you're kind and funny, or great with kids, or even fantastic in bed. No. The only reason I could possibly have accepted your proposal is to get my hands on your family's money."

She sat back in her chair and crossed her arms over her chest, and the straightforward challenge in her stubborn scowl warmed Miles's heart.

Focusing on his brother, Miles said, very seriously, "Your fiancée is absolutely right. I apologize—not only for implying that you're basically a human ATM, but also for not realizing sooner that you've got impeccable taste in women. I should have known that any friend of Greta's would be pretty special. But now . . . Dylan, if I had to comb the globe to find the perfect wife for you, I couldn't do better than the woman at your side."

Dylan stood half out of his chair, planting his hands on the table. He leaned over, eyes narrow and mouth drawn. "What brought on this change of heart?"

"I'm not actually done apologizing yet."

Slumping back down in his chair, Dylan wiped a palm over his jaw. "There's more," he said blankly.

Miles thought about the night before, the way he'd felt while telling Greta about his family, and he knew he had one more apology to make if he was ever going to be able to let the guilt go and move forward to an adult relationship with his youngest brother.

"I want to tell you I'm sorry for abandoning you when Mom and Dad died. I know that's how it felt—and I have no excuse. When you looked at me after the funeral, all shocked and pale, like you still didn't quite understand what had happened . . . but you trusted me to make everything okay again . . ." Miles stopped talking, appalled at the break in his voice.

Across the table, Dylan had that hand over his mouth again, and Penny had stolen a comforting arm around his shoulders. "It's fine," Dylan said hoarsely. "You were halfway through college. It wouldn't have made any sense for you to quit, Mom and Dad wouldn't have wanted that."

"Let the man talk," Penny whispered, leaning her head on Dylan's shoulder. "Now that he's finally making some sense."

That got Dylan to smile behind his hand, and Miles felt the constriction in his chest ease up. The sight of the two of them, so together, so in sync—and the memory of how close to that he'd come with Greta—dispelled the worst of the black cloud of grief.

Miles cleared his throat and pressed on. "You were just a kid, and I was legally an adult. I could have made a different call. But you looked up at me, with all this hope in your eyes. And I just . . . I panicked. I was so afraid I couldn't live up to the responsibility, couldn't take our parents' place and give you what they would have given you. So I ran. And by the time I stopped running, it was too late."

The wooden chair creaked under Dylan as he shifted his weight. Penny lifted her head to look into his eyes, and they had a whole silent conversation while Miles sat there with his guts exposed on the table between them.

Pressing a nudging kiss to his shoulder, Penny moved back to let Dylan stand up. Feeling awkward craning his neck to look up at his kid brother, Miles stood, too, his heart hammering.

Dylan squared his shoulders and held out his hand, reaching out to Miles for the first time in years. "It's not too late."

A heavy-linked chain that had been there as long as Miles could remember finally gave up its hold on his ribs. Drawing in his first clean, sharp breath in ages, Miles shocked the hell out of both of them by grabbing Dylan's hand and using it to pull his brother in for a bone-cracking hug.

"I'm sorry, too." Dylan's thick voice was muffled against Miles's shoulder. "I acted like a jackass for a long time, I squandered every opportunity you tried to give me, and I lived the kind of life I *knew* Mom and Dad would have hated."

"But you figured yourself out," Miles reminded him, pulling back from the hug but keeping his hands on his brother's broad shoulders. "You know all Mom and Dad ever wanted was for us to be happy. And look who turned out to be the smart one, beating Logan and me to the punch."

"I had some help." Dylan turned to smile at Penny, who had tears running down her beaming face.

Miles let go of his brother, sending him into the waiting arms of the woman he loved without a qualm. "Sometimes life's toughest lessons take a while to learn, and we can't seem to make the leap on our own."

Twining her arm around her fiancé's waist with a fond squeeze, Penny arched a knowing look in Miles's direction. "You never did answer Dylan's original question. And not that we're complaining, but . . . why the sudden change of heart, Miles?"

Miles looked into Penny's laughing green eyes, and he knew that somehow she knew. Shaking his head, he backed toward the doorway. "Oh, man. I wish you all the luck in the world with that one,

Dylan. You're never going to get away with a damn thing."

"What do you mean?" Dylan's brows crinkled together exactly the same way they'd done when he was a little boy, frustrated at his inability to tie his own shoelaces. "What's going on?"

Penny did a very convincing angelically innocent face. Miles stuck his tongue in his cheek and held in a laugh.

"What your fiancée—who is too perceptive for my peace of mind, or, frankly, yours—means is that I, too, had some help in figuring things out." Miles cleared his throat, aware of a flush of heat traveling up his neck.

Dylan's grin was wide and delighted. "Soooo, our little Greta Hackley showed you around Sanctuary Island and got you hooked, huh?"

"It wasn't the island, although it's a beautiful place." Miles tucked his hands in his pockets, realizing for the first time that he didn't have his jacket. The knowledge that Greta was wearing it sent a strange, possessive thrill through his bones. "It was all Greta."

"Yeah, she's pretty great," Dylan agreed happily. When Penny poked him in the side, he glared down at her in confusion. "What?"

Arching a brow at Miles, the half quirk of Penny's mouth clearly communicated, *Do you want to tell him, or shall I?*

Miles shook his head. He definitely wasn't saying it out loud to his brother before he even managed to tell Greta how he felt about her. But Penny had no such issues.

"Your brother," she told Dylan with relish, "is withdrawing his objections to our speedy marriage because it has recently dawned on him that it doesn't always take years to fall in love." The smile she sent Miles was softer, although laughter still sparkled at the corners of her pretty green eyes. "Sometimes, with the right person, all it takes is one look."

Dylan's blue eyes went wide with disbelief before a huge grin overtook his face. Crossing the kitchen to clap Miles on the back, he said, "No kidding! This is incredible, we should call Logan up here and open a bottle of champagne or something. What a day!"

A low, bitter bark of laughter made them all turn toward the door that led to the front hallway.

Greta stood in the doorway with his jacket crumpled under one arm, his phone clenched in her right fist, and eyes dark as black coffee in the milky paleness of her face.

Miles started forward instinctively, fear clutching at his chest. "Greta, what happened? Are you okay, your mom—?"

She pitched the phone at him, a perfect curveball Miles managed to catch only by sheer luck and reflexes. "You lied to me," Greta said in a voice like broken glass. "You spun me the perfect fairy tale, a dreamworld made to order, just for me . . ."

Shaking her head, Greta hardened her face until

she looked like a marble statue of the vibrant, beautiful woman Miles loved.

"What happened, you ask?" Greta laughed again, and it was just as painful to hear as it was the first time. "What happened is that I finally woke up."

Chapter Ten

The kitchen was filled with the ear-ringing silence of a detonated bomb. Greta lobbed her grenade, turned on her heel, and left Miles clutching his phone like a lifeline.

Numb with shock and moving on autopilot, he thumbed open the locked screen and scrolled through the most recent texts.

Two from Cleo. The first one about the private investigator made him wince, but it was the second that froze his heart inside his chest.

Boss. Wanted to talk in person about this, but since you're not picking up . . . pls rethink what you're doing with GH. Seducing a woman for info is not worthy of you, and you may regret it. She's different from your usual, you were different around her. Smthg to think about.

In a single devastating glance, Miles took it all in. Greta must have seen the text, and she wasn't an idiot. She'd obviously figured out the truth . . . but she didn't have the whole story.

"What are you waiting for?" Penny exclaimed. "Go after her!"

"Hold on, what was she talking about?" Dylan's heavy hand landed on Miles's shoulder. "Miles. What did you do?"

"You, of all people, know how far I'm willing to go to protect my family." Miles glanced at the dawning horror on Penny's sweet, round face. "I thought Penny was a real threat. I figured her best friend would dish the dirt if I threw a little money around and showed her a good time."

Miles expected Dylan to drop his hand, to back away with his lip curled in disgust. But instead, his baby brother squeezed his shoulder and said, "But Greta showed *you* something instead, huh?"

That brought Miles's head up, finally, and he met Dylan's sympathetic gaze with a sense of wonder. So he hadn't lost everything in the last thirty seconds.

It only felt that way.

"Do you love Greta?" Penny asked abruptly. She still looked upset, but there was a spine of steel running straight up that woman's back. "That's the only real question."

"She doesn't know it," Miles confessed, raw and painful. "But I do."

"Then go tell her," Dylan urged him. "Tell her everything, the whole truth, and don't leave anything out. Then, if you're as lucky as I am, she'll look down into your soul and decide if you're worth forgiving."

"I didn't have to dig all that deep," Penny protested, stepping up to slip her fingers into Dylan's hand.

Miles felt his lips twitch as a tiny spark of hope flickered to life in his heart. "I need to hear that whole story someday, but right now ... I have some groveling to do."

"Yeah, you do," Penny said, but the approving smile she gifted him with made Miles want to hug her.

But he didn't have time. He had to go after Greta—he couldn't stand to leave her thinking the worst of him, and herself, for an instant longer than necessary. The only problem was ...

"Uh, Penny? Can you give me her address?"

Penny's face went slack. "The love of your life, and you don't even know where she lives?"

"Hazards of a whirlwind romance. Address?"

Two minutes later, Miles was racing down Island Road and feeling grateful that Greta's family store was so close to his family's vacation home.

He ran up Main Street and paused to catch his breath in front of Hackley's Hardware. The Hackley family owned the whole building—hardware store downstairs, and a couple of apartments upstairs. Greta lived in one.

And her mother, Esther, lived in the other.

When Miles pushed his way into the shop, he wasn't surprised to find Esther waiting for him behind the counter, as stern and impassive as one of the guards outside Buckingham Palace. But instead of red regimentals and a tall furry hat, she wore a floral cotton shirtdress, a white cardigan, and a forbidding expression.

Miles steeled himself and rolled up his sleeves. He had a feeling he'd have better luck getting past the queen's Royal Guard, but he wasn't leaving here without talking to Greta. "Where is she? I need to see her."

"Greta didn't tell me everything, but she told me enough. So you'll forgive me if I don't give a tinker's damn what you need, Mr. Harrington," Esther said serenely, flipping a page in her crossword book with vicious precision.

Resisting the urge to tear the building down with his bare hands to get to Greta, Miles called on years of experience in delicate, high-stakes business negotiations. God knew, the stakes had never been higher for him.

"Mrs. Hackley," he started, sanding the rough edges off his voice. "There's been a terrible misunderstanding. If I could just have a few minutes alone with your daughter, I'm sure we could work it out."

"A misunderstanding." Esther's razor-sharp gaze raked over him, missing nothing. "So you didn't deliberately set out to betray my daughter's trust in the most despicably calculated fashion?"

Guilt surged like bile in the back of his throat, but Miles kept his body language open and accepting. "I can't deny that when I met Greta, keeping my brother safe was at the top of my mind. Dylan . . . doesn't have the greatest track record. I've had to deal with predatory women looking to score big off my baby brother's frustration and loneliness. So you're right, I was very deliberate and calculated in my efforts to avoid another heartbreak for my brother."

Something flickered in Esther's flat gaze, but if Miles had hoped that appealing to their shared trait of family protectiveness would get him anywhere, he was destined to be disappointed.

"Greta doesn't want to see you," Esther said with finality.

"I understand that." Miles pulled up a rueful smile. "And I don't blame her. But all I'm asking for is a chance to explain. I honestly believe that what I have to say will make Greta feel better—I'm not here to hurt her any worse than I already have."

It was his last-ditch effort before he had to resort to wrestling an old lady to the ground and storming the castle. Miles held his breath.

Esther's lined, careworn face never softened. She didn't betray her thoughts or feelings by so much as the flicker of an eyelash, and Miles had the sudden, brief thought that he ought to hire her to run negotiations for him.

That, or ask her for poker lessons, because when she finally replied, it wasn't the answer Miles had been expecting.

"Greta? Honey, come on out here."

Every one of Miles's senses went on high alert. She was here, listening?

A thump from the back office behind the counter drew Miles's attention, and then there she was gripping the doorway and staring at Esther as if she'd never truly seen her mother before.

"Why?" Greta's question, the pain in her voice, triggered an answering spasm of pain across Esther's face.

She pivoted on her stool to face her daughter, but even in profile, Miles could see that her face was all softness now. "Oh, honey. You need to let him say his piece. Otherwise you'll always wonder."

Greta crossed her arms over her chest. So far, she had refused to meet Miles's stare. "I don't have to wonder. I already know he's a low-down dirty snake."

The words hit Miles like bullets to the chest, stealing his breath and opening up wounds he was afraid would never heal.

"I don't know everything he promised you," Esther said. "I don't know how far back the lie goes. But honey, what if he's telling the truth now?"

The help from an unexpected quarter made Miles stand up straighter, even though Greta was shaking her head as if she couldn't believe her ears.

"Mama. After all the things you've done to keep me safe, all the risks you wouldn't let me take—you want me to take a chance on *him*?"

The anguish and disbelief sliced at Miles. He stepped forward, impatient to get in there, to have his say and make Greta understand, but Esther stopped him with one quietly raised hand.

"No, Greta. I want you to take a chance on happiness," she said, her breath catching. "All the things I did to keep you safe, the treatments and the surgery and keeping you home from college . . . they didn't guarantee that you would be happy. In fact, I have never seen you as happy as you were this morning, waltzing back in here after that crazy, fool trip to New York on one of those death-trap helicopters."

Esther took a deep breath as if to steady herself against the image, one hand pressing high enough on her chest to make Miles imagine that if she were wearing a string of pearls, she'd be clutching them.

"I already told you I was sorry about that," Greta muttered. "It'll never happen again, believe me."

"You're not listening to me," Esther insisted. "I think—maybe somewhere along the way, when you were so sick, I lost sight of what we were doing it all for. Not just so that you would be healthy and keep breathing in and out, but so that you could go on to live an ecstatically happy life, full of laughter and adventures. And love."

The *L* word froze Greta in her tracks, arms wrapped around herself and face turned carefully away from Miles. Esther took advantage of the moment to get down off her stool and give her unresisting daughter a fierce hug.

"Now then," Esther said with a watery sniff. "I'm going to get out of here and let you two have some space to talk. I'll turn the sign to Closed on my way out, so you won't be disturbed. And Mr. Harrington?"

Miles jumped to attention. "Yes?"

Narrowing her eyes at him like a sniper sighting down a target, Esther shook her finger. "I'm happy to call one of my boys back home to help run the shop, or heck, even hire someone. But if you whisk my baby off to see the world without letting her say good-bye to me, I will hunt you down like a dog and shoot you myself."

"Your mother is terrifying," Miles said into the silence Mama left in her wake after marching out of the shop.

No, terrifying is being face-to-face with the man who broke my heart into tiny pieces and has come back for more.

"I don't want to talk about my mother." Greta licked her lips, which felt parched. She hadn't let herself cry, but the tears were building up into a massive storm behind her eyes. "In fact, I don't want to talk to you at all."

"That's fine," Miles said, coming around the counter and looming over her. "You can listen instead."

Greta flinched back, her poor, confused body caught between the still-fresh memories of the night before and the new caution signals her brain was frantically sending out.

His eyes darkened to the blue-gray of hurricane clouds, but he stopped where he was. "Greta."

That was all, just her name. She breathed through the pain of being near him for a long, harrowing minute before it burst out of her in a spew of vitriol. "That's it? That's all you've got for me? And after you worked so hard to persuade my mother to trust you . . . although, what am I even saying? You're an expert at manipulation, I'm sure you didn't even break a sweat."

A muscle ticked in Miles's jaw. "You have every right to be upset. I know this looks bad, but . . ."

"Looks bad?" Greta pushed away from the office door, feeling trapped and needing to move. "It *is* bad, Miles."

He made a frustrated noise and caught at her arm as she brushed past him. The veins stood out in his well-defined forearms, bared by the rolled cuffs of his crisp white shirt and dusted with light brown hair. Greta stared down at the place where they touched, the intersection of their bodies and the contrast between his large, blunt-fingered hand and her thin, bony wrist.

She remembered the way she'd felt under him, feminine and strong, with all the power of the body she'd struggled with all her life suddenly there at her fingertips and hers to command.

Turning her wrist in the circle of his fingers, Greta closed her eyes, overcome with exhaustion. "I can't believe my first time was based on a lie."

Miles dropped her wrist as if her skin burned him. "What?"

The loudness of his voice poked at her. Opening her eyes to glare at him, Greta said, "Don't worry, I didn't hold onto my virginity out of some misguided fantasy—okay, that's actually a lie. It was partly because of that, which I'll own, because that's my own stupid fault for believing in fairy tales. But mostly I was a virgin because everyone around here looks at me and still sees a pale, sickly kid."

Miles reached up with both arms as if he wanted to take her by the shoulders, but he checked himself. Greta told herself she was glad. She didn't want him to touch her ever again.

"That's not what I see when I look at you." His rough voice sent unwanted shivers down the back of her neck.

"No," she agreed, gazing up at him with anger twisting her belly into knots. "You saw a means to an end. An easy mark, so eager to be swept off my feet that I practically threw myself into your arms. I bet you were disappointed I wasn't more of a challenge."

"Nothing about you has ever disappointed me," Miles said, urgency firing his voice. "And Greta, I know it might be hard for you to believe me right now, but you were an incredible challenge. In fact, I found it completely impossible to keep my mind on my goal when I was around you."

"Stop it," Greta whispered, turning away, but Miles wouldn't let her. This time when he reached for her, he ran his hands up her arms with a light touch that nonetheless chained her to the spot.

"Yesterday was the best day of my life," he said, staring into her eyes as if he were trying to read her thoughts. "And last night . . . God, I can't believe you didn't tell me it was your first time. If I hurt you . . ."

"You did hurt me," Greta cried, pushed beyond her limits. "Not my stupid body, I wish everyone in the world would quit worrying about my body, it's fine. But here, inside, the real me."

She thumped a fist against the hollow ache in her chest and bit back a sob. She would not cry in front of him. Greta hadn't cried in front of another person since her first hospital stay, when she was six.

"I know I hurt you." Miles's Adam's apple bobbed as he swallowed. "I never meant for that to happen."

"Oh? What did you think would be the end result of sleeping with me for information and then never talking to me again?"

"Hold on, wait." Alarm widened his eyes. "Sleeping with you was never part of the plan. Remember the guest room? I had it all set up, we were going to have a fun, romantic day, I'd get you drunk at dinner, and you'd spill your guts."

Hating the bitterness in her own voice, Greta couldn't stop herself from hissing, "So I ruined everything by not being able to drink, and you had to go with plan B."

"No, damn it," Miles ground out, looking as if he wanted to shake her. "You ruined everything by making me fall in love with you!"

Chapter Eleven

Greta reared back as if he'd slapped her, rather than declared his love for her, but Miles didn't let go of her arms.

He was through with letting her go.

"That's not true. You're still lying." Her face crumpled slightly. "Why are you still lying?"

"I'm not. There's no reason to," Miles pointed out, almost tripping over the words in his hurry to get them out. "I've already given Dylan and Penny my approval, and thanks to the way you made me see my past in a new light, I think Dylan and I even took a good step toward a real relationship."

As if she'd been turned to stone, Greta stared up at him with huge, bewildered eyes. "That's . . . good. I'm glad. For Dylan's sake."

Miles couldn't help but smile. "Poor Greta. You've been on quite the emotional roller coaster today."

She shivered a little when he lifted a hand to brush her hair back from her face, but allowed the touch. The flame of hope in Miles's chest burned brighter.

"I've never been on a roller coaster," Greta admitted.

"No? You'd love it. If you want, I can call Arturo and tell him to gas up the chopper for a flight to Cedar Point. Best roller coasters in the world."

The light of adventure radiated from Greta's eyes for a short second before her brows drew down. "I can't go anywhere with you."

"Why not?" Miles asked reasonably. "You don't believe me when I say I love you? That I've loved you from the moment you leaned out over the edge of a hundred-story building just to get a better view?"

Her mouth dropped open, and Miles wanted to kiss the surprise off her beautiful face so badly, his fingers cramped with the need to pull her closer.

Instead, he said, "Actually, if I'm completely honest—which I promise to be from now on—I think I fell in love with you from the first moment I set eyes on you. It just took me a day or so to figure it out."

Miles watched her closely. This was the delicate part of the negotiation, he sensed. He'd laid it all out for her, the deepest truth of his feelings, and now Greta had to decide whether to retreat back to safety, or to take a leap of faith and trust someone who'd hurt her.

"I can't . . ." Greta frowned, and Miles's fingers

itched to smooth away the line between her dark gold brows. "I don't understand what you get out of lying about this."

"Best-case scenario?" Miles traced his hands down the length of her arms to trap her cold hands between his. Bringing their twined fingers to his lips, he said, "I could get you."

For one blissful, heart-stopping second, Greta swayed toward him, color blooming in her cheeks and her breath coming fast and light . . . but then she drew back. Fear flashed across her face and she pulled her hands from his grasp. "No! It wouldn't work."

"If you believe I love you, we can make anything work," Miles said quickly. "I can give you as much time as you need to catch up. No pressure, no rush—we can start over and take it slow."

"Right, slow." Greta's smile was bleak as winter, and she wrapped her arms around her ribs as if she'd gotten a chill. "However long it takes me to trust you again . . . you'll just hang out here on Sanctuary Island and let your company go to rot without you."

"There's such a thing as videoconferencing," Miles pointed out. "And we can travel back and forth. I got the impression you enjoyed New York."

"I did love New York. That's the not the point," Greta cried. "I can't leave Sanctuary! It's my home. My mother, the shop—she needs me."

"Your mother will always need you," Miles said, treading carefully. "She loves you. And after what you went through together, the transplant and everything—that connection is unbreakable. I would never want to do anything to harm it. But she did mention there are other options available for help with the store."

Greta was shaking her head hard enough to whip her hair across her cheeks. "No, I can't . . ."

Despair yawned like a chasm beneath Miles's feet, ready to suck him down into the black depths. "Greta. Don't hide behind your mother."

Her head shot up, fire in her eyes, but Miles forced himself to continue. "Please don't say no because you're afraid to leave home. Not you, my wild adventurer. But if you're hesitating because you don't think you can ever love me back . . ."

Pain closed his throat, choking off his words, and he had to look away. A tiny huff from Greta made him glance back at her, though, and the aggravation on her face jump-started his heart.

"You idiot," she breathed, fury reddening her cheeks. "I'm already head over heels for you. What do you think I'm so afraid of?"

Miles whooped and grabbed her, picking her up and twirling her. "You love me?"

"Yes, idiot, now put me down," Greta yelled, laughing.

He set her on the countertop by the cash register, a strategic move that allowed him to step between her spread thighs and keep her close. Resting her elbows on his shoulders, Greta sobered as she stared down at him.

"Of course I love you," she said again. "You couldn't have hurt me so badly if I didn't."

Miles buried his face in her lap, unable to bear the sharp pain lurking in her eyes. "I'm sorry. I promise I'll never hurt you again."

"You can't promise that." A light, tentative hand carded through the hair at the vulnerable nape of Miles's neck. "No one could keep that promise."

Shuddering, Miles straightened and met Greta's worried stare. "You're right. Life is long, and if we spend ours together, it's a given that we'll hurt each other at some point. But I can promise never to hurt you intentionally."

Greta seemed to be holding her breath. "Are you . . . did you just say you want to spend the rest of your life with me?"

"Oh hey, hold on." In a flash, Miles remembered the tiny box he'd retrieved from the wall safe before they left his penthouse that morning. Weird to think if he'd slipped it into his jacket instead of his pants pocket, they might have avoided a lot of heartache.

"Is that what I think it is?" Greta was close to hyperventilating now, Miles noted from the swift rise and fall of her rib cage.

He brushed a loving finger over the black velvet box, then handed it over. "If you think it's my mother's engagement ring, you're right."

Greta's fingers trembled as they flipped open the box, and Miles drew in his breath at the sight of the slim platinum band and princess-cut diamond he'd last seen on his mother's finger.

"It's beautiful." Greta touched the tip of one finger to the sparkling baguettes that flanked the central diamond. "But I can't accept this. Miles, it's too much, you don't even know—"

Miles clamped his hands on her hips. "Yes, you can. I love you, and you love me. Marry me and we'll spend the rest of our lives having adventures and living out your fairy tale."

"The rest of our lives." Greta blew out a breath, and when she met his gaze, the depth of terror in her eyes struck a blow at Miles's heart. "What if I can't promise you more than a few years? Will you still want to give me this ring?"

Miles struggled to control his rising fear. "What do you mean?"

Closing the jewelry box with a snap that made them both wince, Greta said, "Kidney transplants don't last forever. I could get lucky, since my kidney is from a close, living relative—I might have a couple of decades. But it could be less, there's no way to know for sure."

Scrambling to make sense of this, Miles fell back on the problem-solving skills drilled into him as a CEO. "Okay. That sucks. But when it fails, you can get another kidney transplant, right?"

"Or go on dialysis." The corners of her mouth turned down. "Either way, it's going to be . . . pretty awful."

Light dawned behind Miles's eyes. "And you've been living with this sword hanging over your head since you were, what, seventeen?"

Greta nodded, biting her lip. "I couldn't ask or expect you to sign up for that life, never knowing when to expect disaster to strike, but always knowing it's around the corner, waiting for you."

"But don't you see," Miles argued, "that's every life. You think I don't have nightmares about losing members of my family, after what happened to my parents? I do. And one day, unless by God's good grace I die first, it will happen. Disaster will strike like lightning; it's the only guarantee in life. All we can do is choose who we want at our sides when the storm breaks."

"And you want me? A woman with a lemon of a body, who's never done anything with her life and still lives with her mother?"

Miles hooked a hand behind her neck to drag her down for a kiss. "I want you, the woman who conquered her fears and stood on top of the world with me. I want the woman who reminded me that I owe my family more than protection. I want the woman who . . . God. The woman my mother would have absolutely adored. Greta, I want you."

Greta sobbed against his mouth, kissing him back through the tears streaming down her cheeks.

When they came up for air a lifetime later, Miles rasped, "Is that a yes?"

In answer, Greta picked up the box she'd dropped on the counter beside them and opened it. "Put it on me," she ordered in a tear-clogged voice. "Give me my fairy tale ending, damn it."

The band slid smoothly onto the ring finger of her left hand and nestled there as if it had been made for Greta. Blinking away the hot sting behind his eyes, Miles said, "Our fairy tale is a little out of the ordinary."

"How so?"

Kissing her hand, the one wearing his ring, gave Miles a primal thrill of possession. "In our story, the beautiful maiden is the one who rescues the prince. With this ring, you're saving me from a life of nothing but cold, solitary duty and obligation. You and this island gave me back my brothers, my family—and now I get to live happily ever after with you."

Humming happily, Greta locked her ankles together behind Miles's back, curving down to whisper into his ear. "No matter where we go or what adventures we have, we'll always find our way home . . . because, for me, home is wherever you are."

One year later . . .

Miles Harrington stared out over the neat, mani-cured rows of flowering bushes, his heart so swol-len with love he could barely breathe around it.

This whole having-emotions thing was definitely not for the weak and wimpy.

"Nana would have loved this," Dylan said qui-etly as he stepped up beside him.

Miles tactfully ignored the break in his youn-gest brother's voice, because he was considerate like that. And because he hoped Dylan would re-turn the favor. "So would Mom."

Logan straightened from where he'd knelt in the freshly turned soil to examine the rooting of the rose cuttings from their grandmother's garden. "What woman wouldn't like having a public gar-den built in her honor?"

The Harrington Memorial Rose Garden was full to bursting, its winding gravel pathways and romantic stone benches covered with people who'd come to enjoy the dedication ceremony for the brand new park. Miles closed his eyes to the throngs of townsfolk moving placidly through the rose bushes, stopping to exclaim over an exuberant yellow blossom here or to sniff a tiny tea rose there, and simply breathed in the warmth and joy of this special place.

When he opened his eyes, his darling wife was smiling up at him. Even after all these months, it still thrilled him to be able to reach out and draw her into his arms. Miles cherished the way she leaned trustingly into him, the steady balance of their bodies together so much stronger than either of them could be on their own.

"Have you figured out what you're going to say yet?" Greta teased softly.

Miles punished her with a pinch to the rear, which only made her grin. She'd ruthlessly distracted him on the helicopter ride down, taking advantage of their last few hours of total privacy before spending a week on Sanctuary Island with both their families.

"I've got a few ideas." It wasn't a lie; he knew the basics of what he wanted to tell the people of Sanctuary about the Harrington brothers' reasons for donating the park. "Don't worry. I regularly face down hordes of shareholders and board members. I think I can handle one little dedication ceremony."

A musical laugh from behind him prompted Miles to glance at Jessica Bell, Logan's ex-assistant, now fiancée. "I promise Logan won't pass out, at least. Will that help?"

"It's a start," Miles told her, even as his middle brother grumbled that if they didn't get this show on the road, passing out would be the least of his problems. For all that Jessica had done to bring Logan back into the world, get him healthy and help him reconnect with his family, he still wasn't a huge fan of crowds.

Before Miles could take pity on him and step up to the temporary podium the town council had erected for the ceremony, his gaze snagged on a very pregnant woman making her slow, deliberate way toward them through the crowd. He couldn't control the clench in his heart or the worry he knew would be visible in his eyes as he glanced down to check on Greta.

But his sweet wife gave no indication of anything other than pure joy at the sight of her best friend looking round-bellied and serenely content. "Penny, oh my gosh, you're radiant!"

"Hmm. If by 'radiant' you mean 'sweating like a pitcher of sweet tea in July,' then yes, absolutely," Penny huffed, pressing a hand to her lower back. Dylan was at her side in an instant, hovering in that worried, helpless way all expectant fathers seemed to have.

Miles breathed out through his mouth and very consciously did not curl his hands into frustrated fists. He knew a little something about worry and helplessness, even if he and Greta hadn't managed to conceive.

Shoving down the pain of that thought, he reminded himself that today was not about sadness and regret for what they didn't have, but about honoring the gift they'd been given—the chance for love and happiness bequeathed to the Harrington brothers by their parents, their grandparents, and Sanctuary Island.

Be grateful, he reminded himself fiercely. *Only an idiot would ruin a day like today by wanting what might never be.*

"You okay?" Greta tugged him aside for a private murmur. The concern in her bittersweet chocolate eyes tugged at his heart. In the past year, the connection between them had grown and deepened until sometimes it seemed she could read his heart like a picture book.

Determined to live in this glorious moment, with his brothers and their happy wives around him, and his own beautiful bride warm and safe and vital in his arms, Miles nodded. "Just thinking about things."

Of course, that wasn't enough to put Greta off. Gentle and relentless, she searched his expression. "Remembering your parents?"

Part of Miles wanted to grasp at that very plausible excuse for the sudden cloud over his head. It even had the advantage of being mostly true—his parents certainly had been on his mind a lot lately. Ever since Penny and Dylan shared their happy news, in fact.

But Miles had promised Greta a long time ago that he'd never lie to her again. And not only that, he'd promised to be open. As he'd discovered, opening himself and making himself vulnerable was tough. He had to work at it, and maybe he always would. But when he met Greta's dark, understanding gaze, he knew it was worth it.

"Yeah, I'm thinking about Mom and Dad, and how much they would have loved to be here with us today. How much they'd love to see this garden, and the Island Road house, and all three of their boys so happy. Especially . . ."

Without meaning to, Miles felt his stare slide to Penny's pregnant glow and Dylan's proud, terrified smile. Snapping his attention back to his wife, Miles prayed she hadn't noticed the direction of his glance . . . but Greta noticed everything about him.

Her voice soft, she murmured, "You wish your parents were alive to see the next generation of Harringtons."

Miles shrugged, uncomfortable with what that implied. "It's not about carrying on the family name or having someone to inherit the family company. It's just . . . our parents instilled love in us. They taught us how to do it, and even though some of us may have forgotten the way for a while there, we're all back on track now."

I'd give anything to be able to teach my own child how to love.

He bit the words back. His promise to be open only went so far—he wouldn't wound Greta or himself by bringing up the one dark blot on their happy union.

But Greta, as always, heard exactly what he wasn't saying. "You want what Penny and Dylan have."

Guilt raked vicious claws down Miles's ribcage. "I want *you*," he growled. "No matter what comes, whether we're blessed with kids or not, whether we adopt or just act like the most indulgent, spoiling aunt and uncle ever—however our family grows, you're the heart of it. You're my heart. I'll be happy as long as I have you."

Greta leaned up to lay her mouth across his, a searing kiss that Miles felt all the way to the center of his soul.

"But what if you could have more?" she whispered against his lips.

Miles froze, every muscle in his body going into lockdown. "The doctor said, because of your illness—it could take years. It might never happen— . . ."

A slow, secret smile curved Greta's pink lips. "Doctors don't know everything."

He pulled back, afraid to ask, afraid to hear the answer . . . but Greta was looking at him steadily, not a trace of fear in the supple lines of her body. Her courage lifted him up. "What are you saying?"

Joy lit her face like a sunrise as her hand slipped down to her still-flat belly. "I'm pregnant. Against all the odds and after all the heartache, my body finally does exactly what I want it to do."

"We're having a baby." Saying the words out loud shook Miles to the core, an explosion like fireworks detonating his heart and breaking him into a million pieces.

Greta nodded, happy tears dotting the corners of her eyes. "In the spring. I was going to wait until tonight to tell you, but you looked like you needed it now."

Sweeping her up, Miles fought to balance his desire to crush her to him with his new, urgent need to handle her like she was made of fine-spun glass. "You always know exactly what I need."

She laughed in his ear, but it could have been a sob. Miles clutched her tighter and felt his world realign itself around them as happy chatter and the scent of ripe roses filled the air.

He let Greta's toes touch the grass again and they steadied each other for a dizzy moment of perfect connection. There was so much to talk about, so many things to work out, a thousand plans to make and details to consider . . . but when Greta tilted her chin up again, her kiss grounded Miles in the moment. They breathed for a second, in sync and enjoying it.

Miles touched his forehead to hers. "I'll never be able to smell a rose without remembering this day."

"I'll let Cleo know she's got a new shortcut to cheering you up after a crappy meeting."

Laughing, Miles lifted one of Greta's hands and pressed a kiss to her knuckles. "Look at you, giving away all my secrets and ruining my reputation. I'm supposed to be the big, bad, scary boss."

Greta shook her head. "Nope. You're supposed to be happy."

Coughing to clear his tight, scratchy throat, Miles said, "Mission accomplished."

"Uh, guys? I hate to interrupt." Jessica, who'd never met an event she didn't want to organize, appeared to have taken over managing the dedication ceremony. She stepped up with an apologetic smile and tilted her head in the direction of the podium. "I think it's about time to start. If we wait much longer, we're going to lose Logan."

Miles glanced past her to where his younger brother stood, arms crossed and scowling gaze directed up at the sky, while a local dairy farmer talked his ear off. Huffing out a laugh, Miles gave Jessica a nod before squeezing Greta close for one last kiss. For some reason, he was having a hard time letting go of her.

"Go do your thing," she whispered in his ear, a smile audible in her tone. "We'll be right here waiting for you. Daddy."

The promise in that word, and the glint in Greta's brown eyes as she pulled away, gave Miles the shove he needed to get him over to the podium. Holding up his arms to get everyone's attention, he waited for the crowd to turn and gather close.

With a sigh of relief, Logan abandoned his one-sided conversation and moved to Miles's right just as Dylan came forward to flank him on the left. Jessica and Greta joined Penny at the stone bench where she'd settled to one side of the podium, and suddenly Miles knew exactly what he wanted to say.

"If you'd told me a year ago that I'd be standing

shoulder to shoulder with my two brothers, and that all three of us would have found the loves of our lives, I would've laughed in your face. Actually, no. I didn't do a lot of laughing back then—I probably would have sneered, and maybe had you fired. What can I say? I was a bit of a jerk."

"A bit?" Dylan snarked under his breath, with an affectionate shove of his shoulder.

"Back then?" Logan didn't drop his smirk when Miles shot him a mock-angry glare.

"As I was saying," Miles continued with emphasis. "That was the old me. That was before I'd ever visited Sanctuary Island."

There were proud smiles and nods as an approving murmur hummed through the crowd. These people loved their town, and Miles could understand why.

"This island is special," he said simply. "Warm, welcoming, friendly, and so beautiful it feels like stepping into a dream. But it's real. And it's the place where all three of the Harrington brothers found love."

A raucous cheer from the back made Miles grin. He'd recognize Greta's loud-mouthed, boisterous brothers anywhere. "As far as we're concerned, Sanctuary Island is the most romantic place on earth. So to honor that, and also to honor our family's longstanding connection to the island, we decided to donate this beautiful public park to the people of Sanctuary Island. We planted the garden using cuttings from my grandmother's roses—all of these gorgeous blooms came from heirloom bushes lovingly raised by Bette Harrington for the summer home she adored."

Dylan shot him a sidelong glance, the corner of his mouth kicked up into a half smile. Miles clapped him on the shoulder, reaching out to drag Logan into the brother huddle with them. "This island has been good to our family," Miles said hoarsely. "And we wanted to show our gratitude to all of you, and to everyone who comes after. May this garden see many more couples falling in love and planning their futures on Sanctuary Island."

As the crowd broke into cheers and applause and his brothers started shaking hands and laughing with their new neighbors, Miles's gaze found Greta. She dropped the hands covering her trembling lips to mouth the words, "I love you," and Miles felt their impact in his chest.

Sanctuary Island had given them everything: their family, their friends, their future . . . and a love so deep, it was destined to be the true legacy they passed down to their children.

Acknowledgments

These novellas would never have existed without the encouragement of my fabulous agent, Deidre Knight, and the incredible support (both pre- and post-publication) of the folks at St. Martin's Press. Big thanks to Eileen Rothschild and Anne Marie Tallberg for the marketing help, and to Elsie Lyons for creating such consistently gorgeous covers, and to everyone else behind the scenes. And most of all, thank you to Rose Hilliard, who made me rewrite Penny and Dylan's story basically word for word . . . and in the process, taught me everything I know about how to craft a fun, fast-paced, romantic novella. *The Firefly Café* is hers as much as mine.

As always, I wouldn't have made it to The End without my network of fabulous writing friends, especially Kristen Painter, Roxanne St. Claire, Sarah MacLean, Kate Pearce, Bria Quinlan, Tracie Stewart, Ana Farrish, the Writechat gals, Romance Divas, and the ARWA Critique Group. Thanks for all the advice, hand-holding, and cheerleading!

Thank you to my parents for unflagging support, especially the kind that takes the form of bringing over leftovers and walking my dogs when I'm locked in my writing cave under deadline. Mama, I know you love these novellas more than anything else I've ever written, so this book is for you!

I must also acknowledge that my husband would be a saint for putting up with my deadline craziness—if he weren't almost as invested in my career as he is in his own. Even so, Nick, you deserve a big, wet, smacking French kiss of thanks for putting up with frozen pizza, building me a website, celebrating my every success, and just generally being the inspiration behind my enduring belief in true love and happily ever after.